PRAISE FOR

INVISIBLE NO MORE

"Imagine an athlete with the greatness of Patrick Mahomes and Steph Curry, whose backstory is comparable to Jackie Robinson, Warren Moon, Bo Jackson, and Pat Tillman. Now imagine all of it in one 25-year-old. The story of Wilmeth Sidat-Singh is both heroic and heartbreaking. The authors place a much-needed spotlight on a forgotten superstar athlete."

MIKE TIRICO, NBC Sports

"We often hear athletes say they stand on the shoulders of their predecessors, but not until you truly understand their journey is it possible to fully understand the debt and gratitude we owe them for the legacy they left us. I am humbled to be a part of the lineage created by Wilmeth Sidat-Singh. His story transcends the game. He truly is an American hero."

DON McPHERSON, author, educator, College Football Hall of Fame member

"Based on the true life of an extraordinary young man named Wilmeth Sidat-Singh, *Invisible No More* is a testament to the grace and grit of the human spirit. The novel follows Wilmeth from the brutal discrimination of the Jim Crow 1930s and 1940s to his ascension as a brilliant student-athlete at Syracuse University to his tragic death at the age of 25 in World War II. The thread that links the past to the present is a tough, irreverent Black female journalist named Breanna who unearths Wilmeth's long-forgotten story and is changed forever. Readers will be too."

JOAN RYAN, award-winning journalist and author of *Intangibles: Unlocking the Science and Soul of Team Chemistry*

"It takes persistence, courage, and style to move a hero out of the shadows so a new generation can appreciate such greatness. Thankfully, those elements have aligned here."

TIM WENDEL, award-winning journalist and author of *Castro's Curveball* and *Summer of '68*

ALSO BY SCOTT PITONIAK AND RICK BURTON

Forever Orange: The Story of Syracuse University

BY SCOTT PITONIAK

Remembrances of Swings Past: A Lifetime of Baseball Stories

Juke Box Hero: My Five Decades in Rock 'n' Roll (coauthored with Lou Gramm)

If These Walls Could Talk: Buffalo Bills (coauthored with John Murphy)

Playing Write Field: Selected Works of Scott Pitoniak

100 Things Every Syracuse Fan Needs to Know and Do Before They Die

Memories of Yankee Stadium

The Buffalo Bills: My Life on a Special Team (coauthored with Steve Tasker)

Color Him Orange: The Jim Boeheim Story

The Hall: A Celebration of Baseball's Greats (coauthor)

Buffalo Bills Football Vault: The First 50 Years

Syracuse University Football

The Good, the Bad, and the Ugly: Heart-Pounding, Jaw-Dropping, and Gut-Wrenching Moments from Buffalo Bills History

Yankee Stadium: America's First Modern Ballpark, 1923–2008 (contributing author and photographer)

Johnny Antonelli: A Baseball Memoir (coauthored with Johnny Antonelli)

Baseball Memories & Dreams (coauthored)

Slices of Orange: Great Games and Performers in Syracuse University Sports History (coauthored with Sal Maiorana)

Let's Go Yankees!: An Unforgettable Trip to the Ballpark

BY RICK BURTON

Into the Gorge

Darkest Mission

Business the NHL Way: Lessons from the Fastest Game on Ice (coauthored with Norm O'Reilly)

SUBPLOT™
an imprint of Amplify Publishing Group

www.mascotbooks.com

INVISIBLE NO MORE

For more information, please contact:
Subplot Publishing, an imprint of Amplify Publishing Group
620 Herndon Parkway, Suite 220
Herndon, VA 20170
info@amplifypublishing.com

Library of Congress Control Number: 2023912365
CPSIA Code: PRV0723A
ISBN-13: 978-1-63755-863-8

Printed in the United States

To Wilmeth Sidat-Singh. May you never be forgotten.

To Andrew Siegel for your belief in our novel.

ALL AMERICAN
WILMETH SIDAT-SINGH Halfback
SYRACUSE

INVISIBLE NO MORE

A HISTORICAL NOVEL

SCOTT PITONIAK AND **RICK BURTON**

SUBPLOT™
an imprint of Amplify Publishing Group

CHAPTER 1

Buffalo, New York, February 2000

Breanna Shelton smashed her right fist against her desk.

"Dammit!" she blurted, loud enough for the entire newsroom to hear. Her hand swelled. She flexed her fingers to make sure nothing was broken.

"Son of a freaking bitch," she muttered, righting the coffee mug she had knocked over and yanking at a box of tissues to sop up the splattered mess.

"You OK, Breanna?" Erik Allen asked, sheepishly poking his head above the adjoining cubicle. "Can I get you anything?"

"Yeah," she sighed. "How 'bout a new job?"

Erik retrieved napkins from his dump of a desk buried beneath an avalanche of old newspapers, notepads, photographs, phone books, and empty pizza boxes—enough kindling to ignite a bonfire and cause a fire marshal's blood pressure to spike. He handed the napkins to Breanna, then barreled through the newsroom as if possessing a stop-the-presses scoop.

"Here," he huffed, sucking wind upon returning from the cafeteria with a large Styrofoam cup teeming with ice. "Will sting like hell at first, but it should knock down the swelling."

"Ouch!" she shrieked, applying cubes to her throbbing hand.

After a minute or two of torture, the swelling subsided.

"Why don't you and I get out of Dodge?" Erik said. "Looks like you could use a beer or two."

"Try a beer or ten," she grumbled, grabbing her coffee-stained purse and coat.

***

Silk O'Loughlin's Pub had been a divey hangout for ink-stained wretches for nearly seven decades. Named for a flamboyant, immensely popular baseball umpire, whose death from the Spanish flu pandemic of 1918 was mourned nationwide, the bar had been founded by the grandsons of Irish immigrants who had accumulated plenty of dirt beneath their fingernails while shoveling out the Albany-to-Buffalo ditch that became known as the Erie Canal.

Like father and grandfather before him, proprietor Liam MacPherson had a gift of gab and a love of people. He reveled in holding court with the folks who wrote, edited, and printed the stories that had informed Buffalo readers for generations. He especially enjoyed spinning yarns that had been passed down about an old Buffalo newspaper writer by the name of Samuel Langhorne Clemens. Yes, Mark Twain himself had once made a living entertaining readers in the City of Good Neighbors with his pithy, humorous observations of the human condition.

"They said Twain hated deadlines and loved his whiskey," the barkeep known as Mac would tell patrons in a booming voice capable of knocking icicles from eaves. "He was used to novel deadlines, not daily newspaper deadlines, so he took his sweet time writing his humor columns, and that irritated his editors to no end. But none of 'em dared pester Twain to hurry up because he was co-owner of the damn paper. He was their boss. Had the power to fire their arses if need be. Seems Twain married into wealth, and his rich father-in-law gave him money to buy a piece of the *Buffalo Express*. But after a few years, Mr. Twain got bored with his toy. Had bigger fish to fry. So he and his bride sold their interest in the paper and headed to Elmira, where he could devote himself full-time to scribing his great American novels."

Mac loved puns and invariably would end his Twain tales with one that always produced its share of cackles and groans. "They say he was quite a huckleberry," Mac would chortle as smiling patrons heckled him.

O'Loughlin's had a homey, no-pretense feel to it, with sticky, beer-soaked floors and wooden bowls on the bar filled with oversalted peanuts and pretzels to encourage more drinking. At times it could be a loud place—a cacophony of conversations that prompted some patrons to refer to it as the Tower of Babel.

Reporters, editors, and pressmen loved congregating there after the last edition had been put to bed so they could blow off steam and solve the world's problems. Erie County bars were required by law to close their taps and doors by four in the morning, but Mac played dumb, as did the cops who frequented the joint after and—occasionally—during their shifts. Mac had his extended-hours scheme down to a science. A little before four, he would turn off the neon Genesee and Budweiser signs in the windows so as not to call outside attention to the illegal wee-hour thirst-quenchings. That strategy enabled him to keep the taps flowing and the whiskey pouring till the sun rose and the last squinty-eyed patron stumbled out the door.

O'Loughlin's also was a place of no filters. One could say whatever was on their mind, though sometimes there would be consequences, with heated discussions occasionally ending with noses getting in the way of fists. The thing, though, that newspaper folks loved most about O'Loughlin's was its location. It was just across the street from the *Buffalo Express*.

***

"So what gives?" Erik inquired as he and Breanna slid into a booth with a pitcher of Genny. "I saw you rushing out of Stash's office like your hair was on fire."

"I didn't get the Bills beat," she said, filling her mug to the brim.

"So sorry to hear that. Did he say why?"

"He said, 'Honey, you're not ready to cover an NFL team. You need more experience.' That's absolute bullshit. He gave it to Brady Sullivan. Can you believe that? How much experience does Brady have? Hasn't even been here a year. The real reason I didn't get it is pretty obvious. I'm Black. And I'm a woman. In this case, it's two strikes and you're out."

"But—"

"No buts," she interrupted. "You've seen Stash in action. He's always calling me honey, which drives me freaking nuts. And he's clearly not used to dealing with minorities, especially ones who aren't afraid to speak their minds. You're in the staff meetings. Anytime I suggest a story idea he dismisses it, like I should keep my piehole shut and be seen and not heard. Being the only person who looks like me in the department ain't easy when you've got a guy like that for a boss. I'm honestly surprised he hasn't asked me to go fetch coffee or shine his shoes."

She paused to take a huge swig. "Erik, I've been putting up with this crap since I was the only Black girl in my class at those elementary schools in South Buffalo. You're white, so you have no clue what it's like to be called shitty names from an early age and be told you're dumb and inferior just because your skin is a different color.

"And, in your wildest dreams, you couldn't begin to comprehend what it's like to be my older brother, Rasheen. He's gotten pulled over by the police time and time again—not for a crime, mind you, but for being Black. They pull him out of his car and frisk him for no cause, just to break his balls. Can't tell you how many times he's been harassed when he was just minding his own business. Fortunately, he's kept his mouth shut because if you make a peep, these senseless stops can turn tragic in a hurry. America in the year 2000 still has a long ways to go." She could feel her heart racing.

"My parents had to go through that same BS," she continued, the words gushing out like a tsunami. "They did their best to educate us about the ways of the world. They'd say, 'We know how hard this is on you and your brother, and it's definitely not fair, but it's a fact of life, and you're going to have to deal with it. The only way to shut 'em up is growing up to be smarter and better than them. Outwork them. Keep your nose clean. Stay out of the mud. Don't get dragged down to their level.' That's what they always preached.

"Well, I'm telling you, Erik, that turn-the-other-cheek shit is easier said than done. Being Black in this country can be downright exhausting."

Erik was speechless. Sure, he could sympathize and be repulsed by such injustices and unfairness, but Breanna was right. He could never truly comprehend what it was like, because it was a life he hadn't lived—and couldn't live.

"Erik, I've worked really hard at this job," she sighed, her voice now slower and lower. "Busted my ass, handled every assignment thrown my way, even the grunt stuff. I've won some journalism awards, worked well together with you and the rest of the guys. But Stash couldn't give a rat's ass. He's old school. Still views the damn world through that 1950s prism of his."

CHAPTER 2

Stanley "Stash" Malinowski's lens might have been a little more up-to-date than the 1950s, but not by much. He definitely was old school. And prejudiced. He still longed for what he perceived as the good ol' days, when sports staffs were male and as white as a fresh coat of lake-effect snow. He believed a woman's place was in the "fluffy" features department, if in the newspaper at all, writing about the wives of influential men and the latest fashion trends. Leave sports to the guys, just like it had mostly been since newspapers started covering the games people play back in the mid- to late-nineteenth century.

Stash clearly was a product of his times and his old neighborhood, where, while coming of age in the 1970s and 1980s, he had been taught by his police sergeant father and others not to trust those "lazy, welfare-check-cashing coloreds." Never mind that the Blacks who had "pitched tents and infiltrated" Stash's heretofore white hood actually were hardworking middle-class folks, who, just like his family, harbored aspirations for a better life. Their dream was the American dream too. But he refused to see that.

Bigotry usually is an acquired taste, and in Stash's case it had been fed to him in large helpings by his father and his grandfather—passed down from one generation to the next, like some family recipe.

Stash's grandfather, Albert Malinowski, had immigrated to the United States from Poland as a ten-year-old during the depths of the Great Depression in 1933, with little more than the clothes he was wearing. His parents had died a gruesome death when the horse-drawn wagon they were riding in while transporting potatoes to a Warsaw farmer's market tipped over the side of a dirt road and tumbled down a ravine. In the blink of an eye, Albert was orphaned. When the news reached his next of kin—an uncle and aunt in Buffalo—they arranged for him to make the voyage across the Atlantic.

Albert was scared shitless as he boarded the ocean liner swarming with hundreds of strangers bound for a strange land. For the first few nights, he climbed atop one of the bunk beds in the ballroom converted into a barracks and cried himself to sleep. He felt so alone. On the third night, Albert ventured up the stairs and onto the deck. The cool ocean breeze felt refreshing after being cooped up in the stagnant stench of the dormitory ballroom that reeked of urine. He gazed for hours at the luminous stars set against the blackened sky—they had never looked so bright—and tried envisioning how he might fit into this new world his parents often talked about. He remembered how they constantly referred to it as the land of hopes and dreams, even though they'd never been there.

On the fourth day of his journey, Albert became violently ill, vomiting every last piece of rice and every last drop of dirty drinking water that had passed his lips since boarding the ship. Word spread that several passengers had already died, and Albert thought for sure he might join them. Death, he thought, while balled up in a fetal position on his bed, might be a good thing because it would reunite him with his mother and father. Would prevent him from having to continue this venture into the unknown.

Death, though, would have to wait. His vomiting eventually ceased, and

Albert was able to hold down food and drink and slowly regain his strength. On the twelfth day, he awoke to a commotion. People began leaping from their beds and clambering up the stairs to the deck. Albert soon followed to see what the fuss was. He squinted into the morning sun and heard screams of joy. "Look! Look! There she is!" He turned his head and saw a sight he never forgot. There, in full view, was the Statue of Liberty, her copper facade turned green by years of exposure to sun, wind, and pollution. A few people began clapping, and soon a spark had turned into a wildfire. Albert quickly joined everyone else on the deck in applauding the monument they had only read about.

"Outside of my beloved bride, Megan, and of course, the Virgin Mary, Lady Liberty is the most beautiful woman I ever laid eyes on," he would exclaim in an accent still influenced by the old country whenever recounting the moment for his grandson Stash years later. The Statue of Liberty tale invariably was followed by the one of Albert and the other voyagers "herding like cattle" through the huge hall on nearby Ellis Island, where he was "processed" by immigration officers before boarding a train bound for the city with the funny name.

"We had no buffaloes in Warsaw," he'd say, laughing lustily. "I couldn't even pronounce the word at first. I'd say, 'Bufflo.' I'd drop the letter *a*, and people would look at me funny, like I was stupid and dumb. But I got here, and my relatives made sure I had a roof over my head, shoes on my feet, and plenty of perogies and kielbasa to eat, just like in the mother country."

When Albert turned eighteen, his uncle John found him a job in one of the cavernous, block-long steel mills in nearby Lackawanna, where he punched a clock and, in the words of his favorite singer, Tennessee Ernie Ford, owed his soul to the company store for more than thirty years. It was backbreaking, at times, dangerous work, and Albert paid a huge physical and emotional toll forging metal in foundries oppressively hot even in the dead of a frigid Buffalo winter. There were scars on his hands and arms from scalding, and he was hunched over a bit and walked with a slight limp. But he never complained, because he believed he was one of the lucky ones. Many coworkers had lost fingers, hands, and feet. These were pre-OSHA days, when safety regulations didn't go much beyond making sure men wore hard hats and steel-toed boots while working on the factory floor.

Albert figured it was a small price to pay to be an American. Whenever he had a bad shift, he'd remind himself how much better this life was than the place he had fled. He loved telling his grandson, "Only in America, huh, Stash? What a country, huh? You think they're living high off the hog like this in Africa or China or the Soviet Union? I think not. No other place in the world like America, Stash. Everyone who lives here is blessed. And don't you ever forget it."

Albert also liked to tell Stash his happily-ever-after story—the one about meeting and falling in love with a beautiful, blue-eyed, redheaded Irish immigrant from County Cork named Megan Delaney, and how "the Polack and the Mick" got married and raised a large, God-fearing Catholic family of six kids who went to confession every Saturday and Mass every Sunday at Saint Stanislaus Cathedral.

"It's all about God, country, and family," Albert would say, thumping a massive fist against his chest. "We are a family who pulled ourselves up by the bootstraps. We made something out of nothing. We didn't need no stinking handouts. If you wanted something, you worked for it. That's the American way. That's the Malinowski way. Don't you ever forget that, Stash."

CHAPTER 3

Mac arrived at Breanna and Erik's booth bearing another pitcher brimming with beer.

"This one's on the house for my two favorite sportswriters," he bellowed.

They smiled and thanked him. He responded with a thumbs-up before weaving his way back through the crowd to the busy bar.

"Look, I know Stash can be a bear," Erik said, topping off their glasses. "I've felt his wrath too. He's said things to me that have made me cringe, made me wonder if he got off the bus twenty, thirty years ago and never got back on. He's definitely from a different world. And it's a world he is trying in the worst way to hold on to. He probably sees you as a threat. He's clinging by his fingernails to a bygone era."

"Well, that's bullshit," she said, her heart racing once more. "I have a good mind to go across the street and hand in my resignation. 'Here, Stash. Here it is. You can go back to having your lily-white sports staff. Have a good life!'"

"Please, please don't do that, Breanna. I understand you're pissed about not getting the Bills beat, because it's the plum beat, and yes, you were more deserving than Brady. I'd just hate to see you do something rash. Don't give up on the dream. You tell stories that get to the heart. Just stick with it a while longer. People may not change, but times do."

"I don't know," she said, staring into her glass.

***

The following day Breanna was back at her desk, nursing a slight hangover and sore hand, when she heard the voice that never failed to make her blood boil.

"Hey, Breanna, dear. Could you come down to my office?" Malinowski said, leaning over her cubicle. "I have an assignment for you."

Breanna rose slowly from her chair, as if being summoned to the principal's office for some minor misdeed. She grabbed notepad and pen, and rolled her eyes as she trudged past several colleagues and into Stash's glass-walled office.

Behind his large, paper-strewn desk, the walls were festooned with iconic sports photographs and reprints of old newspapers. Two poster-size action shots stood out amid the clutter, grabbing her attention. One depicted legendary Bills quarterback Jim Kelly rifling a spiral through a flurry of snowflakes. The other showed Scott Norwood following through on the failed Super Bowl kick that produced the two most painful and obscene words in Buffalo's lexicon: *wide right*. As she stared at the photos of Kelly and Norwood, Breanna's heart sank. At this particular moment, the pictures didn't represent two seminal Bills performances, but rather how less than twenty-four hours earlier she had been denied the opportunity to cover the team she grew up following—by a man who wished she wasn't on his staff.

"Honey, I have an assignment for you that I think you're going to like," Stash said, handing her some notes he had typed. "It's actually not a sports story. It's more a feature story the managing editor and I thought you'd be perfect for because you're Black."

Breanna squirmed in her seat.

"There's this place in Geneseo, about an hour and change southeast of Buffalo, where they have a warplane museum, and they're going to honor a surviving Tuskegee Airman by the name of Charles Williams with a medal of some sort. I printed out a little information for you about the ceremonies. You can fill in the blanks when you talk to him. Apparently, he was quite the hero in World War II. Shot down something like twenty Nazi planes. We'd like you to drive down to the museum and interview him for a feature we'll run later this week."

"Whatever you say, Boss," she mumbled.

"What was that?!"

"I said, 'Whatever you say, Boss.'"

Stash began turning red. The veins in his neck bulged. He sprung from his chair, stomped to the door, and slammed it shut, startling several reporters standing not far from the glass-walled office some in the newsroom sarcastically called the piranha tank.

"Now, listen here, young lady. You really need to undergo an attitude adjustment. I've grown sick and tired of your uppity behavior. I know you're ticked about us giving the Bills beat to someone more qualified, but this piss-poor frame of mind isn't going to do you any good. I've got copyboys out there who would kill to do this story—or any story, for that matter. I thought the fact this guy was Black would get you fired up, but I guess I was wrong. I suggest you get your keister out of here and drive down to Geneseo and do this assignment justice."

CHAPTER 4

An hour's drive blasting Snoop Dogg, Bon Jovi, and Sarah McLachlan at ear drum–splitting levels helped Breanna take her mind off the man who had become the bane of her existence. By the time she pulled her 180,000-miles-and-still-going-strong Honda Civic into the gravel parking lot at the National Warplane Museum, her attitude had been adjusted. She'd been an inquisitive soul from an early age, loved hearing people's life stories, loved probing what made them tick. As much as she hated to admit it, perhaps Stash and the ME had given her a subject she would indeed enjoy.

Breanna had done a little digging before beginning her drive and was intrigued—not only by the man she was about to interview, Captain Charles Williams, but also by the little she had learned about this group of African American pilots known as Tuskegee Airmen.

A few minutes before the ceremony commenced that early June day in 2000, she walked inside the enormous old hangar housing ten vintage warplanes, including an old P-40, just like the one Williams had flown. She was surprised to see how many people had showed up. Had to be at least two hundred, if not more. A stage had been erected in front of the massive *Memphis Belle* bomber used in the movie that immortalized that plane's vital role in World War II. She couldn't get over the size of the propellers. Must have been at least ten feet high.

Soldiers with cherubic, peach-fuzzed faces stood at attention next to grizzled Vietnam vets with ZZ Top beards and black leather motorcycle jackets bearing more patches than NASCAR drivers.

"Forward march!" barked a drill sergeant in an attention-grabbing voice that sent tremors through the building. A four-soldier color guard unit led Williams, US congressman Colin Highledge, and other dignitaries in a processional down the center aisle to the stage. Soldiers past and present saluted the bespectacled, gray-haired Tuskegee Airman as he walked by, and Williams saluted them back. His lip quivered. He was doing his best to keep six decades' worth of emotions from gushing out.

The color guard stomped to a halt in front of the stage. After a bugler's soulful rendition of "The Star-Spangled Banner" and several vapid speeches and proclamation readings, Congressman Highledge draped a shiny gold medal over Williams's stiff shoulders, and people rose to their feet, their applause reverberating off the metal ceiling, concrete floor, and brick walls. Breanna found herself on her feet, too, clapping. She grew emotional as she watched Williams remove his glasses and dab tears with a red handkerchief.

"I just turned eighty-two," he said into the microphone. "But your warm welcome makes me feel like I'm twenty-two all over again."

He pointed to the bomber behind him and then to the old P-40 fighter plane about twenty feet to his right.

"I think I might put on my old pilot's uniform and take one of these suckers up for a spin—just for old time's sake," he said, eliciting a roar of laughter. "Seriously, though, I can't thank you enough for this tremendous honor and for your kindness. You made an old man feel proud. I will never ever forget this day, nor the guys I once flew beside. God bless you all."

Breanna made note of how, after the ceremony ended, virtually everyone in that old hangar approached Williams to shake his hand and thank him for his service to his country. Many asked to have their photo taken with him and handed him programs and books about the Tuskegee Airmen to sign. One young boy even brought a model of an old P-40 he had glued together.

"Yep, son, that's the one," Williams said, patting the kid on the head.

Breanna stood in the background, observing and jotting more notes. It made her feel good that Williams finally was being given his due decades after his heroics. He clearly was enjoying this opportunity to bask in the glow. Following nearly an hour of adoration, the crowd dispersed, and Breanna introduced herself.

"I'd be honored to talk to you, young lady," he said, shaking her hand. "Pull up a seat."

For the next forty-five minutes, Williams filled Breanna's microcassette tape recorder and notebook with stories about the bravery and camaraderie of the Tuskegee Airmen. She was totally enthralled as he described in meticulous detail close encounters with the Luftwaffe, the Nazi air force once regarded as the best in the world.

"Looking back, the odds were really stacked against us," Williams explained, with a sharpness that made Breanna feel as if he were recounting events from six minutes rather than six decades ago.

"See, the Germans supposedly had the most sophisticated fighter planes ever devised by man, and their pilots were vastly more experienced than we were. In some cases, they had thousands of more flying hours than us. And we were given either hand-me-down, defective, inferior planes, or newly designed planes that hadn't been battle-tested. We became sacrificial lambs, guinea pigs. We were at a huge disadvantage.

"But we were able to overcome because we had the best, brightest, and bravest of Black America in those cockpits. These were accomplished, intelligent men—many of them college graduates with something extra to prove.

I'd argue we had the tightest bond of any branch of the military back then, white or Black."

"Why do you think that was?" Breanna asked.

"Well, unlike the white American pilots or the Brits or the French, we were forced to fight two enemies," he said, collecting his thoughts. "Hitler and Jim Crow. And to be honest, Breanna, there were times when we couldn't tell which opponent was tougher."

Williams stroked the shiny gold congressional medal he'd been given. His eyes glistened as he stared off into the distance.

"Was a different world back then. Whole different world. Night and day. The military was segregated, as was just about everything in America. Don't forget, it wasn't till forty-seven—two years after we won the damn war—that Jackie Robinson broke baseball's color barrier. Schools were segregated. Colleges were segregated. Rosa Parks hadn't made her stand. Hell, we all still had to sit at the back of the bus.

"Colored folk were still getting lynched by them Ku Klux Klan bastards. Those hooded cowards were judge, jury, executioner. Hanged innocent Negroes from trees and made sure they did so in front of wives, kids, mothers, and sisters. Can you imagine being there, watching your daddy being hanged before your very eyes because he supposedly looked at a white woman the wrong way? Beyond horrible.

"And here we were, this tight-knit group of pilots—blood brothers, really. We were all worthy enough to die for our country, but not worthy enough to drink from the same water fountains as the white folks. Whole different world, young lady. Whole different world."

"You really put things into perspective, Mr. Williams."

"You know, young lady," he said, a smile creasing his face, "you remind me a lot of my late daughter."

"Well, thank you."

"She had this way about her, this thirst for learning. Was always trying to figure out what made people tick, ferreting out the truth, getting to the core, the heart of the matter. She'd asked question after question after question. And the more answers she received, the more questions she asked.

"There was many an occasion when she plumb tuckered me out. I'd say, 'Whoa, Doreen! You may have more questions, but I done run out of answers.'"

Breanna chuckled. "Well, thank you again, Mr. Williams. You've been so generous with your time. Loved your stories. You've given me so much compelling material I'm going to have a really tough time keeping it to just two thousand words."

"Pleasure's been all mine," he said, hugging her gently. "You know, I actually live in Buffalo and would love to chat again because there's an even better story to tell about a guy who was far more heroic than me."

"Really? I find that hard to believe."

"No, I'm dead serious. Dude's name was Wilmeth Sidat-Singh, and he was the person who inspired me and hundreds of other Negroes to become Tuskegee Airmen.

"Had the privilege to be at the institute same time he was, and we became best of friends. Sadly, Sing-Sing, as we called him, paid the ultimate sacrifice. And that's a damn shame, 'cause there's no telling how high he might have soared in life. Some of us believe he would have become the first Negro five-star general, maybe even the first Negro president of the United States of America.

"Do some homework on him, Breanna, and get back to me. But don't wait too long, 'cause in case you haven't noticed, I'm no spring chicken."

Breanna smiled, assuring him she would be in touch—and soon.

"It's really a whizbang of a story," Williams added as she began to walk away. "A story that's been lost—how do they say?—in the dustbins of history. Needs to be told. Gotta be told. Might be, for you, the story of a lifetime."

CHAPTER 5

"Wow, Breanna!" Erik Allen said, plopping down the morning edition of the *Buffalo Express* on her desk. "You crushed it, girl. Knocked it out of the freaking park. One A. Top of the fold. Lead story. A jump to two full pages inside."

"Must have been a slow news day," she joked, trying to suppress a grin.

"Slow news day, my ass! I even heard some of the morning DJs talking about it while I was driving to work. You gave Charles Williams his just due. Man's no longer a forgotten hero, thanks to you."

"Thanks, Erik. That's what I'm most pleased about. He's such a sweet guy. And what I wrote apparently was only the tip of the iceberg. There's so much more." She paused for a moment. "Erik, I've been meaning to apologize to you for unloading all my troubles on you a few weeks ago after I didn't get the Bills assignment."

"Breanna, no need at all to apologize. You were really upset."

"Yes, I was, but it was almost like I was taking out my anger toward others on you. You didn't deserve that."

"No worries. I'm just happy you didn't quit, because you're so damn talented."

"Thanks for being a shoulder to cry on and for listening to me vent. You're a good soul."

Just as she was finishing her sentence, Bucky Abramoski, the managing editor, stopped by to add his congratulations.

"Breanna, everyone in our morning editors' meeting was raving about the job you did. Even Stash piped up. And you know how grumpy he can be."

"Thanks, Bucky. That's nice to hear."

"That story really seemed to resonate with people. Don't hesitate to let me know if you come across any similar ideas."

"Well, Bucky, it's funny you should mention that, because when I finished interviewing Mr. Williams the other day, he mentioned another Tuskegee Airman with a hell of a story, and I began doing some research, and I think he's onto something."

"What's it about?"

"It's a long, complicated story, with lots of layers and lots of conflict. It's about a guy who died in a training mission back in 1943 but led quite the life. Was an African American quarterback at Syracuse long before most colleges were even admitting minorities, let alone allowing them to play quarterback and tell whites what to do. Clearly, a pioneer in that regard. Way ahead of his time. Also was a superb basketball player—kind of a two-sport star in the mold of a Bo Jackson or a Deion Sanders. Such a bright guy too—a premed student who wanted to become a doctor. Was a huge hero in the Black community. And on top of all that, he had to hide his blackness, play along with a ruse that he wasn't really Black. Like I said, so, so many layers."

"I'm totally intrigued. What's the guy's name?"

"Wilmeth Sidat-Singh."

"That's different."

"Yeah, there's a story behind that too. I'm supposed to meet with Mr.

Williams to find out more. Only problem is, this may take a lot of interviewing and a lot of digging to tell the story the right way."

"Well, Breanna, I think your timing might be perfect. Warren Buffett recently was in town for his annual visit to see how his beloved and only newspaper was doing, and when I asked him if there was anything he wanted to see more of from the *Express*, he said he wanted to see more compelling stories that haven't been told before. Maybe this Singh fellow might actually be worth a series."

"Wow," she said, rising from her chair. "That would be awesome."

"As your piece on Williams proved, people love these tales about heroes who fell through the cracks, never to be heard from again. I'd say go for it."

"Thanks, Bucky, but you'll have to talk to Stash, because, like I said, this story is really, really involved. To do it justice, it's going to take time and money. It could mean traveling to New York City and DC and Alabama and Syracuse and Detroit to interview people from Sidat-Singh's past. We might be talking several months of work, and I don't know if Stash is going to detach me from my general assignment duties in sports for that long."

"Don't worry about Stash. Like I said, this is the kind of thing Buffett is looking for, and when the richest man in the world talks, even a hardhead like Stash has to listen—unless, of course, he has a career death wish and no longer wants to be employed."

CHAPTER 6

The three-story house at 44 East Utica Street in North Buffalo had seen better days. As Breanna rang the doorbell, she couldn't help but notice all the spots where the paint had either faded or peeled away. Some of the exposed shingles were rotting.

"Welcome to my castle," Charles Williams said, opening the screen door. "Come on in, young lady."

Books and magazines were strewn about. The television was on, but muted, so Breanna couldn't make out what the CNN talking head was opining about on the screen. Williams took her coat and motioned for her to come over to a row of framed photographs on a mantelpiece above the fireplace.

"That's my late wife, Rachel," he said. "Fell in love with her the first time I gazed into her eyes on the dance floor."

"How'd you meet?"

"It was at a club for coloreds, on the other side of town in Tuskegee," he said. "Wilmeth, me, and some of the fellows left the base for a few hours one night. Might even have been in defiance of curfew. See, we were young men in search of libations and female companionship. I remember this quartet was playing Cab Calloway, Duke Ellington, Satchmo—music from our day— and it sounded *real* good. After all the crap we'd been through, we really needed to blow off a little steam. No better place for that than a dance floor.

"Wearing a uniform proved advantageous. Didn't pay for a single drink that night. And I think the ladies liked our fancy threads. I know Rachel did." Williams grabbed the photo so he could examine it more closely.

"Been gone twenty years this June," he said, placing the picture back on the walnut mantel. "Was diagnosed with breast cancer and never got better. Miss her dearly. We had quite the life together. So many good memories."

Williams pointed to another photograph. "This is my late daughter, Doreen, the one I said you reminded me of. Beautiful soul. She's the one who was always asking all those questions, trying to find answers, looking to make the world better."

"When did she die?"

"About three or four years after my wife. She was my rock when Rachel was ill, and then—wouldn't you know it—the same damn thing happened to her. Shattered my world twice over."

"I'm so sorry."

"Hey, what ya gonna do? Life ain't always fair. At least I had those two in my life for as long as I did. A lot of people had it worse. Look at my buddy Wilmeth. Fell in love, but never got a chance to marry or hold a child of his own in his arms.

"Speaking of Sing-Sing . . ." Williams picked up a photo of two men in their pilot uniforms, standing next to an old airplane. "Here's the two comrades in arms. Or should I say the two partners in crime? Man, those were the days. We was young, indestructible. Our entire lives were in front of us, but only one of us got to see how things would turn out."

Williams removed his glasses and dabbed his eyes with his handkerchief.

"Forgive me, young lady," he said. "Funny, ain't it? How a photo can take you back in time?"

Williams and Breanna walked over to the couch and sat down next to a coffee table, where two five-inch-thick scrapbooks were stacked.

"These are for you," he said. "They are filled with photographs and newspaper clippings Wilmeth's mom saved and gave to me. I figured they would be a starting point, give you a good foundation about my brother from a different mother."

Williams opened one of the scrapbooks and gently began turning the pages.

"Whew, was he good!" he said. "Look at this article. It's from when he was at DeWitt Clinton High School in the Bronx. Made first-team all-city in basketball. That's back when the best high school ball anywhere was being played on the playgrounds and gymnasiums of the Big Apple."

Breanna couldn't help but notice the strange-sounding names of the newspapers pasted onto the pages above the articles.

"I'm not familiar with these papers," she said, gazing at articles from the *Baltimore Afro-American*, *New Amsterdam News*, and *Chicago Defender*.

"That's understandable, because they no longer exist. Back in the day, newspapers were it. There was no . . . what's the word? Oh yeah, internet. Got most all your information from newspapers. And there were Black newspapers 'cross the country. They were quite popular with us Negroes because they wrote about us, whereas the white papers pretty much ignored us unless they wanted to write something bad about us. So that's where many of these stories are from. They're from papers that celebrated *us*.

"Now, that's not to say coloreds never got any sports coverage from the white papers, 'cause they did." Williams grabbed the other scrapbook and began thumbing through it.

"Here's what I was searching for. Look at that. A poem about Wilmeth by the great Grantland Rice. Granny was the best-known sportswriter of the time, maybe of all-time, and here he is, this prominent white dude singing the praises of Wilmeth after Sing-Sing led Syracuse to an incredible come-back victory. Whooeee! I'll never forget reading that story. Made him an even bigger hero to many of us because he managed to grab the attention of whites at a time when Jim Crow paid no heed to us, unless it was showing us in a bad light."

Williams reached for a shoebox and an address book and handed them to Breanna. "These are for you too. The box contains the letters I exchanged with Wilmeth and his fiancée and his mom and some of the other airmen who knew him and loved him. There's also letters from Joe Louis, Duke Ellington, and Cab Calloway, and some of his former college football team-mates and coaches—Marty Glickman, Duffy Daugherty, Bud Wilkinson, and others. I think you'll find them quite interesting. They'll give you plenty of insight into just how respected and what a big deal he was."

"Wow, this is all so helpful, Mr. Williams. Looks like you've done my research for me."

"I just think these things will help paint the picture. In that address book, you'll find numbers and addresses I've circled for people you can interview about Wilmeth—friends, relatives, etc."

"Mr. Williams, I'm already intrigued by his story. There's so many ques-tions I wish I could ask him."

"Well, young lady, unless you have a way of conducting interviews through séances, I think you'll be relying on other sources. By the way, I've been sitting here, babbling on like some crazy dude, and I didn't even offer you something to drink. Want some soda or coffee or a glass of water? I'm an old man, so I don't have much else around—unless, of course, you want some whiskey straight." He chuckled.

"No, thanks. I'm fine."

"Well, all right then."

"I'll get these scrapbooks and stuff back to you as soon as I go through everything and make copies."

"Breanna, you can have 'em. See, I won't be needing them. Don't mean to end this lovely visit on a down note, but I should probably tell you that I'm battling the big C. Got stage four pancreatic cancer. My doc tells me I got maybe a month or two before I meet my maker."

"Oh my God! I'm so sorry. Is there anything I can do?"

"Not unless you're a miracle worker and have a wand that makes cancer disappear. No, the only thing you can do for me is make sure Wilmeth's story gets told to as many people as possible."

Williams noticed Breanna's eyes welling. "Here, here, young lady," he said, hugging her. "No need to feel sorry for me. Christ, this old man's had one helluva ride. My only regrets were not having more time with Rachel, Doreen, and Sing-Sing."

Williams peered again at the photo on the mantelpiece of the two young pilots from a lifetime ago. "He was my buddy, my hero, my inspiration. Weren't for Sing-Sing, I never would have achieved what I did, never would have lived the life I lived. And there's a lot of other colored men from that era who felt the same way. So please, please get the word out. Let the world know there's been generations of Black men standing on that cat's shoulders."

CHAPTER 7

Arlington, Virginia, March 14, 2000

Breanna bounded off the Metro stop around 8:00 a.m. and walked hurriedly toward the massive cemetery where presidents, Supreme Court justices, and four hundred thousand military heroes were buried. She'd been there the day before, but there hadn't been time to soak much in because she had been consumed with the emotional task of covering Charles Williams's funeral.

Death had come much sooner than she expected—just three weeks after her visit to his Buffalo home—and it hit her hard. The story she filed about Williams's burial had not flowed easily. In fact, it was one of the most difficult stories she'd written in her still young journalism career. Several times she had to stop typing, her words interrupted by torrents of tears.

Although she'd only spent a few days of her life with Williams, she felt as if she had known him for decades. Part of that had to do with the way she had totally immersed herself in researching his life story. But it also had to do with the bond they formed. Their connection had been immediate—and deep. And then boom. Just like that, it was over. He was gone.

With time to kill before flying back to Buffalo the day after the funeral, Breanna felt compelled to return to Arlington National Cemetery so she could say goodbye without the rush and distraction of newspaper deadlines hanging over her head. She printed out a map at the information building near the cemetery's front gate and spent the next thirty minutes hoofing up and down the undulating pathways that snaked through the endless rows of white tombstones along the vast green expanse. Upon reaching her destination, she took a deep breath and clasped her hands in prayer.

"Mr. Williams, I just want to thank you for coming into my life. I only wish we could have had more time together. And I want you to know, you needn't worry. I'll do as you asked. I'll make sure Wilmeth is remembered."

Breanna patted the gravestone and noticed an empty rifle shell from the previous day's military salute glinting in the nearby grass. She picked it up and placed it in her purse.

There was one more thing she needed to do before departing Arlington for Dulles Airport. She pulled out the second map she had printed and began chugging down another path. There at the base of a hill, near Patton Drive and Clayton Avenue, she reached section eight of the cemetery and found the other tombstone she'd been looking for. She knelt and read the marble carving:

WILMETH W SIDAT-SINGH
DISTRICT OF COLUMBIA
2 LT US AIR CORPS
MARCH 13, 1918–MAY 9, 1943

"Hello, Lieutenant. I'm Breanna Shelton, and I'm a friend of a friend. Guess you could say I'm here on orders from Captain Charles Williams, your old buddy. For all I know, he's probably already briefed you, but just in case he hasn't . . . before saying farewell to this earthly realm, Mr. Williams asked me for a favor involving you. Wanted me to tell your story, but I'm going to need your help, big time, Lieutenant.

"Mr. Williams told me quite a bit about you, and I've been doing a lot of reading and researching. I'm going to talk to your relatives and friends and old teammates—anyone I can track down who knew you even a little.

"But that's not going to be enough, Lieutenant. I'm going to need to go back in time to your time. I'm going to need to get inside your head, understand what made you tick. I've got so many questions that by the time I'm through with you, your head's gonna be spinning."

She rose from her crouch and placed her hand on the weathered tombstone.

"So you better get used to me dogging you the next several months," she said, grinning. "Hopefully, we don't get sick of one another."

CHAPTER 8

Twenty-freaking-five!

As Breanna gazed at the puffy white clouds beneath the plane's wings on her flight back to Buffalo, she couldn't get that number out of her head.

Her age.

Wilmeth's age.

His, though, was frozen in time. He'd be twenty-five forever. And her? Well, she obviously hoped to live long enough to regale children, grand-children, maybe even great-grandchildren with stories about paths blazed, obstacles overcome, dreams realized.

But what if my life ended right here, right now? she thought to herself. *In a plane crash, no less. Just like Wilmeth's.*

For the first time in her young life, she was feeling her mortality. And it was quite unnerving.

Twenty-freaking-five!

She began assessing her own journey. Where she'd been. Where she hoped to go. And how Wilmeth would accompany her on her travels the next several months, if not longer. They'd fly as copilots on this trip back in time. He would teach her about him, and she would pass those lessons on to others through her writings.

Certainly, that number they shared—the one now causing considerable angst—was part of their connection. And so, too, was the skin-color crap they'd been forced to endure. She certainly didn't profess to have it as tough as Wilmeth by any means. After all, no one had forced her to change her identity or drink from "coloreds only" water fountains or live off campus at Syracuse because she was Black. But in some respects, Breanna Shelton's America wasn't dramatically different from Wilmeth Sidat-Singh's America. It hadn't evolved nearly enough. A half century later, barriers persisted. Skin color still mattered. So did gender. And religion. And so many other things that shouldn't have mattered at all.

Breanna thought back to her youth in her mostly white, Irish Catholic neighborhood in South Buffalo. It wasn't easy being one of the few Black families there, but the Sheltons kept a low profile and eventually won over some people. But not all. As she would painfully learn, some hatred, some ignorance, is too deeply entrenched. It simply can't be overcome.

Breanna smiled as she thought about her next-door neighbors, the O'Briens, and how Davey and Meghan would call her their "second daughter," often inviting her on outings for ice cream or trips to Fantasy Island Amusement Park or their camp in the Adirondacks. Breanna became especially close to their biological daughter, Molly. The two friends would stay in touch long after they went their separate ways following high school.

Sadly, not all the neighbors were as welcoming or as enlightened as the O'Briens. In fact, many of them wished the Sheltons had never moved there, because they believed the presence of Blacks had driven down their property values. Some wouldn't even bother to wave to Breanna or her brother or parents. They'd just stare coldly, make the Sheltons feel unwanted, as if they didn't exist—or worse, as if they *shouldn't* exist.

Breanna and her brother were taught by their parents this was the harsh, cold way of the world—that they'd have to put up with it, suck it up. And for the most part, that's what they did. But on those extra-nasty occasions when someone called her an epithet or insinuated she was dumb, Breanna felt compelled to bloody a nose rather than turn a cheek. That got people's attention in a hurry, because she packed a mighty wallop.

Her dad and mom wouldn't be pleased whenever she decided to take matters into her own hands. "Too many ignorant people out there to fight 'em all," they would tell her. "Hard as it might be, you just gotta do your best to ignore them."

Early on, sports became a big part of Breanna's life. It helped her cope with the racial divide, earned her some begrudging respect. She was a natural at just about everything she tried, and depending on the season, she'd be outdoors playing baseball, football, basketball, and street hockey, mostly with and against boys her age and older.

Her athletic genes and love of sports had been passed down from her father. Thomas Shelton had been a high school football legend in Buffalo. He was so good people started calling him Touchdown Thomas, because that's often what happened when he touched the ball.

Recruiters from several colleges in the East courted him heavily, but none offered a scholarship. Some coaches suggested he could "walk on," and if he performed well enough to make the team and kept his grades up, a scholarship would be forthcoming his sophomore year. Hailing from a family of six siblings raised by a single mom meant money was tight, so paying tuition for a year wasn't an option. It also didn't help matters when Shelton got his girlfriend pregnant his senior year of high school. With a wife and son to support, he dropped out of school not long after scoring his final TD and found a job driving an eighteen-wheeler for a grocery store chain. He had promised his mother and the girlfriend, who became his wife, that he'd get his GED, then enroll in a community college. But that never happened. Life got in the way.

To supplement his income, Shelton hawked beer and programs at Buffalo Bills games at War Memorial Stadium, the antiquated concrete bowl known affectionately and derisively as the Rockpile. It was an ideal side job because he had become a huge fan of the team during its nascent rock 'em, sock 'em American Football League days. Over time, the personable, gregarious Shelton formed friendships with several Black players on the team, including star fullback Cookie Gilchrist and wide receiver Elbert Dubenion, whose blazing speed prompted teammates and sportswriters to dub him Golden Wheels.

When the Bills moved from the Rockpile into suburban Rich Stadium in the fall of 1973, Shelton followed as a beer vendor and usher. The rowdy fans who sat in the end-zone section came to love him. Word eventually got out about his high school gridiron prowess and fancy nickname, and soon everybody was calling him Touchdown Thomas, or simply Touchdown. During the Bills' lean years—of which there were many—the diehards would implore Touchdown to put down his beer crate and put on a helmet and shoulder pads and show the professionals how it was done.

Two years after Shelton and a sublime Bills running back named O. J. Simpson helped christen the new stadium, Breanna was born, and during her toddling years, she adopted her father's passion for a football team that had become a source of pride and agony for a beaten-down region. To hear the late-night talk-show comedians blather on in their monologues, one would have thought Buffalo experienced blizzards in July. As a result of being the butt of jokes about lake-effect snow and an economy still reeling from the steel mill closures of the 1980s, Buffalonians bore chips on their shoulders the size of NFL stadiums.

They were chips Shelton and his daughter bore too. With pride.

Shelton's son, Rasheen, never cared much for sports. Jazz was his passion, and he'd spent hours upon hours listening to the riffs of famed guitarists, such as George Benson or Buffalo-born Jim Hall. Though Shelton would rather have spent time shooting baskets or playing catch with Rasheen, he did his best to fuel his son's love of music, even surprising him one Christmas with a brand-new Fender Telecaster guitar. Cost him $250, but he didn't care.

Breanna, meanwhile, needed no coaxing to play ball. She was, in the vernacular of the day, a tomboy, and Shelton was only too happy to have someone he could play H-O-R-S-E with, toss spirals to, and bat against in Wiffle Ball. He took pride that she was like him—someone for whom every sport came easily. And of all the ones she played, she loved football most. But after a few years of Pop Warner, in which she more than held her own against the boys, she was forced to call it quits. No girls were allowed on her schools' football teams, and that irked her no end.

"Daddy, I'm beating those boys' butts," she complained. "Why can't I keep playing until they show they can stop me?"

"Just the way it is, Bre," he said softly. "Nothing we can do about it."

"Daddy, you and mama are always telling me that's just the way it is, like some broken record. It's kind of like when you tell me, 'because I said so.' That's not an acceptable answer."

"You're absolutely right, Bre. Not an acceptable answer. But it's the only answer we got, so you need to move on."

Breanna moved on to basketball, and she did so the way she did most things—full bore. She wound up earning all-city honors at Bennett High School, the alma mater of a former St. Bonaventure and Detroit Pistons Hall of Fame center. Breanna was so good a sportswriter at the *Buffalo Express* began calling her the "female Bob Lanier." A part of her loved the comparisons to the best high school hoopster ever to come out of the Queen City. High praise indeed. But a part of her took the compliment as a dig.

"How would Bob Lanier like it if he were referred to as the male Breanna Shelton?" she groused to Molly one day.

"Well, Bre, look at it this way," Molly responded, "at least they aren't comparing you to some crummy player."

"Yeah, girl, you're right. Sometimes I'm too intense for my own good.

All I see in the sun shower is the damn rain."

"That's all right, Bre. That intensity is what sets you apart."

Breanna's father rarely missed a game and could be heard bellowing above the din of the loudest gymnasiums, exhorting her on and berating any official with the temerity to make a call against his girl. He clearly was living his life vicariously through her. She was taking care of his unfinished business.

It always gnawed at him that he never received his high school diploma, and he was determined to make sure neither Rasheen nor Breanna repeated his mistake. Which is why he was constantly harping on the importance of education and a diploma, reminding them more times than they cared to hear that it was their ticket out. Breanna needed no reminders. She was precocious, learning to read and write before she turned three. Her aptitude for storytelling became quickly apparent. Whenever she joined her dad at Bills games—or any sporting event, for that matter—she'd tell him things about players and strategy that shocked him and the people sitting next to them.

By her senior year, Breanna was being recruited by several major basketball colleges. Lanier even phoned, in hopes of convincing her to become the latest basketball star to go from Bennett to Bonaventure. She was thrilled he'd reached out to her—and was oh so tempted to tell him how there was a part of her that didn't like the comparisons the *Express* sportswriter had made, but she kept quiet and thanked him for taking the time to call.

She ultimately decided on Syracuse because of its famed journalism school.

"Girl, your pappa's so proud of you and can't wait to drive over to Syracuse to see you play," Shelton told her after she broke the news to him about her choice of colleges. "You're gonna do great."

"Thanks, Daddy."

"Now, I know I've told you this a thousand times—and I'll probably tell you a thousand times more—but, girl, you need to remember that basketball ain't going on forever, just like football didn't go on forever for me. At some point, in everyone's career—no matter how great you are—they suck the air out of that dang ball. No more dribbling. No more jumping. No more shooting. Game done for good. Then whaddaya gonna do?"

Breanna knew exactly what she was going to do.

She was going to smash every scoring record at SU. And she was going to write sports for the school newspaper. And she was going to immerse herself in her journalism studies before starting her career as a sportswriter. She might even come back to Buffalo someday and cover the Bills.

CHAPTER 9

Breanna had gotten off to a magnificent start on the basketball court not long after arriving on the Syracuse campus in late August 1993. It was apparent from her first practice she was head and shoulders above her Syracuse teammates. A woman among girls.

"We've got something special here," SU basketball coach Jane Owens marveled to one of her assistants after watching Breanna easily dribble past three defenders and lay the ball into the basket with her left hand. "My, oh my. She could be our ticket to the promised land."

Owens's belief that she was witnessing a once-in-a-lifetime player became more fervent in the coming days and weeks as Breanna continued dominating practices and scrimmages. She was unstoppable.

Then, one afternoon, a week before the season opener against Colgate, Breanna came down hard on her right leg after soaring above teammates for a rebound. Everyone in the gym heard a sickening loud snap, like a tree branch breaking in two, as Breanna crumpled to the floor. Owens blew her whistle to halt play and sprinted over.

"Back up! Back up! Give her some room," Owens yelled.

A trainer came running with an ice pack but quickly realized it would do little good.

"Coach, we better call an ambulance," he advised.

By this time the pain had become excruciating. Breanna started screaming.

"Oh my God! Oh my God! Oh my God!"

Owens and several of her players felt queasy when they saw that Breanna's right foot was facing almost in the opposite direction of her knee.

"It's going to be all right, Breanna," Owens said, gripping her hand tightly while averting her eyes from the misshapen leg.

"Help me! Help me! Please, help me!" Breanna screeched. "Please! Please! Help me!"

The ambulance arrived in a matter of minutes, and medics gave Breanna a sedative before ensconcing her leg in an Aircast and placing her on a stretcher.

"Please call my parents!" Breanna cried out as the medics closed the ambulance door, flipped on the siren, and sped away from the Manley Field House parking lot toward nearby Upstate Medical Center.

Seven hours later, a groggy Breanna blinked her eyes a few times and focused in on her father and a doctor standing next to her hospital bed. The anesthesia was wearing off.

"Daddy, am I going to be all right?"

Thomas Shelton nodded. "Of course you are, Bre."

She looked at the cast that ran from her right ankle to her right thigh.

"Doctor, what happened? Am I going to be all right? Am I going to be able to play again?"

Johnathan Blank, the team orthopedic, clasped her left hand in his.

"Yes, Breanna, you're going to be fine."

"But what about playing, Doc? Am I going to be able to play basketball again? I need to know."

"I would love to tell you yes, but if I did so I'd be giving you false hope. See, this wasn't just a simple tearing of ligaments. You've suffered a horrific injury that severed one of your arteries. You spent six hours on the operating table, and it was touch and go whether we were going to be able to save your leg. Fortunately, we were."

Breanna couldn't believe what she was hearing. Her mouth felt as if it were filled with cotton balls. She sipped from a Styrofoam cup of water.

"I've been at this for thirty years, and I've never seen a leg injury as serious as this one. The good news is, you should be able to walk without a limp after undergoing extensive physical therapy. But—and I know this is tough to hear—you shouldn't try playing basketball again. You'll be too susceptible to this happening again."

Breanna was speechless.

"Try to focus on the good stuff. You'll be able to walk, even run again, as long as there is no cutting involved. You'll still be able to do a lot of physical activity, just not basketball."

Breanna grabbed a tissue from the box on her bed and dabbed away some tears.

"Can we get you anything for the pain?"

"No, thanks, Doc. I'm fine. I'd just like to be alone."

She recalled that conversation with her father about how eventually the air gets sucked out of the ball. She just never imagined it would happen this soon.

***

The four years had flown by swiftly, and as Breanna boxed up her belongings from her seventeenth-floor room in Lawrinson Hall and hugged her suitemates goodbye following commencement in the spring of 1997, she couldn't help but feel nostalgic. Those dreams of becoming the all-time leading basketball scorer in school history had been dashed before they began. But she'd always had a fallback plan, and so, after basketball was taken from her, she immersed herself in her studies, graduating magna cum laude with a dual major in newspaper journalism and African American history.

Friendships she had made would last a lifetime. She'd never forget all the crazy parties in her dorm and at the watering holes on Marshall Street, especially at the Varsity, where she long ago lost track of the number of pizza slices and pitchers of beer she'd consumed. Nor would she ever forget all those late-night hours putting the student newspaper to bed. She became the *Daily Orange*'s first Black female sports columnist and editor, enabling her to compile a robust, clip-filled portfolio good enough to convince the *Buffalo Express* to hire her right out of school.

The racism and misogyny she grew up with in South Buffalo had been prevalent at Syracuse University, too, but most of her classmates were more accepting than her old neighbors had been. Yes, some still sniped when she landed those coveted *Daily Orange* jobs—said she wasn't "qualified" and only got the positions because of her gender and race. It hurt to hear, but she had developed plenty of scar tissue on her soul along the way. She was determined not to let hatred and ignorance derail her ambitions.

The critics could think what they wanted. She knew the truth. She had earned both positions. Nobody had given her a damn thing.

While covering sports at Syracuse, Breanna became quite familiar with the school's rich football history, particularly the tales about the famed running backs who had worn jersey number forty-four. She was especially taken with the poignant story of Ernie Davis, who after becoming the first African American to win the prestigious Heisman Trophy as college's football's top player had his life cut short by leukemia. But in four years on campus, she'd never heard the name Wilmeth Sidat-Singh. It wasn't until that interview with Charles Williams that her education about this lost hero began.

The lessons would be life changing.

CHAPTER 10

Washington, DC, April 10, 1925

"Guess, you showed that jerk Tobias a thing or two, huh, Wil?"

"Yeah, that was sweet, shutting up his big piehole. Dang fool, talking like he was Babe Ruth or something."

"Can you believe that mouth of his? 'Hey, Lil' Willy, serve up dat powder-puff fastball, 'cause I'm gonna knock it all da way to da White House. President Coolidge gonna say, 'Where da hell dis come from?'"

Wilmeth and his best friend, Abraham Lincoln Warren, chortled as they replayed the moment.

"Some rag arm, huh, Wil? Blew three speed balls by him. Swing-miss. Swing-miss. Swing-miss. Bullet Joe Rogan woulda been proud."

Wilmeth smiled at the thought of the three heaters that struck out and shut up leather-lunged Tobias Johnson. The excitement ended a glorious sunrise-to-sunset day of pickup baseball on the stone-strewn dirt lot, next to Lucretia Mott Elementary School, just a few blocks from their row house on 313 T Street in northwest DC.

"Whew, Abe, I'm so thirsty. I'm going to put my mouth under that faucet and drink a gallon of water when we git home."

"Me too."

As the boys turned the corner onto T Street, they saw Wilmeth's cousin Billie barreling toward them.

"Wil! Wil! Wil!" she shouted, gasping for air. "You got to get home right away."

"What the heck's wrong with you, girl?"

"Your daddy's dead, Wilmeth Webb," she said, wrapping her arms around him. "That's what's wrong!"

"What you talking about?" he said, pushing her away.

"He had a big stroke or something while waiting on folks at his pharmacy. Your mama just called the church long distance from Florida and spoke to Pastor Sanders, who just stopped by to deliver the news. Said your daddy fell to the floor like a chopped-down tree. Died immediately."

"No! No!" Wilmeth said, his eyes welling. "That can't be true. You're lying, Adelaide! You're pulling one of them cruel pranks. You want to say you made me cry so you can tell all your girlfriends and have a good laugh."

"No, I'm not. I swear."

"Leave me alone."

Dazed and confused, Wilmeth took off like a triggered bullet, sprinting down the street toward his aunt Bea's house, where he lived during the school year while his parents tended to the family pharmacy in Tampa. The seven-year-old had never run so swiftly in his life. He couldn't wait to get to aunt Bea's so she could put Adelaide's nasty, horrible prank to rest.

"Please, God! Please, God!" he cried out as he ran. "Please, make Daddy OK."

***

Although it had lasted nearly three hours, the funeral seemed a blur. The old Negro spirituals. The booming sermon by Pastor Emmanuel Sanders. The hundreds of folks coming up to him and his mother, telling them what a fine, upstanding man Elias Webb had been—a true pillar of the community, an inspiration to Black folks everywhere.

Wilmeth listened and nodded. He felt numb, disoriented, detached. That image of his father lying in that coffin was seared in his memory bank. He couldn't get over how peaceful he looked, like he was just taking a nap or something. Wilmeth had to keep fighting a powerful compulsion to lean into the casket and shake his daddy awake. What the third grader wouldn't give to catch his father up on how he was doing in school and how he had struck out the neighborhood bully on three straight pitches. Elias Webb would have been so proud. Wilmeth was certain of that. But there would be no more conversations, at least not two-way ones. There would be no waking from this nightmare. This thing known as death was so permanent, so final, and Wilmeth was having a terrible time trying to make sense of it all.

A slight smile creased his face as he remembered those bare-handed games of catch when his daddy regaled him with stories about great Black ballplayers, like Oscar Charleston and Rube Foster. Webb would talk about how they were every bit the equal of, if not better than white legends such as Ruth and Washington's own pitching star, Walter Johnson. Webb mentioned how he had been a fine ballplayer himself, and that if it weren't for an arm injury he might have given Negro baseball a shot too. But God had grander plans.

"Oh, I was right angry with the big guy in the sky when my arm went permanently lame," he told Wilmeth during their last long conversation a few months earlier. "Whew! Did I ever curse him. 'What you doing, Lord, snatching my dream away like that? I didn't deserve that.' Took me a dang long time to stop feeling sorry for myself.

"Learned the hard way, son, that God does everything for a reason, and I guess, in my case, he wanted me to stop relying on my arm and start using my brain. Fortunately, he blessed me with some smarts, and when I no longer could throw that ball through a brick wall, I had to find something new to dream on. If I didn't, I'd wind up moping around like some of your uncles and cousins, who thought they could find life's answers in a bottle of whiskey.

"It all turned in high school. Had this teacher, Mr. Belmont, who took a liking to me. He taught science, and I showed some aptitude for the subject, really liked it. Mr. B encouraged me to look at careers in science. I told him I'd like to go to college, and he suggested Howard University, the all-Negro school right here in the District. So that's where I went, and you know what? While I was there, I decided I wanted to become a doctor, even though there weren't many colored doctors at the time. And I might have become one, too, if I didn't become queasy when it came time to cutting open those dead bodies, those cadavers. Never could stomach that, and if you can't deal with flesh and blood, you can't be a doctor. Simple as that.

"So I was a little lost at that point—just like I'd been when baseball was taken from me. One day I sat down with a guidance counselor. Told him I had wanted to become a doctor because I felt I could really help our people get the medical help they needed, the help they weren't getting, 'cause they were Negroes. And he says to me, 'Eli, there are plenty of professions that help people. If you want to stay in the medical profession, you could become a pharmacist.' I liked the thought of that. That way I wouldn't have to deal with blood. Only cutting I would be doing would be on those little pills.

"Becoming one of the first Negro pharmacists sounded really cool 'cause there were even fewer of them than there were Negro doctors. Being a rare bird, a pioneer of sorts, kinda appealed to me.

"Wil, you wouldn't believe the feeling I had when I graduated. Different feeling than I got from playing ball. When I got that sheepskin in my hand, I thought to myself, *Lordy, Lordy, imagine that? Son of a slave now a pharmacist*. I hope you can have that feeling someday."

"I hope so, too, Daddy."

"There's a saying about God working in mysterious ways. Sure did with me. Took away something I loved and replaced it with something I was meant to be."

In the days, weeks, and months following his father's death, Wilmeth found himself angry at God. Angry at everybody, really. His father had been a good man, a kind man, a man devoted to helping others—and look what happened to him. Cut down in his prime.

"Mama, what kind of God does something like that?" Wilmeth asked Pauline Webb one night.

"Wil, sometimes God calls the angels on Earth back to heaven to help him out, and I guess he needed Daddy at this time."

"Well, I needed him too. Why would he take a father away from his son? Why would he take a man other folks needed too? Why should I worship a God who does something that cruel? To hell with God."

"Wilmeth Webb," she said, raising her eyebrows and voice. "That's blasphemous. Don't you ever, ever talk to the Almighty like that again! Why, he could strike you with lightning."

Wilmeth felt like God already had.

CHAPTER 11

Sports wound up being Wilmeth's saving grace in the aftermath of his father's death. Sandlots and basketball courts became sanctuaries of sorts, places where a fatherless son could take out his anger on balls and peers.

Wilmeth was gifted at everything he tried. A natural. Though average size, he was a man among boys, regardless of the sport. He could throw farther and harder, jump higher and longer, and run faster than his peers. He also could outmuscle them when need be, displaying the strength of a boy twice his size. Those who challenged him to a fight soon regretted it. Wilmeth knew how to use his fists—and use them well.

He also knew how to outthink his opponents. He had an uncanny knack for seeing things unfold on the diamond, football field, and basketball and tennis courts before others could. Seemed like he was always a step or two ahead of people.

Peers took notice. They wanted him on their teams, and they wanted the bat or the ball in his hands when it mattered most. When Wilmeth started getting involved in organized sports, coaches began recruiting him too. He forged strong relationships with several of them. They became father figures who helped fill part of the enormous void left by Elias Webb.

Like his daddy, Wilmeth was an inquisitive sort, and occasionally that curiosity would get him in trouble. Although they had been warned by their elders, Wilmeth and his friends sometimes ventured beyond the Jim Crow boundaries of segregated Washington. They were intrigued to see how the other side lived and visited the historical sites they'd only heard or read about. One early summer morning, Wilmeth and Abe decided to get truly adventurous and walk twenty blocks to take a look at the White House.

"Wonder what it's like inside that big ol' mansion," Wilmeth asked, peering through the black metal fence upon their arrival.

"We'll never know, Wil. Only way a Negro's gonna git inside there is by doing laundry, cleaning rooms, and peeling potatoes."

"Wouldn't it be something if one day there was a Negro president of the United States?"

"Wil, ain't never gonna happen."

"Don't ever say never, Abe. Someday America might change. Someday colored folks gonna live the dream too."

"Boy, you out of your mind."

"No, I'm not. I'm just an optimist."

"Optimist who needs a whoop upside the head. If you really think they're gonna let some Negro in that big ol' house and boss white folk around, then you need your big brain examined."

Wilmeth smiled and shoved his friend good-naturedly.

"Hey, Abe, let's go see that big statue of the white guy you're named after."

After walking several more blocks and reaching the Lincoln Memorial, the boys had built up quite a thirst.

"Let's wet our whistles, Abe."

"Hey, Wil, do you think it's OK for us to drink from this fountain?"

"What you talking about?"

"Well, look at that."

Wilmeth gazed above the fountain. In eight-inch block letters, a sign read: "WHITES ONLY."

"Ah, screw it, Abe. We'll do it quickly. Nobody'll know."

As they took turns slurping water and splashing it on their faces, they heard a ruckus nearby. They turned to see five white teenagers making a beeline toward them.

"What the fuck you doing?" screamed a tall, muscular, blond-haired kid who must have weighed at least two hundred pounds.

"Don't mean any trouble," Wilmeth stammered. "Just getting a drink."

"Boy, you too dumb to read?" sneered another as they circled Wilmeth and Abe.

"Oh, sorry about that. I didn't see it."

"Didn't see it. You must not only be dumb but blind. Sign's as obvious as that monkey face of yours."

"Boy," chimed another teenager, "your fountains are way over there. That's where coloreds drink."

"Oh, you're right. Thanks for letting us know."

"You giving me sass, boy?"

"No, not at all. Hey, we've never been here before, so we didn't know."

The big, blond-haired kid, the gang's ringleader, edged closer to Wilmeth.

"Fellas, I think we should tell the cops that some colored boys took a swig from this fountain. They're probably going to have to put in a new one because this one's contaminated. Wouldn't want anyone catching any Negro diseases."

"Good point, John," piped up another member of the gang. "But before we turn these boys over to the authorities, I think we should teach 'em a lesson or two."

Wilmeth and Abe could feel their hearts pounding as the five boys closed in on them.

"Run, Abe! Run!"

The two barreled through their would-be punishers and bolted down the walk as if they were running for their lives, which they were. The self-anointed vigilantes gave chase, but Wilmeth and Abe were much too fast. After about thirty futile seconds, the gang huffed and puffed to a halt.

By the time Wilmeth and Abe made it back to their neighborhood, they were drenched.

"Wow," Wilmeth said, gasping for air. "I thought we was goners."

"Wil, you think they would have lynched us?"

"Have no idea. And wasn't about to find out."

"Abe, make sure you don't tell anyone about what we did, or we're going to get a licking to match the one we just avoided."

"Don't worry. Our secret."

After catching his breath and composing himself, Wilmeth walked into his row house. A bundle of newspapers were stacked on the kitchen table. His face lit up. He couldn't wait to dig into them. Each Tuesday, they would arrive, like a present waiting to be unwrapped, copies of the *Baltimore Afro-American* and *Chicago Defender* and *New York Amsterdam News* and other weeklies. Wilmeth loved reading them because the writing by Blacks for Blacks made the athletes jump off the page.

Wilmeth's parents had taught him to read at a young age, and he would devour newspapers front to back. His favorite section was the one devoted to sports. He loved reading about his idols in the Negro Leagues and about the African Americans who were making their marks in football, basketball, and boxing. He would show the articles, photographs, and drawings to his friends, and then they would head outdoors and make believe they were Oscar Charleston or Paul Robeson or Jack Johnson.

"One of these days, Wil, they're gonna be writing about you," Abe and the other neighborhood kids would tease. "Gonna be a big picture of you in your Homestead Grays uniform with big headlines saying, 'Wilmeth Sidat-Singh: Sports Hero.'"

Wilmeth would smile whenever they razzed him that way.

He wasn't one to boast, but he had his dreams. And they were big ones. He'd been blessed with brains and brawn. Yes, he wanted to become a sports star. But he also wanted to be more. He wanted to do good too. Not just for himself but for others. He thought about what his daddy had told him during that last long conversation they had, how God works in mysterious ways. Wilmeth was excited about the future. He wondered how his mystery would unfold.

CHAPTER 12

While working in the pharmacy she and her late husband were establishing in Tampa in the late 1920s, Pauline Webb had gained considerable knowledge about medicine, pharmacology, and people in need. That all would come in handy after her husband's death precipitated the closing of their drugstore. She would need to find gainful employment back in DC, and ultimately did so by securing a job as a secretary at Howard University's College of Medicine.

Wilmeth couldn't have been more pleased by this development, because it meant he could continue living in his hometown and spend more time with her. There had been long stretches in recent years when he had been separated from his parents, and he believed there would come a time after they got the pharmacy up and running that he would have to leave his friends and relatives in Washington for good and join his parents year-round in Tampa. That prospect left him torn. On the one hand, he didn't want to leave the District. But on the other, he longed to see his parents more often.

His father originally wanted to set up shop in Washington, but business loans for Black entrepreneurs were nonexistent, so he had to take on a series of odd jobs just to make ends meet. These included delivering newspapers, blocks of ice, and bottles of milk. It was backbreaking work, and it paid little, but Elias Webb had no choice.

One day two men from Tampa visited him with a proposition and a plea. They told Webb there was a dire need in that Florida city for a pharmacist to serve Negroes, something the white-run drugstores refused to do. "There's not a single apothecary in the colored neighborhoods," they told Webb. "We're desperate. People are suffering. Some dying. We'll do whatever you need to make it work. We'll even give you a building rent-free so you and your wife have a place to stay."

Webb thanked the men and told them he would get back to them after talking to his wife. The decision was not clear-cut. DC was home, and as tough as times were for him and his family, they had a great support system of relatives and friends there. Everyone had everyone else's back. He also realized how difficult it would be to start a pharmacy from scratch. He'd be working twelve-hour days, seven days a week, and Pauline would be doing the same.

"It's a huge risk," he told his wife.

"Yes, but it's what you went to school for—it's your calling," she said. "I'll help out. We can make it work."

"But we won't know nobody there. And what we going to do with Wilmeth? He just started school. Neither of us is going to have time to raise him and tend to the pharmacy too. It's not like he's got brothers and sisters. He's an only child."

"We'll leave him here with my sister, Bea. She'll look after him, and he'll have all his cousins. They're like brothers and sisters to him. And he'll have all his friends too. Plus, he'll be able to stay in school, and when it ends, he can come down and live with us until it starts up again."

"Oh, I don't know. My daddy left me when I was a baby. Never knew the man. And I swore I'd never do that to my children. They would have a father."

"But Wilmeth has a daddy. A daddy who loves him. It's only gonna be a year or two. Once we get it going, and we get some help, we'll bring him down permanently. We'll build our life there."

"But what if we don't get it going? What if we fail?"

"Then we pick up and come back home to the District."

Webb hemmed and hawed the next few days, assessing the pros and cons, before finally agreeing with Pauline to give it a go.

It was hard on Wilmeth at first, but he eventually got over his separation anxiety. Frequent letters from his parents helped soften the blow, as did the love he received from his aunt, uncle, cousins, and friends.

Webb and his wife quickly discovered just how enormous the challenges of launching and sustaining a drugstore in an impoverished neighborhood would be. Many patients couldn't afford the medications and other products they needed, and Webb, the Good Samaritan, wasn't about to turn them away. So he allowed them to run up a tab. Though Pauline admired her husband's big heart, she told him they had to start drawing the line, or they'd soon go broke.

Like the rope in a tug-of-war, Webb felt pulled in different directions. The cumulative stress eventually became overwhelming. Several relatives believed it triggered the stroke that killed him.

Fortunately, Pauline and Wilmeth had a large family to lean on following Elias's death. Relatives had played parental roles in raising Wilmeth, and several of his cousins had become the brothers and sisters he never had. Single mother and only child would not go wanting. They would have a roof over their heads and food on their plates. And in time, they would have much, much more.

Roughly a year after Elias's death, Pauline met a Howard University Medical School student who was completing his residency. Samuel Sidat-Singh had stopped by her office to fill out some paperwork.

"I'm sorry," she said, smiling, after he nervously blurted out his name. "Samuel Who-Dat What?"

He laughed. "Sidat-Singh," he said. "But you can call me Sam."

"Well, hello, Sam. Nice to meet you."

"Nice to meet you too. Dean Dixon wanted me to stop by to fill out some graduation paperwork."

"Ah yes. Here it is, Sam. You can take this with you and drop it back here at your convenience."

"Thank you so much, Miss Webb."

"You can call me Pauline."

"Thank you, Miss—er. I'm sorry. Thank you, Pauline."

As he went to leave, Sidat-Singh struggled to get the door open.

"It sticks a bit, Sam. Sometimes have to give the knob a nudge."

"Thank you, Miss—oops. There I go again. Thank you, Pauline. See you later."

"See you later, Sam."

It had been a while since Pauline had experienced the stirrings of romantic feelings. Curiosity piqued, she just had to find out more about this doctor-to-be with the infectious smile, pleasant demeanor, and foreign accent. In the adjoining room, she found his folder in the file cabinet of current students.

Samuel Sidat-Singh

Hometown: New Delhi, India

Schooling: Cromwell Science and Preparatory School, London, England

Honors: Valedictorian

Pauline leafed through a few more pages before stumbling upon his application essay:

First and foremost, I want to attend Howard University's College of Medicine because of its lofty academic reputation. That goes without saying. But my desire goes well beyond that. From the time I was a young boy, I've been inspired by the courage and determination of the American Negro; the persecution they've been forced to endure and the trials and tribulations they've had to overcome based solely on the fact their skin color is not white.

Dealing with discrimination is something I, too, have endured in my own life, though it was of a somewhat different nature. India has long been under rule of the British Empire, and although all men are supposed to have equal rights in our democracy, that hasn't been the case in the Commonwealth. Many natives of India are treated like second-class citizens by the white ruling colonists. Through much of my schooling, here and in London, I've experienced what it's like to be treated differently, inferiorly. Though my skin is not black, it is darker than most of the students I studied with, especially when I was in London. I've been called hurtful names, despicable, demeaning names. I've been made fun of because of my accent and my surname.

So, in many respects, I can sympathize and empathize with the American Negro.

My dream is to come to America, earn a medical degree, and become a citizen of the United States. And I hope to put my degree to work serving people in Negro communities, places where medical care often is denied based solely on the color of one's skin.

Pauline was wowed by Sidat-Singh's essay. Such heart. Such eloquence. It reminded her of Elias. The spark she felt moments earlier was now a full-fledged fire. Though several years older, she was determined to get to know this young man even better. She couldn't wait for him to return with those completed graduation forms.

When he stopped by the next day, Pauline didn't waste any time letting her intentions be known.

"Sam, I hope you won't think I'm being too forward, but I was wondering if you would like to go for a drink sometime."

"Ah, sure. Sure. I would like that."

"There's a bar called the Jefferson Jazz Club just a few blocks from here. If you'd like, you could meet me here after work someday. I finish up at six."

"How about today?"

"Whoa! You don't waste any time, now do ya?"

"Neither," he said, chuckling, "do you."

They wound up having a marvelous time, filling each other in on their respective lives and even taking to the dance floor.

Their conversation continued for another half hour after they left the club, and Sam walked her home. About the only thing that didn't go well was the dirty look they had gotten from the bartender.

"Pay no heed to him," Pauline said. "He clearly didn't think you were dark enough to be with me. To hell with him."

Pauline and Sam's romance blossomed rapidly. Neither was deterred by the disapproval some, including several of Pauline's relatives, expressed about her dating someone who wasn't Black and someone several years her junior. Most of them, though, were happy Pauline had found love again after Elias's tragic death. Even Wilmeth, who had some resentment initially, was won over by Sam's sincerity and kindness. Sam wound up taking Wilmeth to several Negro League and Washington Senators games, where Wil educated him about America's national pastime.

"Reminds me of the cricket we play in my country," Sam said. "You throw the ball and hit it and run from here to there."

After about six months, Sam worked up the courage to ask Pauline to marry him. She said yes. Both were a little anxious about breaking the news to Wilmeth. They worried he might be upset because it was coming less than two years after he lost his father. But Wilmeth had no issues with the timing.

"Mama, I just want you to be happy," he said. "If you're happy, I'm happy. And I'm sure Daddy would want you to be happy too."

Wilmeth even offered to take his future stepfather's surname.

"Are you sure, Wilmeth?" Pauline said. "You don't have to. You can remain Wilmeth Webb, if you'd like."

"Nah, Mama. Sam seems like a good man. Reminds me a little of Daddy the way he wants to help people. Besides, I don't want to constantly be answering questions why my last name's different from my parents. And I kinda like that last name. Definitely different, unique."

Pauline and Sam decided on a small wedding, and he went along with her wishes to hold the ceremony at her church, Washington Free Methodist, even though he was a practicing Hindu.

They didn't bother going on a honeymoon, because money was tight. In fact, between Pauline's meager earnings and Sam's part-time work as a fill-in doctor at Columbia Presbyterian Hospital, they were just getting by.

Near the end of that year, Sam received word there was an opening for a practice in Harlem. He thought back to the calling he had expressed in his med school essay—his desire to serve an underserved community. *This would be perfect*, he thought.

And Pauline agreed. Once again they faced the challenge of breaking life-changing news to Wilmeth. And once again they were anxious about how he would respond.

Although he was going to miss his friends, relatives, teachers, and coaches, he begrudgingly agreed to make the move. The last thing he wanted was to be separated from his mother again.

CHAPTER 13

New York City, 1928

There was a bigness and bustle to Harlem that enticed young Wilmeth from the moment he set foot in Upper Manhattan. The place was alive. As electric as a lightning bolt. Made the District seem like a sleepy hamlet. The ten-year-old couldn't help but gawk at the tall buildings. Easily five times the height of the two-story row houses he was used to back in his old neighborhood. And they went on for blocks, forming concrete canyons for as far as the eye could see. Not only did they block out the sun; they retained the heat, noise, and stench of overflowing garbage cans, wino urine, and automobile fumes. It made for an oppressive sensory urban mix, especially during the dog days of summer.

Early on, Wilmeth entertained himself by staring out his fourth-floor window for long periods of time, marveling at the claustrophobic choreography of shouting pedestrians and honking cars below. Life moved at a faster pace here, and he quickly discovered that a young man needed to be able to adjust on the fly if he wanted to get where he was going.

Wilmeth had arrived in Upper Manhattan at the tail end of the Roaring Twenties and the Great Migration. It was a vibrant, hopeful period, with nearly two hundred thousand Blacks settling into this three-square-mile enclave after fleeing the hell on earth that was the Jim Crow South. Harlem had become a magnet for Blacks seeking a better life, an idea as much as a place. Perhaps this would become the promised land, where Blacks could openly pursue their American dreams in the same manner as whites. Or at least that was the hope.

The Great Migration attracted some of the strongest minds and brightest talents of the day to New York, an astonishing array of Black artists, writers, musicians, scholars, and athletes. This perfect storm would fuel what became known as the Harlem Renaissance, a spiritual coming-of-age in which African Americans transformed social disillusionment into racial pride. One of the era's leading voices, writer Langston Hughes, described it as "an expression of our individual dark-skinned selves." And that "expression" would be celebrated throughout the nation and the world, with whites, most for the first time, embracing this "explosion of Negro culture." It also would be a time when a new militancy sprouted as Blacks began asserting their civil and political rights. "Enough is enough" became their battle cry. They weren't going to just sit idly by and take it anymore.

Wilmeth felt energized by the Renaissance, felt a sense of Black pride he hadn't before. He was optimistic by nature, and this new environment, with all these remarkable Black folk doing their thing in Harlem at the same time, had renewed his hope that African Americans would finally get their just due, that the playing field one day would be leveled, that people would be judged on talent and character rather than skin color.

That's not to say Wilmeth's transition from sleepy DC to the frenetic Big Apple was smooth and seamless. It wasn't. During his first few weeks in the City That Never Sleeps, he missed his old friends something fierce;

he yearned to be with Abe and the rest of the gang. To combat his home-sickness, he'd tag along to the medical clinic Samuel Sidat-Singh had set up just down the block from their apartment at 221 West 135th Street. But those trips got old in a hurry. Soon enough, Wilmeth was bored stiff. And even more homesick. Sidat-Singh realized his son needed something to snap him out of his funk, so he signed him up for a membership at the Harlem YMCA, which was right next door to the clinic. It wound up being the perfect remedy. Sports had always been a great outlet for Wilmeth. And they would be so again, helping him assimilate into his new neighborhood while forging lifelong, powerful bonds.

***

The gym at the Harlem Y was crowded and noisy, the sounds of thumping basketballs, squeaking sneakers, and screeching kids reverberating off the paint-peeling ceiling and subway-tiled walls. Wilmeth walked over to the rack and grabbed one of the weathered leather balls and began dribbling to a vacant rim in one of the corners. He started shooting layups, then moved ten feet away so he could practice outside shots. His first hoist swished through the basket. He retrieved the ball and shot another. Same result. *Swish*. And then another. And another. And another. All with the same successful results.

A slightly built lad around the same age as Wilmeth had been watching from afar. He sauntered over and asked if he could join him.

"Sure," Wilmeth said, extending his right hand. "My name is Wilmeth, but you can call me Wil."

"Hey, my name is Mercer. And you can call me whatever you want."

The two boys laughed. Wilmeth handed Mercer the ball, and he attempted an awkward shot that fell far short of the mark. Wilmeth tracked down the ball and passed it back to Mercer, who bobbled it before taking another futile shot.

Wilmeth retrieved the ball once more.

"Here, Mercer. Watch how I grip and release the ball."

Wilmeth followed through on another shot that dropped through the rim. For the next ten minutes, he tutored his new acquaintance on the fine art of shooting a basketball, and eventually Mercer began making a few shots, though not with the smooth, accurate marksmanship of his mentor.

After Wilmeth stroked several more successful shots, a voice rang out from the other side of the court.

"Hey, hotshots, you guys up for a game?"

"Sure," Wilmeth shouted back.

"Why don't you go ahead, Wilmeth?" Mercer murmured. "As you saw, I'm not very good. I'll just watch."

"Don't be silly. Just a pickup game. Come on."

Mercer reluctantly agreed, and they walked over to the kid who had challenged them to a game of two-on-two.

"John Isaacs," the boy said, extending his hand. "And this is Bill King."

"This is Mercer. Mercer . . . ah . . . hey, Mercer, what's your last name?"

"Mercer Ellington."

"And I'm Wilmeth Sidat-Singh."

"Sidat what?" Isaacs asked, chuckling.

"Sidat-Singh."

"How 'bout we just call you Sing."

"Fine by me."

"You boys can have the ball first," said Isaacs, handing it to Wilmeth.

Wilmeth immediately began dribbling toward the basket, and when both Isaacs and King converged to cover him, he passed to Mercer, who was all alone beneath the hoop. Mercer chucked up a shot that missed the backboard completely, and King grabbed the rebound and laid it in.

"One-nothing, us," King shouted, handing the ball back to Wilmeth. "First one to ten wins."

Wilmeth drove toward the basket, and again both defenders impeded his path. Another pass to an open Ellington resulted in another missed shot and another rebound basket by King.

On their next possession, Wilmeth suggested Ellington start with the ball. As Ellington began dribbling, King stole the ball and passed it to Isaacs for another basket.

"Three-nothing," King yelled. He then turned to Ellington and blurted with a smirk, "Boy, you stink."

If there was one thing Wilmeth never liked, it was a bully. And if there was one thing he'd learned back in DC, it was bullies who needed to be confronted and put in their place. Which is why he immediately stomped over to King and grabbed his right arm.

"Look here, Mercer's just starting out, just learning the game. King, I'm sure you weren't some superstar when you started out. So cut him some slack."

"Get your hands off me, boy."

Wilmeth refused to let go, and when King struggled mightily to escape, he pinned him against a nearby wall. King kept battling to wriggle free but soon realized it was no use. Wilmeth was too strong.

"I'll let you go, you son of a bitch, when you apologize to my friend."

"All right, all right. Cool it. I'll cut your boy some slack."

Wilmeth freed King from his viselike grip, and the game resumed. This time Wilmeth decided to take matters into his own hands. He dribbled quickly toward the basket, and once again Isaacs and King double-teamed him. Only this time he faked a pass to the wide-open Ellington, then spun by his defenders for an easy score.

"Whooee, Sing," marveled Isaacs. "That was one fancy move."

Though Isaacs and King wound up winning all four games, the two-on-two skirmishes were competitive. Ellington even scored a few baskets along the way. By the time they were through, the four boys were bathed in sweat and made a beeline to a water fountain.

"We should do this again tomorrow," King said, offering his hand to Wilmeth.

"Sounds good. See you then."

In the days and weeks that followed, the foursome became inseparable. From that contentious beginning on the Y courts, solid friendships blossomed. Friendships that would last lifetimes.

CHAPTER 14

Although Mercer Ellington loved sports, it was apparent he was nowhere near as talented as Wilmeth, Isaacs, and King. But as that trio would discover, Mercer had other gifts they couldn't come close to matching. He also had a father who just might have been the most famous man in Harlem.

One day, in the spring of 1930, Mercer invited the guys to his family's apartment across the street from the famed Savoy Ballroom on Lenox Avenue and 140th Street. It was there they discovered their friend's celebrity bloodlines. When they arrived, they were greeted at the front door by an affable, smiling man dressed to the nines in a navy-blue pinstriped zoot suit.

"Happy to meet you, fellas. Come on in."

Wilmeth's jaw dropped. There in the flesh was none other than Duke Ellington, King of Jazz. Wait until he got home and told his parents. *Mom, Dad, guess who I met today?*

But the jaw-dropping introductions weren't done.

"Boys, I'd like you to meet a friend of mine who's visiting. This is Mr.

Cab Calloway."

Holy crap, Wilmeth thought to himself. *This can't be happening. Who we gonna meet next? President Hoover?*

But it wasn't a dream. It was indeed happening, and for the next hour or so, the two legendary musicians shared tales with their astonished young fans.

"You boys been awfully quiet. Have we bored you to death?"

"Not at all, Mr. Ellington," Wilmeth said.

"Mr. Ellington," chimed in John Isaacs, "do you think you could play something for us?"

Duke Ellington beamed. "Why sure, young man."

The famous musician walked over to the massive Steinway grand piano that seemed to take up half the living room.

"Boys, I'm going to share with you a new song I've been working on. Now, I'll need a vocalist to assist me here. Mildred, can you come join me?"

Mildred Dixon, a tall, elegant woman, strolled in from another room.

"Oh, hi, boys. You must be Mercer's friends. He's told me so much about you. So nice to meet you all."

"Is that your mom?" Wilmeth whispered to Mercer.

"Yes and no," he replied. "Long story. Tell you later."

"Mildred, can you accompany me on that song we've been working on?"

"I'll try, Duke. But you know I can't carry a tune."

"Oh, don't be bashful. We all know that's not true. You sing like a bird."

"Don't know 'bout that."

"Doesn't matter anyway. Just want to have Cab give it a listen to get his feedback. Plus, it will be nice to have an audience here to try it out on."

Duke practiced a few notes on the piano before proclaiming himself ready.

"And a one and a two and a three."

For the next three minutes, the famed orchestra leader tickled the ivories as only he could, and Mildred did her best to accompany him, scat singing the jazzy, jaunty lyrics as the boys looked on, tapping their feet instinctively to the beat.

When Duke struck the final chords, Calloway and the boys began applauding.

"Duke, you got yourself a winner there," Calloway said, rising to his feet. "That tune's gonna get people jumping and jiving."

"Mr. Ellington," Wilmeth inquired, "what's the name of the song?"

"Well, young man, thanks for asking. You can probably guess the title from the lyrics. Like the song says, 'It Don't Mean a Thing If It Ain't Got That Swing.'"

"Very cool, Mr. Ellington. Like it a lot."

The next day, while walking to the Y, Wilmeth thanked Mercer for the invitation to the impromptu concert, and soon the conversation wandered to other topics, including Mildred Dixon, the mysterious woman who was and wasn't his friend's mom.

"What's the story there, Mercer?"

"Complicated, Sing. Very complicated."

"How so?"

"Well, my real mom left us. Like you, I was born in the District, and we moved to Harlem a few years ago because my dad's band was taking off, and this is where it's at for jazz. Mom agreed to make the move but never took to New York. Too big, too loud for her. District's so much quieter. Suited her tastes better. And her family and friends were there. So one day she decided she'd had enough. Told my dad and me she was leaving, and I had a choice: stay with him or go back with her."

"I can relate."

"Really, Sing?"

"Yeah. See, my dad died when I was really young. And my mom wound up remarrying, and then they decided to come to Harlem because my stepdad was a doctor, and there was a chance to practice medicine here. Probably could have stayed back in Washington and lived with my uncle and aunt if I'd pushed it. But I didn't want to be away from my mom and stepdad."

"I getcha."

"So, Mercer, where does Mildred fit into the picture?"

"Was and is dad's manager. But I could tell early on that she was managing more than my old man's music. Guess they fell in love. And she's been real good to me. Real good. Treats me more like a son than my real mom ever did. So I consider her my mom."

"What's it like having a famous father, Mercer?"

"Mostly cool. Only problem is, you have to share him with everyone else. I know he loves me and Mildred, but to be honest, I think he loves his music more than he does either of us."

"How you feel 'bout that?"

"I understand 'cause I love music too. Guess it's in my blood."

"Do you want to become a musician too?"

"Most definitely. I'm already writing songs. Dad says I'm a chip off the ol' block. Says in a few years his band's gonna be playing my stuff."

"Wow! That would be something now, wouldn't it? I can see it now in big, bold letters on the Apollo Theater marquee: 'TONIGHT AT TEN: THE MERCER ELLINGTON BAND.'"

"I like the sound of that. How 'bout you, Sing? What you wanna do with your life?"

"Guess I'm like you. Not with music, mind you. Couldn't play an instrument or carry a tune to save my life. I think I want to be like my dad and my stepdad. My real dad was a pharmacist. Was helping a lot of Negroes in Florida before passing away. I'd like to go into some kind of medicine. Of course, my real dream would be to play sports for a living, but there ain't much money in it for us."

"What about Satchel Paige? I don't think he's hurting for cash."

"True, but ol' Satch is one of a kind."

"Yeah, he is. Ain't nobody like Satch. But who knows? Maybe someday people will be saying the same about you. Ain't nobody like Wilmeth Sidat-Singh."

CHAPTER 15

Buffalo, March 2000

Breanna knew it was a long shot. Figured the person she was looking for was either an octogenarian with a foggy memory or—worse—dead. But she was determined to leave no stone unturned, even if that meant calling each of the hundred or so John Isaacs listed in the Manhattan phone book.

Fortunately, that wouldn't be necessary, because on the thirtieth call of what she thought would be a futile search she struck gold. Not only was Wilmeth's best friend alive; he was in possession of a memory as sharp as that metaphorical needle she had just discovered in that metaphorical haystack.

"Been a while, young lady, since anyone wanted to chat about my old friend," he told her over the phone. "Would love to talk about Sing. Could spend several days filling up your notepad about him."

"That's fantastic, Mr. Isaacs. Can't wait to sit down with you and have you reminisce. Would next Wednesday morning around nine at the Harlem

YMCA work?"

"Sounds like a plan to me. As long as you call me John. I'll dust off the cobwebs in this old noggin and see you then."

Breanna was thrilled Isaacs had agreed to be interviewed in the place that had been a second home for Wilmeth while growing up in New York City. Being in that building was sure to jog John's memory. And who knows—maybe Wilmeth's ghost would show up, too, to help Isaacs fill in the blanks.

When she arrived at the Y that chilly, windy morning, she noticed a tall, slender man, with a closely cropped gray beard.

"John?" she inquired.

"Yes, I am," he said, handing her a Styrofoam cup of coffee. "Figured you could use some fuel to get the engine revving after having to get up so early to fly in here from Buffalo."

"Why, thank you, John. That's very considerate of you."

"Breanna, I figured we could set up shop over there in those empty bleachers."

"Sounds great. Is that where you and Wilmeth first squared off?"

"Beats me. Was so long ago I can't remember particulars. Heck, I can't even remember what I had for dinner last night. But this definitely is the gymnasium where things happened. That's a fact, though this building's been renovated several times since." Isaacs smiled and pointed to the court.

"Look at that shiny floor these kids play on now. As good as damn Madison Square Garden. Back when we played, the floor was filled with dead spots. More a softwood than a hardwood court. You'd be dribbling and—*thump*—the ball would just plum die; wouldn't come back up to your hand. But nobody bitched about it. We were just happy to have a place to play, especially when it was freezing outside. Having dead spots wound up being beneficial. Forced us to become better ball handlers. Forced us to compensate."

"Nothing wrong with that."

"No, there isn't. Gotta be able to handle the dead spots whether it's basketball or life."

"So just how good a basketball player was Wilmeth?"

"Lemme put it this way—and anybody who ever played with or against him would concur—Sing was so damn good that if he had lived he would have joined me, Pop Gates, Tarzan Cooper, and the rest of the so-called stars from that era in the Basketball Hall of Fame. That's how good he was. Like today's kids say, 'The dude could flat-out ball.'"

"From what I've learned, Wilmeth was pretty good at anything he tried. That true?"

"Got that right. Didn't matter the game. Hoops. Football. Baseball. Tennis. Swimming. Marbles. Checkers. Tiddlywinks. He'd take to it in a hurry, then whup your ass. His talents went beyond his God-given physical abilities. Had as much to do with what was above his shoulders—his smarts, his intuition. Was almost like he was clairvoyant or something. Could see the play happening before it actually did."

"What was he like as a person?"

"Best friend you could ever have. Always had your back. Always doing things to help bring out the best in you."

"Guess that was underscored in that anecdote about the first time you guys played two-on-two here. The way he looked after Mercer, who seemed more music geek than athlete."

Isaacs guffawed.

"Yeah, poor ol' Mercer. Played the piano like a maestro but couldn't play basketball worth a lick. That incident when Sing took Billy King to task for putting down Mercer obviously was the first time I saw Sing sticking up for someone. But it wouldn't be the last."

"What other ones come to mind?"

"One of my favorite Sing stories is how he inspired this girl in our hood. You might have come across her name in the history books—girl by the name of Althea Gibson. Was the first Negro to win that big tennis tournament at Wimbledon. And a helluva golfer too. Althea was considered a tomboy, and the boys really gave her a lot of grief. I think a lot of it was because they couldn't handle her whupping their macho asses.

"Sing was quite the tennis player himself. Once made it all the way to the New York City semifinals. So one day he sees these boys giving Althea the business, telling her to go home and concentrate on cooking and sewing 'cause sports were just for boys. She's in tears, and Sing calls her over. Next thing you know, she and Sing are swatting that tennis ball back and forth, back and forth, back and forth, right there in front of those boys. They weren't about to mess with Sing, because he was several years older, and his rep preceded him. Sing was a lover, not a fighter, but he knew how to use his fists, and did so on rare occasion.

"To make a long story short, Breanna, he'd sent a message to those clowns—and to Althea. From that point on, the boys let her play. And after she won Wimbledon in fifty-seven and got that trophy from the Queen of England herself, Althea came back to the city and was treated like a hero. I'm sure some of those same punks who'd hassled her were in the streets when New York threw a ticker-tape parade in her honor. Don't quote me on this, but she might have been the first Negro to receive that honor."

"Wow! What an amazing story. That's so cool what he did for Althea."

"Yup. Vintage Sing. Always finding ways to inspire and encourage others."

"I heard he had a good sense of humor too."

"Oh yes, he did. Constantly pulling pranks on you. You'd be sitting there, looking away, talking to someone else, and there's Sing, tying your shoe laces together so that when you got up and went to walk you'd trip and fall like some clumsy, dumbass fool. But we got him back, many a time. And he took it all in stride. He could take it as well as give it."

"John, the basketball rivalry that started between you and Wilmeth on this very court continued through high school, didn't it?"

"Indeed it did. Sing was a year older, but we locked horns several times. He played for DeWitt Clinton, which was a powerhouse out of the Bronx, and I played for Textile High School out of Manhattan. His school's nickname was the Governors, and I'd always joke to him that he was the president of the Governors. He got a kick out of that. Sing led those Govs to the city public high school championship in thirty-four, his junior year, and we got the best of them the next year, when I was a junior, and we won it all. One thing I'm most proud of is that we both were named to the *Daily News* all-city team. I think we may have been the first Negroes ever to get all-city honors. To be chosen and see ourselves celebrated in a white newspaper was a big deal."

"Is it true people thought Wilmeth was of Indian heritage and not an African American?"

"Nobody in Harlem thought that. Hell, we all knew he was a Negro. That Hindu stuff was just the doing of some crazy fans and sportswriters. They heard his strange-sounding name and just assumed Dr. Sidat-Singh was his birth daddy. Sing never fed into that. Never. Ever. He was a Negro, and damn proud of it. But you know how they say in your business, 'Don't let the facts get in the way of a good story?' Well, the white newspapers started referring to him as the Manhattan Hindu, and it sorta took on a life of its own. Guess it made him more unique. As Sing learned, many white folk were more comfortable rooting for a guy from India than a Negro from their own country. Crazy when you think about it."

"Did he ever try to fight it?"

"He did. It bothered him. But it was so much different back in the day. Sometimes we Negroes had to play these games in order to compete. Kinda like how Jackie Robinson had to turn the other cheek and take all the shit thrown his way. Got to look at it in that context. Different times."

"I've been reading a lot lately about what Harlem was like back then. You guys were here when the place was really hopping."

"Yes, we were. I tell people I was here for the hop and the flop. Saw it at its peak and at its worst. Place was jumping through the twenties, but the stock market crash brought the locomotive to a halt. Not an abrupt halt but a halt. By the mid-1930s, things got bad. Real bad."

"So, tell me, what was it like in its heyday?"

"Best way I can describe it is Harlem was the capital of the Negro world back then. Every person of color who was somebody was here. Or wanted to be here. All the actors and artists and writers and smarty-pants intellectuals. Colored business was thriving. People were making a decent living. We had a growing Negro middle class. Truly amazing the number of brilliant colored folk here at the same time."

"Great time for music, too, huh?"

"Yes sirree! Jazz was exploding. And knowing Mercer and his famous dad gave us a front-row seat to that world—a seat we wouldn't had otherwise. Got to go to a bunch of the fancy joints where Duke and the others played. Savoy Ballroom. Cotton Club. Apollo Theater. And got to meet all these incredible people. Cab Calloway. Louie Armstrong. Count Basie. Billie Holiday. Josephine Baker. A who's who of Negro America."

"Do you really think the Great Depression in '29 was the beginning of the end?"

"Yep. Hit everyone hard, especially Black folk. But it wasn't until the repeal of Prohibition a few years later that the bottom fell out of Harlem. Before that, whites would come to see Duke, Cab, and the others 'cause jazz was all the rage. And they also came to Harlem to drink our booze in the speakeasies. More available here than in the white bars in other parts of New York. Between the market crash and booze being legal again, there stopped being a reason for the white folk to come. And the money started drying up and the crime picked up and the cops started going crazy on Negroes. Got real ugly, and in 1935, my junior year and Sing's senior year of high school, it all came to a head."

"Was that when the riots broke out?"

"Yep. Harlem went up in flames. Bunch of deaths. Millions and millions of dollars in damage. Looked like a damn war zone, like somebody had bombed the place. People stopped coming, and people started leaving. Drug use and crime exploded. Harlem went from being a place of hope to a place of despair."

"And this was around the time Wilmeth was heading off to Syracuse, wasn't it?"

"Yes, it was. I told Sing, 'You got good timing. You're getting out of here while the getting's good.'"

"How did Wilmeth wind up in Upstate New York instead of one of the colleges in the Big Apple?"

"Because Syracuse was the only place that offered him a chance to play hoops."

"Really? Hard to believe, considering all the success he enjoyed in a high school basketball hotbed like New York. You would have thought he'd receive a ton of offers."

"Different times. Negroes were being recruited to play sports at some white schools, but not like today. It was a trickle, not a flood. Don't know this for a fact, but you could probably count the number of Negroes playing sports at all the white schools on your fingers and your toes."

"Did you get recruited?"

"A little bit. But when the Rens came calling and offered me a contract after we won the city high school championship, I jumped at it. Made something like a hundred twenty bucks a game. Figured with that and a side job, I'd make ends meet."

"Did they offer Wilmeth too?"

"Don't think so. See, unlike me, Sing had a good head on his shoulders. Was a much, much better student. A brainiac. And he had that goal of going into medicine, like his dad and stepdad."

"Wilmeth had become well known in the Harlem community. Received quite a bit of pub in both the Black press and white press. Was it a big deal with him going to Syracuse?"

"It was. Any time a Negro tried to make inroads in the white world, it was newsworthy to Black folk. Inspired them. You could say Sing was carrying our torch when he headed off to Syracuse. And believe me, that torch ain't light. Comes with lots of additional stress and pressure. You're treated differently. You're expected by whites to be this perfect person. Superman. No margin for error. Make even the littlest mistake, and you'll be branded a dumb, worthless you-know-what. You're forced to be twice as good in order to justify your taking away a classroom and roster spot from a white kid. It can be exhausting."

"Truly amazing he could carry that torch without dropping it."

"Really is. Showed a ton more patience and courage than I could have. I woulda punched somebody in the mouth if I'd faced the crap he did. I probably woulda been thrown out of school and into the slammer. But Sing carried on, kept moving forward. You might get him feeling down, but you couldn't keep him that way. He was an eternal optimist. Usually was able to find the good in people. Always believed things were gonna work out in the end. Like Jackie, in some ways. Sing found the courage to turn the cheek and beat the bigots with his endless supply of talent and kindness. Was one special cat. Can still remember hugging him at Grand Central as he boarded that train for Upstate. Feels like it was yesterday."

CHAPTER 16

Late August 1935

"Next stop, Syracuse!" the corpulent train conductor boomed as he wedged through the narrow aisle of the caboose. Wilmeth groggily stretched his arms toward the ceiling before hoisting himself to his feet. It had been nearly seven hours since he and the other Black passengers had crammed themselves into this stuffy, smoky, back-of-the-train car at Grand Central Station on this oppressively hot day. He couldn't wait to get outside and fill his lungs with fresh air.

After working out the kinks and getting his blood flowing, he grabbed the heavy suitcase with his belongings from the overhead bin and plopped it on the floor as the train's brakes hissed and jolted the New York Central car to a halt so harshly Wilmeth had to brace himself to avoid flying down the aisle. When the doors opened, and he walked onto the platform, he heard a loud voice shouting his name.

"Wilmeth?"

"Yes."

"Ike Harrison. I'm gonna be your Syracuse daddy the next four years."

"How do you do, Mr. Harrison?" Wilmeth said, smiling and shaking the burly man's meaty hand.

"No need to call me Mister—Ike will do. Now, boy, let's get cracking so we can get you unpacked and get you some vittles. The missus has prepared salt potatoes for you. They're a Syracuse specialty, and I guarantee ya, they'll fill your gut."

"Sounds, good, Mister . . . I mean . . . Ike. But first can I pay a visit to the washroom?"

"Sure," Harrison chortled. "I bet you need to piss like a racehorse. Men's room's right over there."

As Wilmeth would soon learn, Harrison was a jovial sort, a man with a million stories. As they commenced their fifteen-minute trudge from the train station to the Adams Street apartment where he and his wife lived, Harrison gave Wilmeth a quick history lesson about the neighborhood he'd be calling home.

"You'll be living with us in the Fifteenth Ward. Folks just call it the Ward. Mostly Negroes, like us, though I've read where you're Hindu, ain't you?"

"No, my stepdad's a Hindu. I'm a Negro, through and through."

"I thought you looked like a Negro to me. I just remember reading those newspaper articles calling you the Manhattan Hindu."

"Long story, Ike. I'll fill you in sometime."

"No problem. Doesn't matter a lick to me. Like I said, mostly Negroes in the Ward, though we also have a mix, with some Jews, Italians, Poles, and Irish on the nearby streets. Everybody pretty much gets along. There can be some minor skirmishes from time to time. Nothing too serious. You might get called some names 'cause you're a Negro, but we try our best to ignore it."

"Sticks and stones may break my bones, but names will never hurt me, right, Ike?"

"Yeah, right," Harrison responded.

"So, Ike, tell me about you. You from Syracuse?"

"Nah. Been here 'bout twenty, twenty-five years. Had lived in Samford, Florida, till I was about ten. My daddy's daddy settled the family there after being emancipated following the Civil War. Gramps worked the field, picking tobacco and cotton, and my daddy followed in his footsteps. And when we was young, my brothers and I were out there too. A bunch of sharecroppers."

"That doesn't sound like fun work."

"It was backbreaking and blistering, 'specially when that sun was pounding down on you. That's why you'll never hear no complaints from me when it's cold and snowing in Syracuse, 'cause I just remember how hellish that sun was in those cotton fields. But you know what, Wilmeth?"

"What, Ike?"

"The thing I remember and hate most wasn't working in those fields. It was living in constant fear. Just a different world down there and back then, Wilmeth. Was always hearing stories about bunches of white rowdies getting into the moonshine and coming over to the fields to grab a Negro or two for no other reason than to have themselves a lynching. Was their idea of a good time."

"My heavens. Can't imagine what that's like."

"I'd wake up in cold sweat two, three times a week," Harrison continued. "Kept having nightmares about it happening to us."

"So did that lead to you moving here?"

"It did. One day Daddy couldn't take it anymore after one of his good friends had been lynched. We had some relatives up here in the Ward, and Daddy grabbed his life savings, which wasn't much, and packed us onto a bus. I remembered stories my granddaddy the slave would tell about the Underground Railroad. That's kind of how we all felt when we took our seats in the back of that bus. We were taking a ride in search of freedom.

"And we weren't alone. Every year seems more and more Negroes were doing the same. Our people keep migrating in this direction, seeking a better life. Ain't perfect up here. Not by a long shot. Sometimes the bigotry's just hidden a bit better. You still have to watch where you go. There's some restaurants outside the neighborhood that will make you feel like you ain't human.

"The missus and I were in one place last year, and after we finished eating and paid our check, the owner got mighty angry when he found out a Negro couple had eaten a meal in his establishment. Smashed our plates on the floor. Screamed he couldn't use 'em again, 'cause Negroes had eaten off them. Made a damn spectacle. Humiliated us in front of everybody. Can you believe that crap? Like we'd permanently infected his precious plates with some bubonic plague or something. And he didn't use the word *Negroes* when he was throwing a fit and chasing us out of there, but you get the picture, Wil."

"Yes, sadly, I do."

"That's not meant to scare you. It's better here. Lots better. Less Jim Crow than down in Samford. Some progress being made, and you are evidence of that. You're doing what a lot of Negroes wished they could do. Like ol' Frederick Douglass said, education's the key that can unlock the door. So, Wil, climb that hill overlooking the Ward, and get that sheepskin, because the more Negroes that scale that hill, the better it will be for all Negroes. The missus and me don't have any children, so we're going to treat you like the son we never had these next four years. Gonna do everything we can to help you get that diploma."

"Appreciate that, Ike. I really do."

"There's a handful of young coloreds like you who are attending the university and are staying with host families down in the Ward. So you aren't going to be alone."

"That's good to know."

"And it's been my observation there's some mighty fine good-looking young ladies among that group of university coloreds. Now, please don't tell the missus I said that. She'll smack me a good one if she ever hears my eyes been wandering."

"Didn't hear a thing," Wilmeth chuckled. "Your secret's safe with me."

When they reached the corner of McBride and Adams, Harrison went into full tourist guide mode, pointing out several landmarks.

"Now, that there is the AME Zion Church. Letters stand for African Methodist Episcopal, and since you're not a Hindu—and I suspect a Christian—I'm sure Reverend Thelonious Washington Carver would appreciate you visiting the Lord's house on Sunday mornings.

"And right next to our house of worship is our house of recreation. Wouldn't be surprised if you spend some time blowing off steam there too."

Outside the second story of the large, red-brick building Harrison pointed to, Wilmeth couldn't miss a gigantic sign reading: "DUNBAR COMMUNITY CENTER."

"That and the church really are the heart and soul of this neighborhood," Harrison continued. "All sorts of activities there, 'specially for young people. Dances. Basketball games. Gospel concerts. Arts and crafts. Tons of library books, since there ain't no library in the Ward. The center also has desks for studying, in case you need a break from the Hill. Dunbar's a really, really important place to me because I work there as the rec director."

"Very cool, Ike."

"In your free time, I'd like you to help me out there with cleaning and coaching and counseling some of the kids. That's kind of the agreement I worked out with your parents and the university folks when they asked me about room and board. Need not worry about me piling on too many chores. I'll make damn sure nothing gets in the way of your studies or your basketball, but I know the kids there will get a kick out of having a boy from the Hill spending time with them."

"I'd like that, Ike. Reminds me of the Harlem Y. That was my place. Spent hours and hours there. Kept me off the streets. And out of trouble."

"Great you can relate, 'cause that's what I'm trying to do here. Keep these kids occupied with positive stuff."

Next door to the rec center was a soda shop, and just beyond that was the two-story house where Wilmeth would spend plenty of time in the coming years.

"Welcome to your home away from home," Ike said as they ascended the steps to the porch and the front entrance.

Ike's wife, Thelma, greeted Wilmeth with a bear hug. "Well, well, Mr. Wilmeth, so pleased to finally meet you. Now your room is down that hall and to your right, so just get your things unpacked and come back here so I can put some food into those young muscles. You must be starving after that long train ride."

"I am, Mrs. Harrison."

"Ike probably told you: We're not into formalities here. You just call me Thelma, 'cause you're family."

"OK, Thelma it is."

After placing his clothes in dresser drawers and on closet hangers, Wilmeth feasted on Syracuse salt potatoes smothered in hot butter. Harrison had been right. They were delicious, and after eating three spuds, two pork chops, and some greens, he was full.

On his walk through the neighborhood, he spotted a playground with a sunbaked dirt basketball court. He told the Harrisons he was going to check out the court, maybe shoot a few baskets, then chug up the Hill to stroll around the campus he'd seen only in photographs and postcards.

"Sounds good," Thelma said. "Just be back before dark, 'cause bad things can happen once the sun goes down."

"No problem, Thelma. I promise I'll be back before the sun sets."

At the park, Wilmeth saw a teenager shooting some baskets and walked over to introduce himself and asked if he could join him.

"Hi, my name is Wilmeth."

"Hi, I'm Jacob. Jacob MacAlister."

"Mind if I shoot a few with you?"

"Not at all."

And so for the next half hour, Wilmeth and the thirteen-year-old took turns shooting baskets and conversing.

"So you really gonna play basketball up there on the Hill?"

"That's the plan," Wilmeth said, dribbling on the concrete-hard dirt before letting fly a twenty-footer that fell through the netless iron rim attached to a rotting piece of plywood.

"I thought they didn't allow Negroes up there."

"Well, there aren't many of us, but they made an exception for me."

"That cool. Maybe someday I'll climb that Hill and play up there too."

"No reason why you can't, Jacob. Just make sure you hit the books and take care of your schooling. Can't make that climb if you don't got the grades. Can't just be about basketball."

After swishing another twenty-footer, Wilmeth shook Jacob's hand and thanked him.

"Where ya going?"

"I'm going up that hill. Got a few days before classes start. Figured I get the lay of the land since I never set foot on campus."

"Good luck, Wilmeth. Be rooting for you. So will everyone else in the Ward."

"Thanks."

Founded by the Methodist Church back in 1870, the campus on the bluff was known first as Piety Hill, then simply the Hill. And as Wilmeth hoofed up toward majestic Crouse College standing sentinel at the summit, he thought to himself the nickname surely fit the landscape.

"Woof!" he muttered after reaching the peak. "Not gonna have to worry about staying in shape climbing that mountain every day."

It was a warm summer evening, and as Wilmeth walked across the quadrangle—a wide green expanse bordered by a half dozen academic buildings—he noticed a handful of students frolicking about. He smiled and waved at a group of boys tossing a football around, but they neither smiled nor waved back. Unnerved by the icy response, he averted further eye contact and continued walking toward Archbold Stadium and the gymnasium. The gates to the massive concrete bowl and gridiron were open, so Wilmeth ventured inside to take a look.

The massive edifice reminded him of the photographs he had seen of the Roman Colosseum. Or of Yankee Stadium, which was just across the Harlem River, about six blocks from his Upper Manhattan home. He began descending the rows of steps, and when he reached the bottom, he walked across the track circling the field and leapt over the fence so he could walk on the grass. Off in the far end zone, he saw two towers that gave the place the feel of a medieval castle. He envisioned what a rush it must be to be on this grass, looking up and seeing the place packed with roaring spectators on a Saturday afternoon.

Once done fantasizing, he scaled the fence and the rows of seats and walked past the beige-brick gymnasium. The door was unlocked, and he poked his head inside. Down the hallway, he saw the sign for the main door to the basketball court and pushed it open. Once again his mind wandered. He visualized the stands being filled, and him sinking shots and driving by defenders and passing the basketball to open teammates for easy scores. He dreamed of fans chanting his name.

His fantasy ended abruptly, when a stentorian voice out of nowhere scared the bejesus out of him.

"Hey! What the hell are you doing?"

"Nothing," Wilmeth stammered as he turned to see a security guard in uniform. "Was just checking the place out."

"Well, you don't belong in here," the guard shouted, waving his billy club. "Get your trespassing ass out of here, or there's gonna be trouble."

"Yes sir. Yes sir," Wilmeth stuttered before sprinting through an exit door on the opposite side of the court.

His heart was racing, just as it had when he and Abe had run for their lives after drinking out of the whites-only water fountain a decade or so earlier in DC. Rather than jog across the quad and run the risk of more icy stares, he chose the less traveled route. His detour took him to the far side of Crouse, and he decided to descend the hill there, even though this slope was steeper than the one he had scaled to reach campus.

As he started his trip downward, he tripped over a tree root and began tumbling. Round and round he spun, finally crashing to a halt against the trunk of a large oak tree, about half way down the hill. He hadn't been hit this hard since Jameson Hilbert rammed him to the ground during a sandlot football game back in Harlem a few months earlier. Fortunately, the collision with the oak hadn't broken anything, just left him with a few bruises to his chest, arms, and ego. Dizzily, Wilmeth rose to his feet, brushed off the grass and dirt, and waited until he regained his bearings before resuming his trek to the bottom.

Back on Adams Street, he paused to look back up at Crouse College. He hoped the tumble he'd just taken was not an omen of things to come during his next four years.

CHAPTER 17

The adjustment from his old world to his new one had not been easy, but a few months into his first semester at Syracuse in 1935, Wilmeth was feeling good, like he could handle things. Even all the cruel, stupid obstacles that came from being Black in an America where Black folks were still fighting to reverse the results of the damn Civil War. His freshmen classes certainly were more challenging than high school, but he didn't feel overwhelmed. He was doing well in all his subjects, remarkable in some respects, given the prejudice he'd encountered from several professors. Though disheartening, particularly at a place where people were supposed to be enlightened, Wilmeth just did what he'd been conditioned to do: kept quiet and tolerated it. His parents, as well as old friends John Isaac and Pop Gates, had warned him such obstacles might arise.

"Keep your eye on the basket, not the defender's hand in your face," Gates told him, employing a basketball analogy.

And that's what Wilmeth did.

He had gotten to know the handful of other Black SU students living in the Ward. There was many a morning when they would trek up the hill together, comrades in arms exchanging war stories about something stupid and mean they had experienced on campus. Wilmeth had made many white friends too. Sure, there were still some who wanted nothing to do with him, who glared at him with their "you don't belong here" looks and spewed epithets and racist taunts loud enough for him to hear. *Sticks and stones*, he reminded himself. *Sticks and stones*.

Basketball practice began in November, and since first-year students were not allowed to play varsity sports, he was assigned to the freshman team and Coach Walter Gustufsen. Gustufsen was a stern taskmaster, an inflexible thinker. It was his way or the proverbial highway. So, whenever Wilmeth deviated from his plans with either a fancy pass or a long shot, Gustufsen would stop practice and lay into Wilmeth for what he perceived as showboating.

"Singh, that crap might be OK for the folks you've spent your life playing basketball with, but we stress intelligent basketball here," he would yell. "Either get with the program or get some bench."

Wilmeth wanted to answer back. Wanted to point out to Gustufsen that the fancy pass often was a more effective pass. Instead, he bit his lip. He would suppress his creativity for the time being.

In scrimmages between the freshman and upperclassmen, it quickly became apparent to varsity coach Lew Andreas that Wilmeth was a special talent, already the best player on the floor. In many ways, Wilmeth reminded Andreas of Vic Hanson, the three-sport star who had helped the Orangemen win a basketball championship a decade earlier while also captaining the football and baseball teams.

"Never seen a kid this fast—quick as a cat," Andreas told Gustufsen. "Moves faster with the ball than most of our guys move without it. Like a blur."

"Yeah, but he's got a little bit too much of that New York City playground flash and trash in him," Gustufsen bristled. "Showboats with that fancy dribbling and those fancy passes. Got to pound that stuff out of him and make him become more disciplined."

"I hear ya, Walt. No place for Negro ball in the college game. He's a talented lad, and if he stays within our scheme, he should be OK. If he goes off on his own, there's gonna be trouble."

CHAPTER 18

Around this time, Wilmeth had become smitten with one of his English Lit classmates, and the feeling was mutual. With long, flowing blonde hair, apple cheeks, and a killer smile, Nan Maris had this "sweetheart of Sigma Chi, all-American girl" look about her and a personality to match. She didn't lack for suitors, but Wilmeth, with his handsome, chiseled features, deep intellect, and engaging sense of humor, was the young man who caught her eye—the young man she wanted to get to know better.

They both realized the inherent dangers of being seen together because racially mixed relationships were beyond verboten. Something as simple as walking to and from their classes together might be frowned upon, even reported to SU disciplinary officials. That could result in immediate expulsion for Wilmeth, and Nan would be branded with some kind of scarlet letter—*NL*, for Negro Lover—and be told to leave school too.

They had to be as discreet as possible. One day, before class, Wilmeth handed Nan a note, which she read later while alone in her dorm room.

Hey Nan. I have an idea for a secret meeting, where we can enjoy each other's company and not be seen by anyone. How 'bout we head to Oakwood Cemetery on the outskirts of campus for a picnic next Tuesday at 3? I know it's not exactly the most romantic of places, but there's a section that's heavily wooded with a stone outdoor fireplace. Let me know what you think? Wil

Nan could feel her heart pounding. She wanted so badly to be alone with Wil, and this sounded like a good way to do it. The next time they were in class, she surreptitiously handed him a note saying they were on, and the following Tuesday she showed up in the cemetery and found Wil placing logs on a fire.

"This is so cool," she said, hugging him.

"Hopefully, it's so *warm*," he said, chuckling. "Don't want you to be cold."

Nan groaned and smiled at his corny attempt at humor. It was one of many things she found endearing about him. They sat down on a blanket and began munching on sandwiches Wil had brought from the Harrisons. For the next two hours, they talked and laughed and had a grand old time. She told him how she was from Hoboken, New Jersey, just across the river from Manhattan, and how she dreamed one day of performing on Broadway. He told her of his dreams of becoming a surgeon and maybe playing a little professional basketball on the side.

"Sounds like we got some pretty cool dreams, Wil."

"Gotta have hopes and dreams, Nan. As important as food and oxygen, as far as I'm concerned."

"Fuel for the soul, Wil. Of course, you left something out."

"What's that, Nan?"

"Love. Love's the most important thing of all."

"Yes, it is. Yes, it is."

After a few seconds of silence, Wilmeth summoned the gumption to ask a question he'd been dying to ask since the moment they met several weeks earlier: "Nan, do you mind if I kiss you?"

She blushed and said, "Of course, Wil. I thought you'd never ask."

Wil nervously gave her a peck on the cheek.

"I want a real kiss, Wil." And with that, she pulled his head toward hers and kissed him on the lips.

"There," she said, beaming. "That's better now, isn't it, Wil?"

"Much better for sure, Nan. Just one problem."

"What's that, Wil?"

"I just can't stop at one. I'm hungering for more."

She pulled his body close to his, and they kissed again, only this time Nan didn't stop at his lips. This time she penetrated his mouth with her tongue.

"They call that French kissing, Wil," she said after they had come up for air. "You like?"

"I like," he said, giggling.

They embraced and kissed some more.

"Whoa," he said, after coming up for air a second time. "Better stop right here before we reach the point where we can't stop."

"But I don't want this to end, Wil."

"Me neither, Nan. But the sun's beginning to set, and I better put this fire out and walk you out of these woods so you can get back to campus while it's still light out."

"Can we do this again, Wil?"

"You betcha. But we're gonna have to come up with some other places to hold our secret rendezvous. Because once that snow starts flying, we're not gonna want to be outdoors."

Fortunately, the weather remained unseasonably mild in the coming weeks, and Wilmeth and Nan continued their secret soirees in their secret place. Each time they met, the hugging and kissing became more intense, and it became increasingly difficult for these two teenagers in love to control their raging hormones.

"One of these days, Wil, we'll go someplace where I can take care of you, and you can take care of me."

"That day can't come soon enough."

"I know. Just be patient, my darling Wil. We'll figure something out."

Wilmeth had never felt this way before, and he was loving being in love for the first time in his life. Though he and Nan had been together for just a short time, he felt like they were old souls who had known one another in a previous life. He couldn't imagine life without her.

Wilmeth practically floated down the Hill to the Ward after their latest tryst, but sadly his euphoria didn't last. Upon opening the door to his house, he saw Ike and Thelma sitting in the living room, looking none too pleased.

"Young man, we need to talk," Ike said. "Sit down."

"What's up?" Wilmeth said, slunking into the nearest chair.

"You know darn well what's up."

"No, I don't."

"Don't act like me and the missus are stupid."

"Seriously, I don't know what you're talking about. What's going on?"

"A white girl with blonde hair is what's going on."

Wilmeth's jaw dropped.

"You mean Nan. What's the big deal?"

"What's the big deal?! Come on, Wil, you know what's the big deal. Where I came from, Black boys got hanged just for looking the wrong way at a white girl. Got to break this off immediately. Can't see this Goldilocks ever again."

"But I really love her."

"I don't give a hoot. Plenty of Negro girls you can fall in love with. Stick to your own kind."

"But—"

"No buts. You're playing with dynamite here."

"How did you find out about Nan anyway? We were discreet. Didn't hook up on campus."

"Got a call from Mr. Andreas. Apparently, someone saw you guys in the cemetery."

Wilmeth placed his head in his hands.

"It's over, Wil. It's over. Too much at stake here, son. Keep at this, and you'll blow it all. They don't want Negroes up there on the Hill as it is. So don't give 'em an excuse to expel you. Go see Mr. Andreas tomorrow before practice and apologize. Tell him it will never ever happen again. You hear me?"

"I hear ya."

Wilmeth stormed to his room, slammed the door, and began sobbing.

That night he put his feelings down on paper and handed the note to Nan when he showed up for English Lit the next morning.

"What's wrong, Wil? You look horrible."

"Someone snitched on us."

"Oh my God."

"I gotta go."

"But class will be starting soon. Can't we talk?"

"Gotta go," he said, doing everything in his power not to cry as he bolted out of the classroom.

After exiting the Hall of Languages, he began sprinting across the quad and beyond. Had no idea where he was headed. Just needed to keep moving as fast as possible in hope he could somehow outrun the hurt.

Once class ended, Nan read the letter and started crying so hard she could barely breathe.

Hey Baby,

I wish I never had to write this. I'd dreamed of a day when we could be together forever, but just like that play we've been reading in class, we appear to be star-crossed. Just change the names from Montagues and Capulets to Negroes and whites, and you'll have our modern-day Romeo and Juliet story. Never gonna forget you for as long as I live. You'll always have a piece of my heart.

Love, Wil.

CHAPTER 19

When it came to sports, Wilmeth had always been a man for all seasons.

In the spring and summer, his attention turned to baseball and tennis. In the fall, he played football, and in the winter months, basketball. But when he arrived at Syracuse, he intended to stick to basketball. He figured that's what Lew Andreas had recruited him to play, and he didn't want to rock the boat. He also surmised it was best to concentrate on one sport while he acclimated to college life—a life in which he would face a rigorous premed course load and the challenges of being one of a handful of Black students on an almost all-white campus.

During the first semester of his sophomore year, in the autumn of 1936, one of his classmates asked him to play on their intramural football team. Wilmeth said he would, "If you let me throw the ball."

"Well, that depends on how well you throw it," responded Bradley Shaw.

"You've seen me on the basketball court," Wilmeth boasted. "If I can heave a basketball from one end of the court to the other, I'll have no problem throwing that football all over the field. The aerodynamics will be even better because of the football's shape. I should be able to chuck it longer and faster."

"You're on, Wil. The other dorm teams just try to run the ball all the time because they don't have anyone good enough to sling it. Plus, they figure, like most, that bad things happen when you pass. They'll be shocked when they see us putting it in the air. They won't know what hit 'em."

And so Wilmeth played intramurals that fall, just to satisfy his sports appetite till the start of basketball practice in November. It would provide a fun and fruitful pastime as he and his Sadler Hall teammates dominated their competition on the way to a campus championship. Unfortunately, one of their vanquished foes filed a protest with the dean of students just after the season ended. They claimed the title should be forfeited because Wilmeth was not a resident of Sadler Hall. Dean Sebastian Folger sided with the aggrieved.

"Can you believe that shit, Wil?" Shaw bitched after hearing the news.

"Yes," sighed Wilmeth. "Unfortunately, I can."

"But it ain't right. How you supposed to be eligible to play for us or any other dorm team when you aren't even allowed to live in any of the dormitories? That's ludicrous."

"Welcome to my world."

Despite the unjust decision, something really good had come from Wilmeth's intramural pursuits. It had rekindled his love for the game. And it had opened a new door.

One afternoon that fall, Roy Simmons Sr. was strolling across the quad toward Archbold Gymnasium when he noticed a young man unleash a fifty-yard pass during an intramural game. "Wow!" the Syracuse varsity's assistant football coach said to himself as he detoured toward the game to get a closer look. "Who the heck threw that bomb?"

As he watched the action unfold, the man known to everyone on campus as Simmie realized the possessor of the thunderbolt arm was none other than Wilmeth, one of the Orangemen's up-and-coming basketball players. Although it was just a game of touch, it quickly became apparent to Simmie's trained eye that Wilmeth was as adept with an oblong ball as he was with a round one. After watching him deliver one spiral after another, the coach interrupted the game.

"Singh, you got one hell of an arm there," he said.

"Thanks, Coach."

"I'm dead serious. You don't belong here on the Quad. You belong over there." Simmons pointed toward nearby Archbold Stadium.

"Uh, I don't know about that, Coach."

"Well, I know. You're better than anybody we got on the varsity right now. You need to get your ass over there and play football for us next year."

"But Coach Andreas brought me here to play basketball."

"Who the hell says you can't play two sports? Hell, I played football and lacrosse and started the boxing team when I was a student here. Just give it some thought, and in the meantime I'll tell Coach Andreas and Coach Oz we spoke. And I'll give 'em both my eagle-eyed scouting report."

As Simmons walked away, Wilmeth's teammates and opponents patted him on the back and started hooting.

"Hey, Wil, I want a finder's fee," Shaw chortled. "Or at least some free tickets to the games. Don't forget us when you become a football hero."

"Eat shit, Shaw. I didn't say I was gonna do it. Coach Simmie asked me to give it some thought, and I will. Now let's get back to concentrating on the game at hand."

Wilmeth hadn't realized just how much he missed football until he started playing intramural ball that fall. And while the touch game was fun, he longed to play tackle again. He missed the contact, the sense of excitement—and at times fear—one could only feel when trying to advance the ball down the field while being chased by men attempting to cause bodily harm. Still, Wilmeth wondered if he would be able to juggle the commitments to two sports while maintaining his grades. Keeping a robust grade-point average was imperative if he wanted to get into med school and follow in his father and stepfather's footsteps.

He also was concerned about what position he'd be allowed to play. Passing halfback was his preference and what he was best at, but he knew he'd be the only Black on the squad. Would the all-white staff, headed by first-year head coach Ossie Solem, allow a Negro to play a high-profile position that would require him to "boss" white players around? Would those players even listen to him? Or would they sabotage his efforts by going rogue? What if they decided not to block for him? What if they didn't run the patterns they were supposed to? What if they didn't come to his defense when opponents gang-tackled him and sucker punched him and attempted to gouge his eyes out and twist his ankles and knees in directions they shouldn't go?

Wilmeth had heard the horror stories about dirty tactics employed against Paul Robeson, William Henry Lewis, William Tecumseh Sherman Jackson, Oz Simmons, and other pioneering Black football players on predominantly white college teams. Like them, he likely would face discrimination from all directions. The press. Alumni. Fans. Administration. Opposing players. Even his own teammates and coaches. Wilmeth didn't doubt for a second he had the skills to excel and flourish, but he realized he wouldn't be able to succeed in this ultimate team sport without others having his back. If it was going to be Wilmeth versus twenty-one others on the gridiron, forget about it. He stood no chance. He'd get maimed. Or worse.

"What you got to understand is, they don't want the Negro out there in the first place, muddying up *their* game," Ike Harrison told him later that evening on the steps of their Fifteenth Ward porch. "Some—maybe a lot of them—are gonna try to beat the snot out of you even after the play's done. Some gonna want to stage a gridiron lynching, if you will. They're gonna pound you in hopes you'll run away like the inferior coward they believe you to be. So you gotta ask yourself, Wilmeth: Is it worth it? Am I gonna lose life and limb playing their game? Or can I make it work? Can I win over enough of my teammates? Tough call. And one only you can make. I'll say this much: basketball sure feels a lot safer."

Over the next several days, Wilmeth grappled with the decision. Back and forth, back and forth he went.

He finally decided to pay Coach Simmons a visit to discuss it further.

Simmie was quite the character—a gregarious sort with a bushy white mustache, a Gerson pipe, and a million stories. And unlike the other coaches, he went out of his way to get to know all the athletes on campus, not just the football players. He got to know them as people, not just as what-can-you-do-for-me athletes. Although Simmie hadn't coached him directly, Wilmeth had run into him several times at Archbold Gymnasium and always enjoyed their conversations. Never once did he feel the coldness he had experienced with other coaches at Syracuse. The ones who weren't colorblind. The ones who tried to make him feel inferior because he was Black. Simmie actually listened to what Wilmeth was saying. Looked him in the eye. Seemed genuinely interested. He felt like a kindhearted person one could confide in, and Wilmeth hadn't experienced many white people like that in his life.

"Hey, Coach," Wilmeth said, knocking on the partially open metal door in the bowels of the gymnasium. "Got a minute?"

"Sure, Singh. Come on in, and shut that door behind you so we can have some privacy."

Wilmeth sat down on the chair in front of a desk Simmie shared with several other coaches.

"Coach, I was thinking about what you said the other day, and I'm really interested in playing football, but I got some concerns."

"Like what?"

"Well, first off, there's the time commitment. Don't get me wrong—I'm willing to put in the time. Pride myself in working as hard as anybody. But I'm premed, and I am taking twenty credit hours a semester, and the courses aren't basket weaving."

"I understand. But you seem like a very disciplined, organized young man. I think you know how to juggle a schedule and get a bunch of things done."

"I think I do, but it's only going to get more demanding when I'm an upperclassman, and this is my priority."

"Again, understood. I think you can handle all those demands. I really do. What else is bothering you about this?"

"Well, I also worry about how I'll be received."

"You mean because you're a Negro?"

"Yeah, exactly. I'd be the only Negro on the roster."

"I hear ya, Singh. I hear ya. This is how I see it. You got talent—loads of it. And it's the kind of talent that can help Syracuse win some football games. And once you get out there on the field, that talent and your personality are gonna take over. If you are moving that football down the field and winning games, then believe you me, even the lunkheads will come around. People can be selfish. They want to know what you can do for them. And the way I see it, you can do an awful lot for them."

"But it's more than them just accepting me. What if I'm in a position where I'm running things out there? They going to accept being told what to do by a Negro? And would Coach Oz have faith to put me in that position in the first place?"

"I don't see why not. You're in a similar position on the basketball court, and Coach Andreas is comfortable with you making decisions out there. And you're the only Negro on the basketball team, right?"

"Yeah, that's right, but this is different. Football's big man on campus, and instead of making decisions for myself and four others, I'd be making decisions for myself and ten others on the field. I just need to know because in every sport I play I thrive when I've got the ball in my hands, and I'm the decision-maker out there. I want to make sure Coach Oz would be comfortable with that because I really don't want to play if he wants to convert me to some other position."

Wilmeth paused and thought about discussing the fear factor too. About how white teammates and opponents might resent him because of his dark skin and take extraordinary measures to hurt him. But he decided not to bring it up.

After absorbing all Wilmeth had said, Simmie leaned back in his chair and folded his arms behind his head.

"Singh, lemme tell you a story about gaining acceptance. It's a story from personal experience, and you might be able to relate to it in some small way.

"I once was this big-shot player who the great Amos Alonzo Stagg recruited out of a high school in Michigan to play for his powerhouse teams at the University of Chicago. You no doubt heard of Stagg. Outside of Knute Rockne, and he's gone, he's probably the most famous football coach in America.

"Well, I was pretty full of myself, thought I could get away with anything. During Thanksgiving break my freshman year of college, I head home to watch my high school alma mater play the defending state champs in Lansing, Michigan. And my old team isn't doing so well, and I'm pissed about that. So, at halftime, I suit up for them. I have this big second half and score the touchdown that helps us secure a 7–7 tie."

"Next week, I'm back on campus in Chicago, and Stagg calls me into his office. The shit has hit the fan by this time because a newspaper outed me as a high school ringer. Stagg tells me, 'Boy, you've got too much school spirit, and while I admire that loyalty to your old high school, I got no choice but to kick you off the team.' I also got kicked out of school.

"I'm distraught because I think I've thrown it all away, but someone suggested I head to Philadelphia and try out for the University of Penn. So I pack a suitcase and hop aboard a freight car without anybody knowing I'm hitching a ride for free. Halfway to Philly, I get off at Syracuse and head over to the football practice. See, a friend suggested I visit with Chick Meehan, the football coach here at the time. He was aware of who I was and told me to put some pads on for that day's practice and show him what I got. Well, he liked what I showed enough to enroll me the next day. And over the next three years, we won a ton of games, including an upset of a Nebraska team that was the only squad that ever beat Notre Dame's famed Four Horsemen.

"So, Singh, you're probably wondering what the hell's the point of this long-winded story, aren't you?"

"Um, yeah, Coach, I am. To be honest, you've kind of lost me. Don't know where you're heading with this."

"Well, the guys were extremely resentful of me when I showed up out of nowhere and was immediately given a job. They called me Hobo and a lot of things much worse. For the first few weeks, they engaged in a lot of dirty tactics. Twisting my arms and legs after tackling me in practice. A few even tried poking my eyes out when I was at the bottom of the pile. One of the pranksters shat in my shoes. I was pretty alone and isolated at first—to the point I was thinking about hopping onto another train to see if things might be better for me at Penn.

"But I stuck it out. And little by little, they grudgingly started accepting me. They saw what I could do for them, how I could help the cause. So the moral of this gasbag's story is this: I believe you can show these guys the same thing. You can make everyone around you better. You can win them over. But I'd be lying to you if I said you weren't going to have to put up with some shit—maybe even a lot of it—along the way. You definitely will. And you probably won't win over everyone. I didn't. There are some guys who will go to their graves resenting me. To which I say, 'Screw 'em.'"

Wilmeth began to smile. "Well, Coach, I think you convinced me. I think I want to give it a shot."

"That's great, Singh. Just so you know, there's some good eggs on this team. There are plenty of guys here who come from poor backgrounds. Some guys who have to take crap, too, because they're Irish or Polish or Italian or Jewish. I think they'll be on your side from the start. Coach Solem is set in a lot of his ways, but he's also a very innovative guy. He'll eventually get over his reservations about you being a Negro when he sees all the creative things he'll be able to do with someone of your abilities. I just wanted to be frank with you, but I have faith in you. I've seen you on the basketball court. We've chatted before, so I have a decent feel for who you are. You're battle-tested. You've probably been dealing with this kind of crap since you came out of your mother's womb. You know all about how to persevere, how to succeed when the odds are stacked against you."

Wilmeth got up from his chair, shook hands, and thanked him for his time. When he reached the door, he remembered one other thing he had wanted to discuss.

"Coach?"

"Yes, Singh?"

"I'm sorry to take up more of your time, but there was one other thing."

"What's that?"

"It's this Hindu stuff, Coach. Started back when I was playing basketball in New York City, and it's continued on here. 'Cause my name's different and 'cause a lot of people aren't accepting of Negroes, sportswriters and coaches and administrators keep telling people I'm a Hindu, like I'm from India."

"Yeah, I can see why that would bother you."

"It got so bad here that someone in the athletics department even suggested I dress up in Indian garb and take some pictures so that they could promote me as a Hindu star. Thought it would be good publicity, something they could market. I told 'em no way I'm doing that. I'm a Negro and proud of it. I'm not going to act the lead in some dang minstrel show."

"I don't blame you, Singh, for putting that idea where the sun don't shine. That's bullshit."

"Coach, why do I have to keep playing this charade?"

"Really wish I could help you out with this. I really do. If I had the power, I'd make sure the university and society stopped this nonsense. Unfortunately, it's beyond my control. Sadly, it seems people are more comfortable playing this game than doing what's right. My only advice would be to play along because I'm fearful there are some real ignoramuses in positions of power who won't give you this chance otherwise. You know what I'm talking about. Hell, even the chancellor's a bigot. I've seen the memos where he and the director of admissions don't want any Negro students. They think coloreds are mentally inferior, not deserving to attend a white university. Singh, I can't pretend to know how I would react if it were me in your shoes. I'd probably punch somebody in the nose because that's how I'm wired. But I wouldn't suggest you take that course of action. You probably have to continue the ruse. In the meantime, take full advantage of the education you're receiving here, and maybe someday you'll be part of a reckoning and help show America the error of her ways."

CHAPTER 20

October 16, 1937

The bus trip back from Ithaca was loud and boisterous. All that was missing were victory cigars and celebratory bottles of champagne.

"Big Red, my arse!" bellowed Duffy Daugherty, the pugnacious, undersized lineman whose blocking and tackling had set the tone in that afternoon's upset of national football powerhouse Cornell.

"Screw the Big Red! How 'bout the Big Orange!" roared teammate Phil Allen. "Guess the boys from Syracuse University showed those Ivy League prima donnas how the game's played, now didn't we? Don't those pricks know the sun always sets orange?"

A beaming Harold "Babe" Ruth rose from his seat and shouted for his teammates to pipe down for a moment.

"OK, boys," he said, moving into the aisle. "I think it's time we serenade our vanquished opponents in song."

"And a one. And a two. And a three," Ruth crooned into a make-believe microphone.

"Far above Cayuga's waters.

There's an awful smell.

Some say it's Cayuga's waters.

We think it's Cornell."

Players began pelting the would-be lounge lizard with balled-up paper cups.

"Sit down, Babe," yelled John Schroeder, a hulking two-way tackle.

"Don't quit your day job," shouted Roger Mabie, the team's manager.

Near the back of the bus, Wilmeth and Marty Glickman were laughing so hard they were having trouble breathing.

"I'm gonna pee my pants," Wilmeth said, gasping for air.

"I hear ya," responded Glickman. "Good times, hey, Sing-Sing?"

"Yeah, Marty. Really good times."

After a few hours of revelry, the team bus pulled into the crushed-stone lot next to Archbold Gymnasium, which overlooked the concrete Roman Coliseum-like stadium where the Orangemen played home football games. The rowdy players tumbled out the door and began grabbing their duffel bags from the storage compartments beneath the bus. Before they could haul their gear into the nearby locker room, Coach Ossie Solem gathered everyone for some final words.

"Men, I just want you to know how proud I am of you. No one gave us a snowball's chance in Hades—that's 'hell' for you guys who aren't up on your Greek mythology—but thank goodness you were too either too stubborn or too dumb to listen to the naysayers. You delivered quite a message today. Not only can we play with the big boys; we can beat the big boys. In a hostile environment, no less."

Before Solem could say another word, Daugherty shouted, "You got that right, Coach!" And soon he and his teammates were pounding on the side of the bus and hooting and hollering like a bunch of wild men.

"All right, all right!" Solem shouted, raising his hands to quiet them back down.

"We're three and oh, and we got a chance to do something special this autumn if we all stick together. We're a family, and we need to make sure we keep having one another's back. All for one and one for all."

"You got that right, Coach!" Daugherty boomed once more.

"E pluribus unum," screamed Schroeder.

"OK! OK!" Solem shouted, again trying to restore order. "Now, go out and have a good time tonight, men, but keep your wits about you. I'm not spending my hard-earned cash bailing any of you clowns out of jail.

"Let's all huddle together. Duff, you got the biggest mouth, so break it down for us."

Daugherty the ham was more than happy to oblige.

"OK, men. Join hands together. You know the drill. Repeat with me. One! Two! Three! Win!"

Although it had been a long, long day, it was clear the boys from Syracuse were still operating on full testosterone tanks. The victory had energized them, and it was Saturday night—party time. The downtown bars were beckoning, and their hormones were raging. They were ready to paint the town orange after one of the school's biggest victories in years.

"Hey, guys," bellowed Ruth, "let's take a roll down ol' Piety Hill."

"Great idea, Babe," said Allen.

Soon several of them were rolling, dizzily like little kids down the steep, grassy knoll upon which Crouse College stood. As they regained their bearings at the base of the hill and brushed the grass and leaves from their clothes, they noticed the chimesmasters were ringing out the Syracuse fight song from the Crouse bell tower.

"Howdaya like that?" Allen said. "They're playing our song."

Before continuing down the block toward downtown, Daugherty commanded his comrades to stop and began pulling bottles from a bag.

"Here, boys," he said as he began dispensing the six-pack of Utica Club beer to Wilmeth, Allen, Ruth, Glickman, and Schroeder. "I got some presents for you. These UCs have been sitting in my locker all day, so they might be piss-water warm, but beer is beer, and they'll get the night started."

"Hey, Duff, you got a bottle opener?" asked Schroeder.

"Oh crap! I don't."

"Well, how the hell you suggest we open the bottles? With our teeth?"

"Hold on! Hold on!"

Daugherty unfastened his belt and removed the strap from his pants.

"Hey, Duff, we didn't mean no harm," Allen shouted. "No need to whip us."

"Believe me, Allen, I wouldn't need a strap to kick your ass," Daugherty said, prying the caps off the bottles with his belt buckle.

"Duff, you're a freaking genius."

"Just putting my college education to use."

"May I propose a toast," Ruth said, raising his Utica Club skyward. "To the boys from Syracuse!"

"Here! Here!" they said in unison before chugging their suds and continuing on their merry way.

"Where we going, by the way?" inquired Allen.

"Hotel Syracuse," Daugherty responded.

"Why there? Their prices are too high for my sorry-ass, starving-student's budget."

"The price will be just right when they find out we are football players, and we just kicked Cornell's keister. Plus, you forget that I grew up here in the good ol' Salt City, and we Irishmen know everybody. The proprietor's a good friend of my dad's. Mention the name Daugherty, and it's like handing him a blank check.

"So you needn't worry, Allen, you cheap bastard. You won't have to spend that first communion money that's been accruing interest since you were twelve. Boys, those taps are gonna be flowing like Niagara tonight. You'll be drinking for free."

After a few more blocks of ball busting, the boys from Syracuse found themselves at the front door of the grandiose hotel that had been built in the Roaring Twenties—the building known as the Grand Lady. It was *the* place to be and to be seen in Syracuse—the place where US presidents and world-class entertainers stayed when visiting Central New York.

"They tell me, Duff, that my namesake—the great Babe Ruth—downed twenty-four mugs of beer in an hour when he was in town with Lou Gehrig for that exhibition baseball game last fall."

"Well, let's see if you can top that tonight, Babe Jr."

As they prepared to enter the front door, Wilmeth told Daugherty and company to have a good time.

"Sing-Sing, where the hell you think you're going? Aren't you gonna join us?"

"Nah, I think I'm going to call it a night."

"Whaddaya mean you're gonna call it a night? Got a hot date? Or now that you're a big star have you become too damned important to drink with us?"

"Not at all, Duff. It's just that . . . well, you know."

"Know what?"

"Come on, Duff, you know why I can't go in there."

"No, I don't. Educate me, Dr. Sing-Sing."

"I can't go in there, because I'm a Negro. And they don't like serving Negroes. The only Negroes in there are the ones cleaning the rooms and doing the laundry and peeling the potatoes."

"Sing-Sing, you forget," chimed in Schroeder. "They don't think you're colored. They think you're a Hindu, and they don't have any problems serving Hindus. That's what they've read in the papers, and that's what they believe, even if we all know it's bull. Nobody's gonna give you guff in our presence. If they do, we'll trash the place, floor to ceiling."

"John, I ain't a Hindu, and I'd appreciate it if you wouldn't call me that."

"All right, all right, Mr. Negro. I didn't mean no harm."

Wilmeth lunged toward Schroeder, but Daugherty and Allen grabbed him before he could throw a punch.

"Relax, Sing-Sing!" Daugherty shouted.

"Let me go!" Wilmeth yelled.

"All right. All right, Sing-Sing. Nobody meant no harm."

"I'm outta here."

Though he still felt an impulse to body-slam Schroeder to the sidewalk, Wilmeth decided to walk away.

"Suit yourself, Sing-Sing," Allen said as he and the others headed into the hotel.

Wilmeth took deep breaths to calm himself as he hoofed down Salina Street. In no time at all, he'd be back in the Ward, back in the place where he slept and ate and was treated like an equal—and in some cases, like a hero. Especially by the young Black kids who aspired to play like him on the big basketball courts and football fields.

After a few blocks, his fury subsided, and he began smiling. Other than Schroeder's ignorant comment, it had been a good day. So good that for several hours he really did feel like one of the boys from Syracuse. The football game couldn't have gone any better. Not only had the Orangemen upset the Big Red but Wilmeth had been given more responsibilities by the coaches and had executed the game plan flawlessly. On that raucous bus ride back, he had laughed so hard he had almost wet himself. Rolling down that steep grassy hill with his teammates made him feel like he was back in elementary school without a care in the world. And the suds he swigged with Duff and the guys, though room-temperature warm, never tasted so good. In those moments, he had lost himself in joy. Didn't feel like a Black man. Or a Hindu. But rather, like any man and every man. One of them.

The smile, and the good thoughts, though, would not last long. Reality had slapped him upside the head when he reached the entrance to that swank hotel. As much as he would have loved going into that bar and continuing to be one of the boys from Syracuse, he knew he couldn't. He remembered what John Isaacs advised before he departed Harlem for Syracuse. "You need to be a good Negro up there—the best Negro you can be—because if you have one slipup, even the slightest one, it's over," Isaacs had warned. "They'll send your Black ass and your dreams packing in a New York minute."

Wilmeth understood if he joined the guys in that bar and something happened, he'd be blamed. The missteps wouldn't be excused as boys being boys. It would be seen as a *boy* being a *boy*, screwing it up for the white guys. And the racists who never wanted him on their lily-white campus in the first place would have had a field day. "Told you so," they would have spewed. "Better off without those troublemaking Negroes."

And so Wilmeth kept walking—away from that world and back to the world where he didn't have to pretend to be someone he wasn't.

CHAPTER 21

"Hey, Sing-Sing, did you see the papers? We're ranked seventeenth in the country. And they're talking about you—the only Hindu college football player in the land."

Wilmeth gazed at the stack of papers in Daugherty's locker.

"You're a star, Sing-Sing. *New York Times. Washington Post.* Can I have your autograph?"

"Eat shit and die, Duff," Wilmeth said, grinning broadly as he grabbed one of the sports sections.

The Syracuse football team was indeed garnering national recognition after knocking off Cornell, and so was their "Hindu" star. Wilmeth was not the bragging type by any means, but he did take pride in seeing his name in the paper, though he could have done without the Hindu references he'd been pegged with since his all-city basketball days at DeWitt Clinton High School, when some sportswriters began calling him the Manhattan Hindu.

He was excited about Syracuse potentially improving its 1937 record to

4–0 that Saturday and climbing even higher in the polls. But that wasn't his only motivation. That week's game against the University of Maryland in Baltimore also would be a homecoming of sorts. It was a chance not only to return to his birthplace—the place he called home the first seven years of his life—but also a chance to play in front of several close relatives for the first time in his college career.

He was especially excited about seeing his aunt, Adelaide Webb, again and giving her a bear hug.

"Addy was more like a big sister than an aunt to me," Wilmeth told Daugherty. "She was always bragging on me to people, telling me I could become anything I wanted if I just kept my nose clean and to the grindstone."

"Is that right?" Daugherty said as he strained to pull his tight practice jersey over his shoulder pads.

"When I first came up here, I was really homesick. On more than one occasion, I thought about packing my suitcase and hightailing it back to Harlem. But every time I felt that way, I'd get a letter from Addy telling me how proud she, the family, and the old neighbors were of me. She said a lot of people in the old hood were living their dreams through me. That I'd been given an opportunity a lot of people would kill to have. So my clothes stayed in the dresser and that suitcase in the closet."

"So what you're telling me, Sing-Sing, is that not everyone there Saturday will be rooting against us."

"Oh yeah, Duff, we'll definitely have some supporters from the Webb side of the family. And mark my words: Even though they'll be heavily outnumbered, you'll be able to hear 'em. Loud and clear. Especially Addy. She's loud and proud. Ain't nobody gonna tell her to pipe down."

Wilmeth plopped down on his stool and began reading the *Washington Post* story more closely. Back in March, during the basketball season, the newspaper interviewed him for a short feature in which he confirmed he had never been to India. That tidbit became the headline of a story that pegged him as "presumably the only Hindu basketball player in the United States."

Playing the mistaken identity game was draining. There were times when Wilmeth wanted to scream from the top of the Empire State Building that he was neither Indian nor Hindu but rather Black and Christian. And damn proud of it too. But he'd been warned by Isaacs to keep his mouth shut and keep living the lie white sportswriters, coaches, and officials created about him because that's the only way he'd be able to get his college education and continue playing sports in 1930s America.

He couldn't help but notice this latest *Post* article had identified him as a "full-blooded Hindu." There also were two mocking references to him as "sit-down-Singh"—a juvenile and unfunny play on his surname.

"What an asshole," Wilmeth muttered, tossing the paper to the floor.

CHAPTER 22

Baltimore, April 2000

On Breanna's list of people to interview, Charles Williams had circled Sam Lacy's name, writing in caps next to it: "ABSOLUTE MUST!" She was astounded to learn Lacy was still cranking out a weekly column at age 96 for the *Baltimore Afro-American*, still coming to the office three times a week in his role as sports editor. She couldn't wait to meet him, because Lacy had known Wilmeth well and was involved in a seminal moment in his life. He'd be able to fill in so many missing details.

But she also was excited because she wanted to pick his brain about what it had been like covering Jackie Robinson's barrier-shattering 1947 season with the Brooklyn Dodgers, and the indignities Lacy and other Black sportswriters faced while crusading for racial equality in sports and society. Theirs was a lesser-known story of heroism against odds nearly as daunting as the ones Jackie faced.

"Ms. Shelton, Mr. Lacy is expecting you," a receptionist told Breanna when she arrived in the lobby of the *Afro-American* offices. "You can meet him in his office on the third floor."

"Thanks. Where's the elevator?"

"I'm sorry, but there isn't one. We joke this building was constructed before the invention of elevators. You'll have to take the stairs."

As Breanna hoofed up the three flights—thirty-six steep steps in all—she wondered how a nonagenarian like Lacy negotiated this staircase three times a week. Even though she was in good shape, barely twenty-five years old, she was huffing and puffing halfway through her trek.

There, at the top of the stairs, stood a wiry man, short and slim, with chiseled facial features inherited from his mother, a full-blooded Shinne-cock Indian.

"Good morning, young lady," Lacy said.

"Good morning, Mr. Lacy," she replied.

"You can call me Sam. I'd shake your hand, but as you can see from this old codger's gnarled fingers, seventy years of pounding the keys of an old Underwood did a number on me. Got so bad I had to stop using my type-writer. These days I scribble my column longhand and have somebody else type it into the system. Sometimes I need to do some interpretation of my Sanskrit for them. One of my reporters told me, 'Good gracious, Sam, my doctor's prescriptions are more legible than this.'"

Lacy and Breanna chuckled.

"Moral of the story, young lady—don't get old. And make sure you hire somebody to take dictation."

"I'm just impressed you're still pumping out columns after all these years," she said as they made their way to his office.

"Well, some people my age play Scrabble. Or do crossword puzzles. I write and still manage to play a little golf. My game's about as good as my typing. Nonexistent."

On the wall behind Lacy's huge metal desk was the J. G. Taylor Spink

Award for meritorious contributions to baseball writing that he received two years earlier, making him just the second Black scribe to earn a spot in the writer's wing of the Baseball Hall of Fame in Cooperstown. Next to the plaque was a photograph of Lacy, resplendent in suit and fedora, standing next to Robinson at Ebbets Field in Brooklyn before a World Series game in 1956.

"Wow! This stuff is awesome," Breanna said, peering at other photographs, including one of tennis legend Althea Gibson after she became the first Black to win Wimbledon in 1957.

"We all talk about Jackie, Joe Louis, Hammerin' Hank Aaron, Muhammad Ali, and now Tiger Woods, but that win by Althea is as significant as any achieved by a colored athlete," Lacy said. "Doesn't get the due it deserves. Althea had it tougher than the guys. Faced the double whammy of being colored and female. And had to compete in a sport that was the epitome of whiteness and privilege."

Breanna nodded. She could relate, in her own small way.

"Didn't mean to ramble," Lacy said. "Now, you said on the phone you wanted to talk about Wilmeth Sidat-Singh, the man who wasn't allowed to show his true colors."

"Yes, but before we talk about Wilmeth, I want to know more about you—what it was like being a Black sportswriter in the late 1930s. I would imagine, like Wilmeth and the Black athletes, you writers had to deal with a lot of stuff too."

"Yes, we did," he said, handing her a copy of his autobiography, *Fighting for Fairness: The Life Story of Hall of Fame Sportswriter Sam Lacy*. "This is for you. It's got details about what those times were like, but let me try to paint the picture for you.

"We had to put up with the same baloney every Negro had to endure. No Negro was immune. Jim Crow was everywhere, and I mean everywhere. Even in the supposedly enlightened North, although up there it was more subtle, more disguised.

"Wendell Smith, Joe Bostic, me, and some of the other Negro writers would go to cover Brooklyn Dodger games, and we'd be denied access to the press box. Whites only. At some ballparks on the road, they'd stick us out with the colored folks, in the Jim Crow fan sections they roped off in the outfield bleachers at every park. Believe you me, we aren't talking good seats. They'd place us so far away you'd need binoculars.

"Other times they'd put us up on the roof. I didn't take too kindly to that, because I was scared of heights. Not my idea of a good time, 'specially when the wind howled or the rain was pelting you.

"The Baseball Writers Association of America wasn't much help at first. So, when I complained to Mr. Rickey—Branch Rickey, the Dodgers' general manager who was the mastermind behind the Jackie Robinson experiment—he said, 'Sam, don't you fret.' And Mr. Rickey arranged for me to sit at the end of the Dodgers' dugout for some home games. That really pissed off a bunch of the white writers, to which I said, 'Too bad.'

"Like Jackie and the other Negro major leaguers, we couldn't stay in team hotels or eat in the same restaurants or drink from the same water fountains as whites. Had to stay in homes of Negro families. Wound up being a blessing in disguise because it gave us access to Jackie and his wife, Rachel, something the white reporters didn't have. So our stories were richer in detail. A lot more human."

"From doing a little reading about you, Mr. Lacy, you weren't afraid to take a stand and take on the white establishment."

"I don't think what I was doing was anything brave or noble. It was just about righting wrongs, or as my book says, fighting for fairness. And sometimes that irks people on both sides. I fought for baseball and everything else in our society to be integrated and allow for equal opportunities. Now, some of the Negro League owners and players didn't like that. See, they were OK with the status quo and thought integrating Major League Baseball would ruin the Negro Leagues, which it did. But putting the Negro Leagues out of business wound up being the best thing that could happen, even though it caused pain for some at first.

"Clark Griffith, the owner of the old Washington Senators baseball team, also wanted to maintain the status quo because, in his heart, he didn't want colored boys playing with whites, and, oh, by the way, he was making a ton of money renting out his ballpark to Negro League teams. He argued integration would put four hundred colored guys out of work. That ticked me off. I wrote in my column, 'When Abraham Lincoln signed the Emancipation Proclamation, he put four hundred thousand Black people out of work.' Needless to say, Mr. Griffith didn't like my response."

"You were persistent."

"Darn right I was. I believed if we kept pounding away, pounding away, pounding away, like sledgehammers to rocks, we'd eventually get all the sports integrated."

"What kept you going?"

"I'm an eternal optimist. If you're born Black, you know when you wake up in the morning the day ahead can't be any worse than the one before. So you take a positive attitude from there. All Blacks have a birthmark of optimism."

"Although you're best known for crusading to integrate baseball and your coverage of Jackie, the story you wrote about Wilmeth before Syracuse played Maryland in 1937 really launched your career, didn't it?"

"Did indeed. Biggest scoop I ever had. Most controversial too. Got a lot of people riled at me, especially in the colored community, and that's where my bread was buttered. Those were my readers, my people. Probably the only folks happy with me were the bigots running the University of Maryland and their football team.

"Wasn't my intention, but I did something they were incapable of doing. I stopped Wilmeth Sidat-Singh dead in his tracks. What I didn't stop was their bigotry and hatred. And that was too bad, 'cause that was the purpose of my story. To shame them into doing the right thing, but they didn't. And sadly, Wilmeth wound up paying a heavy price."

CHAPTER 23

Baltimore, October 23, 1937

Wilmeth and Duffy Daugherty awoke early, got dressed, and headed down
to the hotel lobby to kill time before breakfast and the bus to the game.

"Hey, Sing-Sing," Phil Allen said, sprinting over with a rolled-up newspaper. "Did you see this?"

Wilmeth unfolded the copy of the *Washington Tribune* and gazed at the
bold headline at the top of the page. There, in large type usually reserved for
war declarations or presidential deaths, blared a banner headline: "NEGRO
TO PLAY U OF MARYLAND; THEY CALL HIM A HINDU."

"Holy shit!" Wilmeth said.

"Sophisticated Maryland University's tradition stands to be knocked
into a crooked hat Saturday," read the lede to the unbylined story written
by Sam Lacy. "For behind the scenes stands a Negro. {Sidat-Singh has been}
exploited by local dailies as a Hindu, obviously for the purpose of explaining

the presence of the dark-skinned footballer in the visiting backfield.

"And now—oh, horrors—{Maryland} must match wit and brawn, shoulder to shoulder, with a colored person. What ironical tricks are being played on the poor unsuspecting Nordics!"

As Wilmeth continued reading, several people huddled around him.

"What's all the commotion, boys?" Coach Ossie Solem exclaimed upon arriving in the lobby. "Something in that paper I might want to read to the troops to fire them up in the locker room before kickoff?"

Wilmeth handed the paper to Solem without saying a word and slinked slowly away.

"Coach, it's from the Negro newspaper in town," Allen said.

Solem took a look at the headline.

"Oh my goodness," he said softly. "Why don't you guys go to the banquet room and grab some grub? I'll see all of you on the bus in a bit."

Solem tracked down Lew Andreas, the school's athletic director, at the other end of the lobby.

"Lew, I think we have a problem."

"What's going on? Somebody break curfew last night?"

"Take a look at this."

Andreas's eyes bulged as he read the headline.

"Holy moly. This is not good. Not good at all."

"What are we going to do?" Solem inquired.

"Don't know," Andreas responded. "Ossie, you know how these things work. Maryland, like most southern schools, doesn't have any Negro players. Hell, they don't even have any Negro students. And there's this understanding, this gentlemen's agreement, that they won't play any teams who have Negroes on their roster. We know that and the other northern schools know that when we sign on to play these games south of the Mason-Dixon Line."

"Ossie, we got a guaranteed contract for thirty grand to play this game, and we absolutely got to have that money if we want to keep our sports programs going. The Great Depression's been a killer—put us on the brink. Been a few times when the chancellor's threatened to shut sports down completely, but I've talked him out of it—sold him on the idea they're especially important right now to school spirit and morale. We're in quite a pickle here."

"Lew, this is a Negro newspaper. So maybe the folks at Maryland haven't seen this. Maybe we go to the stadium, play the game, and then they'll have to pay us because we'll have fulfilled our contractual obligations."

"Let's pray that's the case."

Any hopes of that happening evaporated a few hours later as the Syracuse players went through their pregame warm-ups on a field that had been turned into a quagmire by the torrential downpour pelting the East Coast. Hoisting an umbrella, Andreas sloshed across the field to say hello to Maryland athletic director Swede Eppley.

"Hey, Swede, how's it going?"

"I'd be doing better if I had an ark," Eppley grumbled.

Before Andreas could continue their idle chitchat, Eppley pulled a rolled-up newspaper from his trench coat and handed it to his Syracuse counterpart. It was a copy of that morning's *Washington Tribune*.

"Lew, don't know if you saw this or not, but we have a problem that's going to need to be resolved—and resolved in a hurry. Your boy is an issue."

"Yeah, I did see this, Swede."

"Lew, you signed that contract, so you know about that gentlemen's agreement we have. We don't play against Negroes down here."

"Yeah, I know, I know. But couldn't you make an exception here? Would it really be so bad if Wilmeth played?"

"It wouldn't be if he was who you guys said he was—a Hindu, not a Negro. We don't play against Negroes on our turf. Simple as that. Been our policy forever, and I don't see it changing here in the foreseeable future. Certainly not today."

"Look, Swede, almost all your fans are white. They don't read this newspaper. It's printed for Negroes. Nobody's gonna know."

"You saw it, and I saw it, so who's to say a lot of other white folks haven't seen it too? Put yourself in my shoes, Lew. If my boss, Curley Byrd, caught wind I bucked policy and let our boys play against a Negro, he'd fire me on the spot."

Eppley wasn't being hyperbolic about Byrd, who had been at Maryland forever—first as a student, then as a coach and athletic director, and now as school president. Byrd was a staunch segregationist and had even made public comments about his stances, which had been lauded by Maryland alumni and donors.

"This is the South, Lew, and we do things different down here," Eppley continued. "Either No. 19 sits, or we don't play. You'll forfeit the game, and you won't be cashing that check. A deal's a deal."

Andreas realized he was fighting a hopeless battle. Eppley had to answer to Byrd, and the chancellor wasn't going to budge.

"OK, Swede. Guess we have no choice but to bench him."

Andreas shook Eppley's hand, then sloshed over to Solem to break the news.

"I can't believe we're doing this, Lew, especially less than an hour before kickoff. You're a football guy. You know what the hell I've been developing here. Each week we've been building more of our attack around Wilmeth. Now you want me to bench him? That's bullshit!"

"Yes, it is, but we got no choice. Money talks. Wilmeth can always play next week, when we're back at Archbold. It's just one game. We'll survive."

CHAPTER 24

New York City, April 2000

Marty Glickman welcomed Breanna to his Manhattan apartment just a few weeks after she interviewed Sam Lacy in Baltimore. She'd read where Glickman had gone out of his way to make Wilmeth feel like one of the guys on the football team, even arranging for him to live on campus his senior year.

"I believe there were only between a half dozen to a dozen Blacks enrolled at Syracuse University at the time, and they had to reside off campus—those were the prejudiced but accepted rules of the time," Glickman said, delivering his words in a staccato cadence familiar to longtime New York sports fans who remembered him as the play-by-play announcer for Knicks basketball and Giants and Jets football.

"Well, me, Duffy Daugherty, Phil Allen, and some of the other guys didn't think that was right, so we took it upon ourselves to put together a makeshift dorm for about twelve of the football players, including Wilmeth, on the uppermost floor of old Archbold Gymnasium. Roy Simmons Sr., who was a boxing, lacrosse, and assistant football coach and a gem of guy, got some bunk beds for us, and we hunkered down near the weight room, which really wasn't much of a weight room back in the day.

"The only bad thing about the place was it could get hotter than the blazes in the early fall and colder than Antarctica during the winter months. And the closest bathroom was four floors below, in the football locker room. That could cause some problems, particularly if you had to go pee in the middle of the night. So, boys being boys, we came up with a system. We'd open up a window and take a whiz."

Breanna chuckled.

"Yeah, it was pretty crazy," Glickman continued, grinning sheepishly. "In the fall and spring, the groundskeepers couldn't figure out why the patch of grass below our 'relief' window was always yellow. And in the winter, the snow beneath the window was always yellow too."

"Hey," Breanna said, after composing herself. "When Mother Nature calls . . ."

"Indeed," Glickman replied.

"Marty, from what I've read and the people I've talked to, you seemed to be the closest to Wilmeth. Why was that?"

"Oh, a number of reasons, I suppose. First off, you could not help but like Wilmeth. Had an infectious personality. Very charismatic. Loved to laugh. With others. At himself. Extremely popular on campus. The coeds would swoon over him because he was so damn handsome. Of course, in those days, there were social mores against interracial dating, so Wilmeth did his best not to cross the line, though I know he did on at least one occasion. And it broke his heart.

"Wilmeth also was smart as a whip—no lame courses on his class schedule. I remember several times going to him for help with my science and math courses. He tutored me through a class or two. And he did the same with a few other teammates. Very generous in that way."

"Marty, did any of the guys resent him because he was Black?"

"Yeah, there were a few Neanderthals on the team. But they were in the minority. The majority of us had the utmost respect for him—his character, his ability, his smarts. How could we not? You can't fake it out there on the field. The cream rises to the top. He was so talented, and we all knew he gave us the best chance to win.

"Wilmeth had a cannon for an arm and great instincts. He was doing things out there with the passing game that people hadn't seen before, including pump fakes and an occasional no-look pass that would fake defenders out of their jocks.

"Fortunately, we had some innovative coaches—guys like Solem, Bud Wilkinson, and Biggie Munn. They weren't afraid to go against the grain and tailor plays to take advantage of Wilmeth's extraordinary skills. Sing-Sing allowed us to be daring and bold, to throw the ball at a time when most coaches still believed two out of three things could go wrong any time you put it up in the air—either it falls incomplete or gets intercepted. With Sing-Sing, the good far outweighed the bad."

Glickman paused for a minute.

"I think the biggest reason I might have been closer to him than the others was our shared experiences. We both were forced to learn how to deal with prejudice. He faced stuff because of his skin color. I faced stuff because I was Jewish. Racism and anti-Semitism were rampant at the time. Still are, I guess."

"Did you guys ever talk about that?"

"No, we really didn't. Nor did we need to. Our empathy for one another was unspoken but deeply understood."

"Ever discuss with him what happened to you at the Berlin Olympics in 1936—how you weren't allowed to run in that relay race because you were a Jew?"

"No."

"Why not?"

"Because it was something I was trying to bury in the deep recesses of my mind. The wounds were still too fresh, too painful. I was trying my damndest to forget about it, even though that was impossible."

"Two years ago, the US Olympic Committee tried to make amends by presenting you with a plaque in lieu of the gold medal you almost certainly would have won. Did that help in some small way?"

"Yeah, it did, with the emphasis on the word *small*. But one of the hard lessons I've learned in life is that you can't undo the past, no matter how hard you try. I have two huge regrets. That certainly was one of them."

Glickman peered into the distance. Breanna's questions seemed to reopen old wounds and transport him back fifty-four years. Suddenly, he no longer was in his Manhattan den festooned with broadcasting awards and inscribed photos from the likes of Marv Albert, Bob Costas, Mike Tirico, and the other Syracuse men he inspired, helping the school earn its reputation as Sportscaster U.

He was eighteen again, sitting in the locker room of the massive Berlin Olympiastadion, listening to his coach break the news that broke his heart.

Avery Brundage, the racist, anti-Semitic head of the United States Olympic Committee, had just met with Adolf Hitler's minions. The Führer, they told Brundage, was furious. Jesse Owens, the Black sprinter and jumper, had blown Hitler's theory of Aryan superiority to smithereens, winning three gold medals in events the German chancellor's fair-haired, white-skinned boys were supposed to dominate.

The last thing Hitler wanted was two "Jew boys"—Glickman and teammate Sam Stoller—rubbing salt in his wounds. The message had been conveyed to "Slavery Avery," and he agreed not to humiliate Hitler further. So the day Glickman and Stoller were scheduled to run their legs in the four-by-one-hundred-yard relay for the gold-medal favorites, US track and field assistant coach Dean Cromwell informed the two they were being replaced in the lineup. No reason was given, but Glickman, Stoller, and everyone else on the team knew why they had been benched.

"Marty? Marty!"

"Oh, I'm sorry, Breanna. Just got stuck in the past for a moment or two."

"No, problem. I know it must be painful recounting this."

"Yeah, it is. Built up a lot of scar tissue through the years, but it still eats away at me. I obviously was furious with Hitler and the Nazis—that goes without saying. They were horrible, despicable people. But I may have been even angrier with Brundage and the other US officials. They proved to be spineless cowards. Jellyfish. Had neither the backbone nor the morals to stick up for Sam and me. They might as well have been wearing brown shirts and swastikas too.

"It's funny, but Jesse stood up for us. Told Cromwell we deserved to run. And that spoke legions about Jesse's morals and integrity. He stood to benefit from us sitting because that gave him the opportunity for a fourth gold medal, but he was willing to forgo that because he wanted to do the right thing. Of course, Cromwell wasn't about to listen to him, a Black man, or us, two Jews. Case closed."

"You mentioned you had two huge regrets. I'm assuming the other one was what happened in Maryland in 1937, right?"

"Bingo! See, the one in thirty-six, I couldn't have done anything about that. Totally out of my control. But the incident in thirty-seven, I could have and should have taken a stand. Kind of ironic, isn't it? Here I am, this guy who made quite a career for himself through the things he said over the course of thousands and thousands of broadcasts. But it was what I didn't say that haunts me to this day. Kept my damn mouth shut, and I'll carry that silence to my grave."

CHAPTER 25

Baltimore, October 23, 1937

After completing their calisthenics and kicking and passing drills, the soggy, mud-caked Orangemen returned to the locker room to towel down and warm themselves with cups of coffee before heading back out for what they believed would be a victory against Maryland that fateful October afternoon in 1937.

Wilmeth removed his drenched leather football helmet, grabbed a towel, and sat down next to Glickman. The two had become close that season, developing a chemistry on the field, with Wilmeth's accurate arm and Glickman's lightning-quick feet creating a potent combination.

"Gonna be a sloppy one out there today, Sing-Sing," Glickman said, sipping his coffee.

"Could be to our advantage, Marty," Wilmeth said.

"How so?"

"Slippery grass makes it tougher on the defender. Ballcarriers and receivers can juke and cut and force tacklers to slip when they try to plant their feet. They slip or fall, and you're off to the races."

"Good point."

"I hope the coaches stay aggressive with our offense and keep forcing the action. Keep doing what got us here. No time to become gun-shy."

"Hey, Sing-Sing, I heard you've got a bunch of relatives here. Did you get a chance to see them yet?"

"Not yet, but I'm hoping to be celebrating with them briefly after we whip these Terrapins."

Glickman smiled and patted Wilmeth on the shoulder pads.

Just then Solem and Andreas walked into the locker room, their fedoras and trench coats soaked from the downpour.

"All right, men, pipe down and listen up. Mr. Andreas has something to say."

Nearly two decades earlier, Andreas sat where these players were. A standout in both basketball and football at Syracuse, he stayed on to coach hoops at his alma mater and recently had taken on the added role of athletic director. He recruited Wilmeth to Syracuse to play basketball and had reluctantly agreed to allow him to play football, too, after Simmons's discovery during an intramural game. The news he was about to deliver involving his best basketball player wasn't going to be easy.

"Men, I want to start out by saying you guys are off to a great start, and a big reason you've been successful is because you've put the team first. You've shown a capacity to overcome obstacles. When one man goes down, another one steps up to take his place. You've adjusted to tough challenges and stuck together.

"And you're going to need to do that again today because we have a little bit of unexpected adversity tossed our way. Coach Solem and I received some bad news this morning. Unfortunately, because of circumstances beyond our control, Wilmeth is not going to be able to play today."

Several players began to grumble.

"What are you talking about?" shouted Daugherty. "Whaddaya mean he can't play? He's not hurt. He's as fit as a fiddle."

Andreas squirmed.

"And we want to keep him that way. We put him out there, there's no telling what might happen. These southern boys definitely will try to hurt him on every play. They'll assault him. Use dirty tactics. Late hits. Pile-ons. You name it."

"Let 'em try that crap," shouted Phil Allen, "and those southern boys will wish they were never born. We'll go through them like Sherman through Atlanta."

"Silence!" Andreas screamed.

The players were caught off guard. They had never heard the mild-mannered Andreas raise his voice like that before. The room grew quiet.

"Coach Solem and I are just trying to do what's best for Wilmeth. He's not playing, and that's that. End of discussion."

As Andreas stomped out of the room, Wilmeth slunk back on his stool. He felt as if all the air in his body had been sucker punched out of him. He grabbed a towel and wrapped it around his head.

Glickman sat in stunned silence. His heart began racing. Berlin all over again. Benched by bigotry. "Stand up, Marty! Stand up!" raged a voice inside his head. "Tell 'em if Wilmeth can't play, you aren't playing either! Get your ass up, Marty! Say something!" But another voice inside him joined the debate. "Stand up, Marty, and you're through! Solem and Andreas are anti-Semites, and they're backed by another more powerful anti-Semite— the chancellor. Make a stink about this, and they're going to call you a troublemaking Jew boy! They'll throw you out of Syracuse. You'll never get that degree. You'll be done, Marty. Stay seated, Marty! Stay seated!"

The second voice, louder and more pronounced, drowned out the first. And so he sat. And Wilmeth sat. And Syracuse played, but their hearts clearly weren't in it as Maryland slogged out a 13–0 victory in the muck and mire.

Wilmeth spent the entire game on the bench, towel wrapped around head, feeling naked and humiliated for all the world to see. He thought about the "one-for-all-and-all-for-one" comments Solem spewed following the victory against Cornell. Seemed like utter bullshit at this moment, words hollow and hypocritical. Neither his teammates, coaches, nor school stuck up for him when he needed them most. He felt alone. And used.

After showering and dressing, he trudged out of the locker room, head down. Soon he heard voices calling his name. He looked up and saw his uncle, aunt, and cousins.

"You OK, Wil?" Adelaide asked. "We were hoping you'd be out there. You hurt or something?"

"Nah," he sighed. "Just circumstances beyond my control."

"Yeah, we know all about those circumstances," his Uncle Benjamin Henley bellowed. "Ran into that sumbitch Lacy the other night in a bar, and he bragged he had a big scoop about you. If I knew that little weasel was gonna stir up shit like this before the game, I would have knocked his teeth out."

Wilmeth didn't say a word.

Adelaide wrapped her arms around him.

"Don't let the world wear you down, Wil," she said. "Your time's gonna come. You gonna make 'em all pay. Whole story ain't written yet."

"Thanks, Ade, but I'm done with all this baloney."

"Whaddaya mean? You're done?"

"I'm through. I'm done. Experiment's over. I'm coming home with you guys, going back to the District where I belong."

"Don't blame you in the least, son," Henley said. "Enough is enough. Loyalty 'sposed to be a two-way street. Syracuse U showed you today what they think of you. Screw 'em."

"Yeah, Uncle Ben, screw 'em," Wilmeth said.

Adelaide felt his pain, but there was no way she was going to let him throw it all away.

"You come too far, Wil. You can't quit now. This is bigger than you, boy. This is about all those kids in the District looking up to you, thinking you're a hero. You've been given a gift and an opportunity. May not look like a golden opportunity, 'specially now, but you got to keep plowing forward. You got a chance to open some doors. For you. And for others."

"Well, Ade, today that damn door got slammed in my face. Shut tight —and me and all those kids you're talking about in the District are on the outside looking in."

"I get that, Wil. Believe me, I get that. And there's sure to be other doors slammed in your face too. But you got to find some way to get 'em unlocked and get back inside."

"Sorry, Ade, but my mind's made up. I'm outta here."

"Look," she said, grabbing him by the shoulders. "You don't think your daddy and stepdaddy had some doors slammed in their faces? What if they had quit?"

Wilmeth's eyes began watering.

"Wil, do me a favor. Get on that bus to the train station and get on that train back to Syracuse. Give it a few days to think it over. Try looking ahead. Try focusing on the bigger picture. And if you get back to Syracuse and you feel like you can't do this anymore, then we'll welcome you back with open arms."

Adelaide hugged him with all her might, then pushed him in the direction of the team bus.

Wilmeth took a deep breath.

"All right. All right. I'll head back, but I ain't making no promises."

She smiled and kissed him on the cheek, and Wilmeth slowly boarded the bus for the train station to begin the longest, loneliest trip of his young life.

CHAPTER 26

The advance stories in the *Washington Post* and *New York Times* had made a huge deal of Syracuse's emerging gridiron star. The hype about Wilmeth being the only "Hindu" playing college football only added to the intrigue.

But in the postgame accounts following his bigoted benching during the 1937 Maryland game, Wilmeth's name wasn't even mentioned. Was he injured? Was he sick? Had he broken curfew? Had he gotten into an argument with his coach or punched a teammate? Inquiring minds wanted to know why the Syracuse star hadn't played a single snap and had spent the whole game anchored to the bench. But neither the *Post* nor the *Times* provided answers.

The man of the hour had become the invisible man.

Wilmeth who?

His name, though, was front and center in the *Washington Tribune*'s postgame coverage. The four-deck, attention-grabbing headline above Lacy's game coverage cleared up any mystery.

Gridiron Star Ousted From Maryland Game
Wilmeth Sidat-Singh Removed Following Discovery By Maryland
Authorities That He Was Not Hindu
Tribune Exposes Foreign Ruse
Players On Orange Eleven Sulk As Coach Is Compelled To Comply
With Demands of Host

Lacy pulled no punches in his lede:

An unsullied football record went by the boards here today as racial bigotry substituted for sportsmanship and resulted in the removal of the spark-plug from the machine which was Syracuse University's football team.

***

Breanna read the words aloud in Lacy's Baltimore office six decades later in 2001, she wondered what many had.

"Sam, don't mean to be rude, but did you ever consider waiting until *after* the Maryland game to break the news? That way Wilmeth could have played."

Lacy stared at her sternly.

"You aren't the first person to suggest that, young lady. Like I mentioned, I took a ton of abuse. Whew, you should have seen some of those letters to the editor! Nasty as can be. Full of venom, ripping me a new you-know-what. Some people called me a traitor to my own race—asked how could I do such a thing to one of Washington's finest, no less.

"And I'll tell you what I told them: your anger's misdirected. People love shooting the messenger 'cause they don't like the message. I wrote a follow-up column defending my stance—not that I needed to do any defending. I reminded folks that those white adults at Maryland were the people they should be angry with. Sam Lacy didn't say Wilmeth couldn't play.

The University of Maryland did. If they had been the decent, God-fearing Christians they claimed to be, they would have said, 'Let the kid play. Let everyone who deserves to play, play.' But they were racists and hypocrites."

"Did Wilmeth ever tell you he was angry with you for doing that?"

"Not really. His family was really ticked off. Wanted me fired. Wanted to run me out of town. But Wilmeth never said he was upset. And I wound up talking to him many, many times after that, and we became friends, and you might say business partners. I was the one who worked out the deals for him to come back to DC to play pro basketball and semipro football."

"Did you try to interview him after the game to get his thoughts?"

"I did. I did. But neither he nor Coach Solem wanted to be quoted. I could understand why Wilmeth wouldn't want to say anything, because if he had, he'd be done there. They'd kick him out. But Solem and his bosses proved to be cowards. Let's be clear here: Maryland was at fault, but Syracuse wasn't an innocent bystander in this."

"Years later, when Wilmeth was playing basketball and football and working as a cop in DC, did you talk to him in greater detail about the outing?"

"Tried to, but he didn't want to revisit it. Wanted it to stay buried. And I understood why and respected that. Only thing he said was, 'That's just the way things are in this country. Nothing I can do about it but move on.' Again, he was between a rock and a hard place."

"Would you have spoken out?" Breanna said. "Would you have played the ruse that people had concocted since his high school days?"

"Tough questions. Tough questions. I probably would have shot my mouth off because that's my nature. I'm a troublemaker. Always have been since my playing days at Howard. I've always agitated for change. But not everyone approaches everything in the same way. It's easy for me to say I would have done this or that, but you do have to view things in the context of the times. And you have to understand consequences. Wilmeth was a bright, bright guy, and I think he thought he'd bring about change through his actions—and he just might have done that had he lived because the sky was the limit for him."

"Did you turn him into a civil rights cause?"

"Oh, I don't know. Suppose you could look at it that way. Colored folks were angry Singh hadn't been allowed to play. And my story got play in all the Negro newspapers throughout the country. Sadly, the white press totally ignored it. So much for journalistic integrity, huh?"

"So no regrets breaking that story?"

"Nope. None whatsoever. No question it really hurt Wilmeth not to play that day, but I believe he actually felt some relief getting outed. Think about it: I had liberated him. Set him free. He no longer had to live the lie. He no longer had to be a 'Hindu,' even though sportswriters and others kept that false narrative alive in the weeks, months, and years that followed. That outing allowed him to finally be publicly who he was privately—a Negro."

Lacy paused for a few seconds to gather his thoughts.

"You know what they say: the truth shall set ye free. Always write the truth, young lady, even when it's painful."

CHAPTER 27

Shut-eye had been near impossible during the six-hour train trip back from Baltimore following his benching. Wilmeth's brain kept churning and chugging like the locomotive engine hauling him and his teammates northward.

He had done a lot of staring out the window—a lot of soul-searching. He kept wondering if he had made the right decision boarding the train. Maybe he should have listened to his heart and told Coach Solem and Lew Andreas to screw off after they failed to stand up for him. None of his teammates would have blamed him if he'd quit on the spot and gone home with his uncle and cousins for good. Better to go someplace where he was loved and wanted than return to a place that seemed to love and want him only on its terms. Wilmeth kept thinking back to his aunt's pep talk.

"Don't let things wear you down. Your time's gonna come. You gonna make 'em all pay. Whole story ain't written yet."

After arising groggily the next morning in his bedroom at the Harrisons, Wilmeth put on his suit and tie and walked to the nearby AME Zion Church for Sunday services. The vast majority of the churchgoers were unaware of the humiliation he'd suffered the day before. News didn't travel fast—and that was fine with him because he was in no mood to relive yesterday's agony.

The church was packed and sweaty on this unseasonably warm November day. Several men removed their suit coats and loosened their ties. Many fanned themselves with their programs. Reverend Thelonious Washington Carver commenced his sermon, and soon everyone's attention was on his charismatic words, not the annoying heat. Back and forth the slender pastor paced, his booming baritone reverberating off the mint-green walls and ceiling.

"As we Negroes know all too well, life isn't always fair. And sometimes your faith in people and in God Almighty himself gets severely tested because of that unfairness. But, my brothers and sisters, all will be revealed one day, and with it will come understanding why God put you through these tests. We must maintain belief without evidence. We must keep the faith and 'run the race,' even when it feels as if we are walking into a great fire that's about to consume us."

At a pew, near the back of the church, Wilmeth closed his eyes and raised his hands.

"Amen, Brother Carver," he said softly. "Amen."

After the service ended, Wilmeth walked to a nearby park, where he noticed a bunch of young boys in Sunday-go-to-meeting clothes tossing around a raggedy football. They immediately recognized Wilmeth.

"Mr. Singh! Mr. Singh! Can you throw the ball to us?"

Wilmeth smiled.

"Sure," he said, and soon the boys were taking turns fielding spirals from the man they called the Hero on the Hill.

After about fifteen minutes of pitch and catch, Wilmeth plopped down on a bench. The boys gathered round.

"Mr. Singh! Mr. Singh! How did you do against Maryland yesterday?"

"Not so good, I'm afraid. We lost thirteen to zero."

"What happened, Mr. Singh? What happened?"

Wilmeth paused and stared up at the clouds.

"Well, boys, some days things just don't go your way, and you have no control over the circumstances. It's frustrating, but you got to deal with them. When things don't go your way, you got two choices: You can quit. Or you can try again."

"You ain't gonna quit, are you, Mr. Singh?"

"Nah, son," he said, spinning the brown ball round and round in his hands. "I ain't gonna quit. Like Brother Carver said in his sermon, you need to keep believing, even when life punches you in the face. So I'm gonna heed the good brother's advice, and I suggest you do too. I'm gonna try again."

Wilmeth trudged up the Hill that afternoon to Carnegie Library and began researching one of his zoology projects. His soul was still aching—and would for some time—but he figured if he buried himself in his studies, it would take his mind off his troubles. Come hell or high water, he was going to get that damn sheepskin. "They used me," he muttered to himself. "And now I'm gonna use them."

The next day he was back in classes and back in uniform. Before practice, Duffy Daugherty and Phil Allen stopped by his locker and told him how sorry they were about what had happened, and after they headed to the practice field, Marty Glickman paid a visit.

"Sing-Sing, I—ah—I . . . don't know what to say."

Glickman had grown up with a stuttering problem, and although he had worked hard to conquer it, the affliction occasionally returned when he felt stressed.

"Nothing needs to be said, Marty. They made a choice. You made a choice. And I didn't have a choice."

Wilmeth finished tying his football cleats and looked up at Glickman.

"What's done is done, Marty. I'm going to do my darnedest to look forward, not back. I'm going to try not to let my yesterdays use up my todays."

Wilmeth rose from his stool, grabbed his leather football helmet, and headed out of the locker room. He was intent on burying the past as deeply as he could. Beneath a pile of dirt as high as Everest if necessary. Glickman was hoping to do the same.

When Wilmeth took the practice field for the first time since the benching in Baltimore, his teammates—and unapologetic coaches—couldn't help but notice an intensity, almost a fury, they hadn't seen from Wilmeth before. And that was saying something, because he had always been a fierce competitor during practices and games, a player who never held anything back.

Although he had told Glickman he was going to do his best to look forward, it was apparent his anger from two days earlier was fueling his present. At one point, after a particularly hard tackle in which Wilmeth temporarily separated a teammate from the ball—and his senses—Coach Solem blew his whistle and motioned for Wilmeth to join him on the sidelines.

"What'd I do wrong, Coach? It was a clean hit. A lot cleaner than many of the ones I've had to take."

"Yeah, Singh, it was a clean hit, a good hit. But you seem a little too fired up right now. You need to spend a little time with me on the sidelines while you cool off."

Wilmeth was tempted to tell Solem, "I spent enough time with you on the sideline against Maryland. I want to play. And I've earned the right to play." But he kept his mouth shut.

Wilmeth closed his eyes and took some deep breaths. Though he had every right to be angry, he realized Solem was right. He knew he needed to settle down, regain his bearings.

"Coach," he said, after about a minute of meditation. "You're right. Lost my head a little. Sorry about that."

"No problem, Wil. I'd be mighty angry, too, if what happened to you happened to me. Believe me, that decision wasn't mine. Geez, I'd be nuts not to want my best player on the field. Between you and me—and this has to stay between you and me—that decision was made above us both. As hard as that crap was for you to deal with, we've got to move forward— got to show the people who made these rules they were wrong. Channel that anger toward this week's opponent. Take it out on Penn State. Now get back in there."

Wilmeth's intensity would serve him and the Syracuse football team well the next two Saturdays. The Orangemen beat rival Penn State, 19–13, on a late-game thirty-seven-yard interception return for a touchdown by Wilmeth, and then, a week later, clobbered Western Reserve, 27–6. Both victories came at Archbold Stadium in front of large crowds.

In their next game, Wilmeth held his own in a 6–6 tie against power-house Columbia and its much-ballyhooed, all-American quarterback Sid Luckman. The season ended on a down note, with a 7–0 loss to neighboring Colgate, but it nonetheless had been a grand bounce-back campaign for the Orangemen, who finished with a 5–2–1 record one year after winning just one of eight games. Solem's creative coaching had contributed to the turn-around, but the biggest catalyst was Wilmeth, whose arm, legs, vision, and smarts provided the Orangemen with a weapon, the likes of which college football had never seen.

CHAPTER 28

Although Lew Andreas had cowardly capitulated to Maryland's demands to sit Syracuse University's best football player a month earlier, Wilmeth managed to put any animus aside once the 1937–1938 basketball season began. It had always been Wilmeth's nature not to let things fester or to hold a grudge. He preferred to focus on making things better, figuring bitterness would do him no good and just shackle him further. He had enough obstacles as it was. Why add more?

Andreas had his prejudices regarding race, but he also was driven to win. And he wasn't about to let anything, including his own biases, get in his way of racking up as many coaching victories as possible. And that meant eventually counting heavily on Wilmeth, a cerebral, improvisational athlete who was doing things on the court that no one else could, things that had never been tried before on white-only teams. Yes, Wilmeth had a style all his own. To his credit, Andreas was starting to see its boundless possibilities and was trying his best not to suppress them.

One of Wilmeth's innovations was the crossover dribble.

"This kid's faking people right out of their jockstraps with his quick change of direction," Andreas marveled to a fellow basketball coach midway through that season. "You think you've got him covered, and the next thing you know, you're stumbling to the floor like a clumsy fool watching him dribble by you. Has all these fancy moves. And handles the ball like it's attached to his hand with a string."

Wilmeth also introduced the no-look pass. At first this brand-new tool drew the ire of Andreas and some of Wilmeth's teammates because they weren't prepared to catch passes out of nowhere. One teammate was none too pleased when he caught one of Wilmeth's unanticipated tosses with his nose rather than his fingers.

"Stop your showboating, Sing-Sing," he grumbled while tending to the blood gushing from his nostrils. "Your uppity tactics ain't doing us any good."

Wilmeth walked over and apologized, then tried to explain that they all could benefit greatly from no-look passes. At first they dismissed him. Thought he was just being selfish, playing what they derisively called "Negro ball." But as practices went on, they realized he was right. No-look passes were not merely fancy, but functional, enabling the Orangemen to catch unsuspecting defenders off guard and score easy baskets.

"Never seen anything like him in all my years in basketball," Andreas said, shaking his head in amazement. "Kid's a magician."

A magician forever in search of new tricks.

Wilmeth was constantly tinkering, constantly seeking an edge, even if it went against conventional wisdom. He loved the creative aspect of everything, especially sports. There were times when he fancied himself a scientist conducting experiments out there—the field and the court his laboratories. In sandlot baseball games, he would try different grips in hopes of delivering pitches that befuddled batters. Same thing on the football field or basketball court, where he would attempt different moves, passes, and shots. As his no-look passes demonstrated, the advantages he sought were not merely for himself but for the entire team. He wanted everyone to succeed.

"Man was laying the foundation for Michael and Magic Johnson and Larry Bird and Pistol Pete Maravich and so many others," his old Harlem and Washington basketball teammate Pop Gates would tell Breanna years later. "Gotta remember how primitive basketball was back in our day. Center jumps after every basket. No rules about having to get the ball over half court in ten seconds. No shot clock, so if you got a lead early, you could just sit on it, play stall ball, run the clock out.

"I believe some of the stuff Singh and a few others introduced or cultivated helped make the game more exciting and led to some major rule changes. It's kind of what happened in baseball after the Negro Leaguers got a chance to play in the white majors. Cats like Jackie Robinson and Willie Mays and Hank Aaron brought speed and quickness and daring to the games, made baseball more exciting. Same thing with Singh. Guy was a pioneer in a lot of respects. Way ahead of his time."

Wilmeth's sterling skill wasn't the only thing that conjured connections to Michael Jordan.

"When Singh was driving to the basket, his tongue often hung out of his mouth," Gates said, chuckling. "First time I saw Michael on the tube, I said, 'Well, I'll be. Just like Singh.'"

Syracuse's stature as an eastern collegiate basketball powerhouse would continue during the 1937–1938 season as the Orangemen went 14–5. One of those victories occurred at Madison Square Garden in front of Wilmeth's relatives and Dr. James Naismith, basketball's inventor.

Wilmeth also was excelling in the classroom, though he occasionally encountered a professor who thought it beneath him to teach a Negro.

Despite the humiliation of the Maryland football game benching, it had been a good year overall. Wilmeth's athletic prowess and infectious personality had endeared him to his fellow students, even ones who had never been around a Black person before. In fact, he became one of the most popular kids on campus—so popular that the school's magazine, *The Syracusan*, ran a full-page feature about him, emphasizing his medical studies and aspirations as much as it did his sports feats. It boasted how Wilmeth was more interested in a sheepskin than a pigskin.

"Don't know how to explain it, but there's something special about Sing-Sing," his football teammate Duffy Daugherty told the magazine writer. "Some people are like storm clouds when you're around them. Bring everyone down. Sing-Sing's just the opposite. Like the sun, he lightens up everything. Makes everyone and everything feel better and brighter."

During that junior year, Wilmeth switched his major to zoology—one of the most demanding of the premed curriculums—and he couldn't wait to return to Harlem and accompany his father on house calls and spend time working in a hospital emergency room. He had made up his mind to become a surgeon rather than a general practitioner. Samuel Sidat-Singh couldn't be prouder and told Wilmeth as much when he arrived home following the spring semester.

"Wil, I was a little worried when you decided to try to play two sports on top of your studies," he said. "Thought it was going to be way too much to handle. But you've shown yourself to be not only an outstanding student, football player, and basketball player but also quite the juggler."

Wilmeth chuckled.

"Thanks, Pops. So glad I didn't act on impulse after that crap in Maryland. Kept thinking 'bout what you'd told me about keeping my eye on the big picture instead of the now. Also thought about all the good Daddy Webb did with his pharmacy and how much I learned from watching him and you working in the ghettos, helping people others had turned their backs on. I want to do that too."

"Warms my heart, son. Really does. And I know Daddy Webb would be proud to hear that too. Look, there's going to be more challenges for sure. More stuff you're gonna have to put up with. But you're resilient. You've overcome so much in your young life already. It's what's made you the fine young man you are. It's all falling into place, Wil. All falling into place. Sky's definitely the limit."

CHAPTER 29

It had been a fabulous, restorative summer back home in Harlem, truly a summer Wilmeth was sad to see end. Working part-time in hospital emergency rooms and assisting his stepfather with patients during July and August 1938 had stoked his desire to go to medical school. It also cemented his ambition to become a surgeon. But it wasn't just work that had him pumped. Chumming with neighborhood buddies had been replenishing too. Good for the soul. The pickup basketball and sandlot football games, plus a heavy dose of tennis that saw him make it all the way to the semifinals of the New York City men's amateur tournament, sated his competitive desires, helped him keep his athletic skills fine-tuned.

His fancy footwork also was on display at the smoky, always hopping Cotton Club, where Wilmeth and his friends danced the night away to the jazz riffs of Duke Ellington and his band. Not surprisingly, Wilmeth was a natural on the dance floor too. Light on his feet and quick to pick up the latest moves, he was in high demand as a dance partner, with women always swooning over him. One night three of them actually got into a fight while vying for his attention, and his buddies didn't let him hear the end of that.

"Hey, pretty boy, can I have the next dance?" John Isaacs mocked as Wilmeth and the rest of his entourage headed home following the female fracas.

"I want to Bojangle with my handsome Casanova," chimed in Mercer Ellington.

"You guys just jealous 'cause you all ugly as sin and got two left feet," Wilmeth responded.

The merriment of the most enjoyable summer of Wilmeth's young life ended late that August when it came time for him to again climb aboard the northbound New York Central. And although Wilmeth wished the good times in the Big Apple could have gone on forever, a part of him was happy to be returning to Syracuse for his senior year. He was looking forward to going out with a bang. In the classroom. On the gridiron. And in the gym.

Ossie Solem had revitalized interest in Orange football, and there were hopes and expectations Syracuse could become nationally relevant again, maybe even push for a Rose Bowl invitation, like the two the school received a generation earlier but turned down. Wilmeth figured to be an integral part of those plans, as Solem and his staff spent their summer plotting ways to become even more creative incorporating this superb athlete's unique but still raw skills.

Because he had not played organized football in high school and only one year of varsity ball in college, there still were things Wilmeth needed to master. But he'd always been a quick study, and Solem had reached a point of trust where he even sought Wilmeth's feedback, particularly in the passing game. Wilmeth had spent extra time that summer tossing the pigskin to friends, and his improved arm strength was evident at SU's first football practice in the fall of 1938.

"Wow, Oz," assistant coach Bud Wilkinson marveled to Solem afterward. "Did you see those throws?"

"Of course I saw 'em. Have to be blind not to."

"Like a high-powered rifle. Those sports scribes can talk all they want about Luckman, but Sid's got nothing on this kid. I think his arm is even stronger."

"Could be. Nice weapon to have in our arsenal, huh, Bud? Gotta feeling it could come in handy down the road."

Though Wilmeth had done a good job not getting consumed by past injustices, he was only human and couldn't help but notice that Syracuse's second game of the season would be a rematch against Maryland. Only this time the teams would meet at Archbold Stadium, meaning the Terrapins couldn't force him to be benched again because there was no "gentlemen's agreement" north of the Mason-Dixon Line.

Syracuse opened the season with a 27–0 thrashing of Clarkson University. As expected, Wilmeth was unstoppable, but early in the fourth quarter he tweaked his right ankle. It was still sore and swollen when practice resumed that Monday, but Wilmeth insisted he'd be good to go against Maryland.

"Don't care if they have to amputate the damn thing," Wilmeth told Daugherty. "I'm playing. Wouldn't miss this one for the world."

Solem understood Wilmeth's fervent desire to play, but the coach was focused on the bigger picture. Decimated by injuries, Maryland would arrive in Upstate New York with barely enough healthy players to field a full team. They would be huge underdogs, likely beatable even by Syracuse's second- and third-stringers. Though Solem, like all coaches, preached to his players the importance of not looking past any opponent, privately he wasn't practicing what he was preaching. The following week's game against eastern powerhouse Cornell would pose a far more daunting challenge. For SU to have any chance whatsoever of upsetting the Big Red again, they would need Wilmeth to be healthy.

The prudent strategy was obvious to Solem: rest Wilmeth against the overmatched Terrapins; give him several more days to heal. But the decision wasn't as clear-cut as it seemed. Given the circumstances of what happened in Maryland the year before, Solem knew full well Wilmeth would resist sitting out.

"Bud, we're damned if we do; damned if we don't," he lamented a few days before kickoff. "You've seen Wil out there. Still hobbling. We both know we can clobber the Terps without him. But he'll never forgive me if we try to sit him, even if it's in his best interests. Damn. If it were any other team, he might go for it. But in his eyes, this isn't any other team. Got a personal score to settle, and I get it."

"Well, Oz, how 'bout seeking a compromise?"

"Whaddaya mean?"

"Let him play and get a few licks in, then rest him the rest of the way."

Solem stared at the Xs and Os he had written on his chalkboard.

"Hmm," he said, after a few seconds. "Not a bad idea, Bud. He'll probably still be ticked at me. He'll still want to play the full sixty minutes, but maybe, just maybe, we can reason with him. Get him to buy what we're selling."

That Friday Solem called Wilmeth into his office and told him his plan. As expected, Wilmeth raised a stink.

"Can't do this to me again, Coach. Not against this team. Not after what they did to me. Put yourself in my shoes. How would you react?"

Solem fidgeted in his chair. He knew Wilmeth was right, but he felt he couldn't budge, even if it seemed like he was piling on.

"Wil, I'm just trying do what's best for you and best for the team in the long run."

"You mean just like last year, Coach? Was that best for me? Best for the team too?"

"Sorry, Wil, but sometimes leaders have to make hard decisions. I need you—the team needs you—more against Cornell than Maryland."

After a few more minutes of give-and-take, Wilmeth realized nothing he said was going to change Solem's mind. The debate was over.

"Coach, you obviously have your mind made up. But if I do what you want, can you promise me one thing?"

"What's that, Wil?"

"If this isn't a romp, you'll let me keep playing."

Solem smiled.

"You gotta deal, Wil."

As it turned out, Solem got what he'd wished for. The Orangemen romped, and the rout was even more lopsided than he had envisioned. Wilmeth played a few series, completed a couple of passes, broke off a few good runs, then sat. The day actually would belong to Marty Glickman, who clearly was channeling the anger he felt toward himself and Maryland for what they had both done to Wilmeth the year before. The Olympic sprinter wound up scoring three touchdowns, including one on an eighty-yard dash as Syracuse rolled to a 53–0 drubbing in front of twelve thousand spectators.

Maryland had brought a fifty-piece marching band but only twenty-three players to Archbold. A few more Terps wound up suffering injuries during the game, and things became so dire Coach Frank Dobson was forced to suit up one of the team's student managers at halftime to play guard because Maryland ran out of replacements.

Solem had no such attrition issues. He wound up playing all fifty-three players that day, meaning Wilmeth and most of the other starters, even the second-stringers, spent the second half as spectators.

When the final gun sounded, Wilmeth sought out Glickman, and the two men embraced.

"Thank you, Marty."

Glickman smiled and patted his teammate on the head.

"Doesn't make up for last year. Nothing ever will. But it sure felt good to stick it to those bastards, didn't it?"

"Did indeed, Marty. Couldn't have happened to a more deserving bunch of bigots. Can't wait till my friends and relatives back in DC read all about it in the newspapers."

With decisive wins in their first two games of the 1938 season, the Orangemen were on a roll, right where they wanted to be. But those cakewalk victories would be quickly forgotten and dismissed if they didn't defeat unbeaten Cornell. This would be the sternest of tests, and for the second straight week, the Orangemen would find themselves embroiled in a retribution game. Only this time their opponents would be the ones seeking revenge. Cornell's Big Red would be seeing red a year after their neighbors had handed them their only defeat of the 1937 season.

CHAPTER 30

"Hey, Sing-Sing, you hear the news?"

"Yeah, Duff. I did. You one ugly cuss."

"Ha ha, Sing-Sing. Good one. Better stick with medicine, my man, 'cause with material like that, you got no chance on Vaudeville."

"So what's the big scoop?"

"Granny's coming."

"Your grandmother's coming to the game?"

"No, you numbskull. Granny Rice—as in Grantland Rice, world's best-known sportswriter."

"You're kidding me. What's he coming to little old Syracuse for? Thought he only goes to the big events—World Series, Joe Louis fights, Kentucky Derby, Notre Dame football."

"Well, Sing, we think he's coming here to write hosannas about Cornell. Believes the Big Red is loaded with all those stud players back. They're unbeaten and got a score to settle with us after we kicked their asses last year."

"Probably thinks he's picked the perfect game to tout them nationally 'cause he figures they'll put a whupping on us."

"Yup."

"Well, you know, Duff, we could always ruin his story for him. Make him sing our praises instead."

"My sentiments exactly."

In a time when newspapers reigned supreme as the main disseminators of information and influencers of opinions, Grantland Rice had no equal. By the end of the Roarin' Twenties, he had become as famous and powerful a celebrity as Babe Ruth, Jim Thorpe, Jack Dempsey, Bobby Jones, and Red Grange—sporting Gods he helped mythologize with his florid prose. His syndicated sports columns ran in more than a thousand newspapers across the country, and he also edited and wrote his own widely circulated sports magazine and narrated the highlight films shown in movie theaters everywhere. His readership was expansive and devoted. Easily in the millions. What he wrote had impact. His mere presence at a sporting event gave it a stamp of great importance. If Granny's there, it must be huge.

Having him in the Archbold Stadium press box that unseasonably warm mid-October afternoon in 1938, tapping away on the keys of his trusty Royal Classic, afforded Syracuse a golden opportunity. And on that day, Wilmeth would do as he and Daugherty had hoped: he would force the legendary sportswriter to change the narrative, scrap his story. Amid the rubble of crumpled-up paper yanked from Rice's typewriter carriage, a new tale would emerge. A new legend would be born as sport's preeminent mythmaker introduced America to Wilmeth Sidat-Singh.

***

Feeling immense pressure to emerge victorious and hold on to regional bragging rights, both Solem and his Cornell counterpart, Carl Snavely, became increasingly paranoid in the days leading up to that October 15, 1938, game.

So much so that they ordered their respective practices closed to all outsiders. Their distrust for one another was so deep they even stationed a few security guards around their practice fields to ferret out potential spies. The guards were armed with billy clubs and binoculars.

The clandestine preparations merely added to the game's hype—and attendance. Shortly before kickoff, nearly twenty-five thousand spectators had congregated in Syracuse's concrete bowl of a stadium, and most wore short sleeves because the sun was shining brilliantly as the temperatures climbed into the low eighties, about thirty degrees above normal.

"Hoo-wee, Duff! Gonna be a scorcher," Wilmeth howled during pregame warm-ups. "You and the boys are going to need about twenty beers instead of your normal ten to rehydrate after this one."

"Hopefully, we'll be imbibing those brews for celebratory reasons, not just medicinal purposes, if you know what I mean."

"All right! All right! Knock it off, you clowns!" barked Solem, who seemed more tense and agitated than normal. "Get your focus where it's supposed to be, or you're going to get your keisters handed to you."

Up in the press box, there was a stir once Rice showed up. His fellow sportswriters stopped by to say hello and pay homage, and after Rice had settled in, a student spotter from SU's athletic department worked up the nerve to introduce himself.

"Is there anything I can get you, Mr. Rice?"

"How 'bout a good story to write about?"

The student giggled nervously. "We'll see what we can do, Mr. Rice."

"In the meantime, kiddo, you can grab me a beer."

Rice had, as Wilmeth and Daugherty surmised, come there that afternoon with his story already constructed in his head. The game, the famous sports scribe figured, would be a foregone conclusion, mere window dressing. Cornell would win easily, and Rice would write about how the unbeaten Big Red was the team to watch that fall.

"Hoping for an easy day," Rice told Burdick Kimball, a *New York Times* columnist seated next to him on press row.

"I hear ya, Granny. Faster we write, the less time we spend in this hotter-than-hell press box and the more time we spend in that hotel gin mill."

"Exactly," chortled nearby *New York Herald-Tribune* writer Matt Lindsley. "Got to have your priorities right. You know the credo: never let your writing time cut into your drinking time."

For the first fifty-one minutes of the game, the plot unfolded as Rice had hoped. The Big Red dominated, bottling up Wilmeth, Marty Glickman, Phil Allen, Harold "Babe" Ruth, and the rest of the high-powered Syracuse offense. With nine minutes left to play, Cornell's 10–0 lead seemed safe. The Orangemen looked lethargic and spent, worn down by the blistering sun and Big Red gang tacklers playing with payback in mind.

And so Rice and his fellow scribes clickety-clacked away on their typewriters, paying scant attention to the game and more attention to their watches. Deadlines, even for first editions, seemingly would not be a problem. Complete stories would be filed early back to respective newspapers via the Western Union ticker tape with no need for revisions and additions.

Desperation time clearly had arrived on the Syracuse sideline as Solem pulled Wilmeth aside.

"It's now or never, Wil. Got to let 'er rip. We're gonna throw our way down the field. And then throw some more. You ready?"

"Been ready for a lifetime."

With roughly six minutes to go, the sweat-soaked Syracuse fans finally had something to cheer about as Wilmeth flung a thirty-five-yard touchdown pass to Ruth to cut the deficit to 10–6.

"Here we go! Here we go!" Wilmeth screamed as he pounded several of his teammates on the shoulders. "Look out, everyone. The boys from Syracuse are back."

The euphoria didn't last long. Maybe fifteen, sixteen seconds. That's how long it took for Cornell's Kenny Brown to bob, weave, and sprint 94 yards for a touchdown with the ensuing kickoff. The extra point sailed between the uprights, giving the Big Red a 17–6 lead.

"How'd you like that play, boys?" Brown said as he jogged past several Orangemen on his way back to the Cornell bench.

"Shut the fuck up, you prima donna!" Daugherty shouted.

"I feel for ya, Daugherty," Brown continued, egging him on. "Has to be tough knowing you and the rest of you lowlife boys from Syracuse will be working for us someday."

SU captain James Bruett quickly grabbed Daugherty by the shoulder pads and shooed him toward the home-team bench.

Solem looked as if he had just been run over by all eleven Cornell players.

"Nail in the coffin," he muttered to himself. "We're toast."

Things indeed looked dire, but Wilmeth wasn't ready to give up. He scooped up the next kickoff and raced past midfield before being hauled down by three Cornell players. Two snaps later, he connected with Ruth in the end zone again to cut the deficit to five points. The Orangemen had a glimmer of hope. But only three minutes remained. If Cornell gained a first down on its next possession, it could run out the clock and secure the win.

"Come on, guys," Wilmeth implored. "Got to do something—anything— to get that ball back. Get me that ball back, and I guarantee you we'll win."

"I got an idea," Allen said.

"What's that, Phil?" Daugherty grumbled. "You gonna bribe 'em to fumble?"

"Just wait, Duff. You'll see."

Two snaps later, Cornell running back Vinnie Eichler bulled around left end and appeared to have gained enough yards for the first down. But as Eichler was about to be tackled, he heard someone yell, "Here, Vinnie. Give me the ball."

Mistakenly believing it was one of his teammates, Eichler lateraled the ball—right into Allen's hands.

Syracuse had regained possession.

And hope.

On the next play, Wilmeth made good on his guarantee, tossing a touchdown pass to Allen to give Syracuse a 19–17 lead.

"Where there's Wil, there's a way!" Daugherty screamed as he jumped into Wilmeth's arms.

"How 'bout Phil?" Wilmeth responded. "Outfoxing those Ivy League boys with a little trickery. Who would have thought those eggheads would fall for that?"

Cornell was unable to gain any yardage on two desperation plays after the kickoff following Syracuse's go-ahead touchdown, and the referee fired the final gun.

Game over. Miracle completed. Legend launched.

Thousands of sweat-drenched fans poured out of the stands and onto the field. Chants of "Sidat-Singh! Sidat-Singh!" thundered throughout Archbold as Wilmeth and his jubilant teammates trotted up the steps leading to the locker room. Before walking through the door, Wilmeth stopped to take a final look at the celebration below. Off in the distance, the bells from the Crouse College tower clanged as the Syracuse fight song rang out far above Onondaga's waters.

In the Archbold press box, Rice and the other knights of the keyboard scrambled to compose new stories. Though their writing time was going to cut seriously into their drinking time, none of them were complaining. Least of all Rice.

"Holy cow! I don't believe what I just saw," he said. "Don't know if I've ever witnessed a greater college football game or a greater individual performance than this one. And believe me, I've seen a few memorable games and players in my time."

CHAPTER 31

Syracuse, October 16, 1938

"Whooee! Whooee! Rise and shine! Give God your glory, glory!"

"What's all the commotion, Ike?" Wilmeth asked, rubbing sleep from his eyes.

"What's all the commotion?! Why, you's all the commotion, that's what!"

"Look at these newspapers, Wilmeth. Sidat-Singh this. Sidat-Singh that. In big, black, bold, "FDR WINS ELECTION" headlines. You're a hero, boy, and the missus and I couldn't be prouder."

Wilmeth stared at the stack of newspapers Ike had plopped on his bed.

Man, he thought to himself. *Still feels so surreal. Like some out-of-body experience. Did this really happen? To me? Wilmeth Sidat-Singh?*

At church later that morning, everyone and their brother came up to Wilmeth, shaking his hands, patting his back, telling him how much he had lifted their spirits and pride.

"A boy from the Ward done good," yelped a large woman before planting a kiss on his cheek.

Perhaps no one was more excited than Pastor Carver, who devoted his sermon to Wilmeth. "Now, just in case you've been living in some cave and haven't heard, one of the congregants from AME Zion had himself a pretty good day up there on the Hill yesterday afternoon," began Carver as the parishioners oohed and aahed. "Brother by the name of Wilmeth Sidat-Singh did us right proud. Threw that pigskin all over Archie and beat them boys from Ithaca."

Wilmeth appreciated the acknowledgment but couldn't help feeling embarrassed. He didn't want to be the center of attention. Didn't want to be a spectacle. Particularly not in church. But there was no escaping it, especially when Pastor Carver asked Wilmeth to come up to the pulpit and say a few words.

"Ah . . . ah . . . thanks for asking me to say something, Pastor, but . . . ah . . . but ah . . ."

"Speak up, Brother Singh. Don't be shy. They told me you're a college boy, so I figured you could string at least a few words together."

Wilmeth grinned as the pastor and congregants roared with laughter.

"I just want to thank each and every one of you for taking me in and making this colored boy feel at home when he showed up here from Harlem four summers ago. You made me feel welcome, always had my back, always encouraged me that I could make it up there, on that Hill. Definitely want to thank Ike and Thelma Harrison. They been father, mother, big brother, and big sister to me. Kept me on the straight and narrow, and there were a few times when I really needed a good kick in the pants.

"You know, people on the Hill ask me where I'm from. I tell 'em three places: Harlem, the District, and the Ward. The Ward's been my home away from home. It—and you all—are always gonna be a part of me."

As Wilmeth walked back to the pew amid a roar of applause, he recognized one of the boys he had played catch with in the park a year earlier after the devastation of his benching in Maryland.

"So glad you didn't quit, Mr. Singh," he whispered.

"Me too," Wilmeth replied, stroking the young boy's head. "Me too."

In the coming days, Wilmeth would be stunned to learn just how far and wide his story had traveled. From sea to shining sea. His name wasn't merely plastered in headlines in the Syracuse newspapers but in sports sections across the land. It was a testament to Wilmeth's stunning performance and to the power of the press. Or, more accurately, the power of Grantland Rice.

America's most famous sportswriter could barely contain himself. His story, which would appear in more than a thousand sports sections, overflowed with purple-prosed hyperbole and tortured metaphors:

> A new forward-pass hero slipped in front of the great white spotlight of fame at Syracuse today. The phenomenon of the rifle-shot event went beyond Sid Luckman and Sammy Baugh. His name is Wilmeth Sidat-Singh, a Negro boy from Harlem wearing an East Indian name with the deadly aim of Davy Crockett and Kit Carson.

Rice concluded his account by writing:

> In the course of this exterminating rifle fire, Sidat-Singh completed five passes in succession for a total of 158 yards and three touchdowns. If there is any passer who has surpassed this record, coming from behind, I can't recall it in the ancient annals of the game.
>
> It was one of the most amazing exhibitions of machine gun fire I've ever seen, where the odds were all the other way.

Rice was hardly the only one gushing. Other scribes were too. And newspaper headline writers had a field day, with clever proclamations such as "IT DON'T MEAN A THING IF IT AIN'T GOT THAT SINGH," and alliterations like, "SINGH'S SLINGS SINK CORNELL." Wilmeth enjoyed the clever allusion to his friend Duke Ellington's classic song—the same song the jazz master auditioned for Wilmeth and friends years earlier.

Rice was so captivated by what he had witnessed that he couldn't let it go. In fact, he continued to write about it in the days that followed, even publishing a poem about Singh a fellow sportswriter had sent along:

The sons of Syracuse now yell at a new, exotic saga.

Of a magic spell that entranced Cornell in the vale of the Onondaga.

The shades of night were falling fast and the score was 10 to zero.

When Sidat-Singh, the wizard, passes six times to become a hero.

By some mysterious, dervish art he could rifle a pigskin bullet.

From the scrimmage heart or a spinner's start to the runner left free to pull it.

Then Wilmeth Sidat-Singh, in sooth, just thrice did loose his missile.

To Herr, to Balmer, then to Ruth and they heard the touchdown whistle.

That made the score stand six to ten, but fullback Brown like lightning soon struck again.

Through the orange men with a field-length run that was frightening.

But there stood Sidat-Singh once more, cool as a cobra striking.

In place of Ruth, he made Allen score with a pass through Peck, the Viking.

So, on Piety Hill, the great chimes rang—they peal in ancient splendor.

For the sorcerous wing of Sidat-Singh—black-artful, bitter-ender.

But in Ithaca now the sad boys ring their charge on a bitter theme.

"Did you see that thing? That's Sidat-Singh—the Syracuse walking dream.

Wilmeth had been covered extensively by the historically Black newspapers since his days as a rising scholastic hoops star at DeWitt Clinton. He'd also received some play in the mainstream white press, but never to this extent. This was gangbusters. Blew him away, especially the comparisons Rice had made to Baugh and Luckman.

Baugh already was a big-time football hero. Had led the National Football

League in passing yards and guided the Washington Redskins to a title. And Luckman was projected to follow suit. A contemporary of Wilmeth's, he was regarded as the nation's finest passer and a top pro prospect. To have America's most powerful sportswriter—a white man from the Deep South, no less—write that a Black man had done something not even football's biggest white stars had done meant something to Wilmeth. And to other Blacks.

It got Wilmeth to thinking about possibilities.

"Wouldn't it be something, Ike, if they really did give me an opportunity to play ball in the National Football League?" Wilmeth mentioned to Harrison one night at the dinner table. "Me being able to sling it around for pay, just like Slingin' Sammy Baugh."

Harrison smiled and shook his head. "Yeah, that would be something. No doubt in my mind you'd hold your own. Apparently, no doubt in Mr. Rice's mind, either, and that's saying something because that cracker from Tennessee rarely writes about Negroes. Of course, there's no Negroes in the NFL or Major League Baseball or on white university teams in the South."

"Shame, aint' it?" Wilmeth sighed, picking at Thelma's butter-smothered salt potatoes with his fork while dreaming dreams that wouldn't be allowed to walk or run.

CHAPTER 32

The influential stories by Grantland Rice and his fellow scribes had pushed the heretofore unranked Orangemen all the way up to tenth in the national college football polls in early autumn of 1938, but they would come tumbling down from that high perch after suffering upset losses the next two Saturdays. Despite two touchdown passes by Wilmeth, the Orangemen lost 19–12 to Michigan State on the road, then were throttled by Penn State, 33–6, at Archbold as the Nittany Lions gained an astonishing 489 yards on the ground and limited Wilmeth to just five passes, two of which he completed for 31 yards.

On November 5, the Orangemen hosted next-door neighbor Colgate in what the locals regarded annually as the "game of the year." The Red Raiders had held the upper hand in the series lately, with thirteen consecutive wins, and were hoping to continue their "HooDoo Hex." The night before the game, students from SU rented a plane and dropped orange dye into the lake on the Colgate campus. Colgate students retaliated by sneaking into

Archbold Stadium and painting a maroon *C* at midfield. They also splashed paint on the Saltine Warrior statue on the quad.

The game had taken on such outsized importance that it resulted in the firing of Syracuse hero Vic Hanson as head coach following the 1935 season. This despite the fact Hanson had posted a robust win-loss record overall. Failure to beat Colgate was a mortal sin, and he was jettisoned. Solem was well aware what was at stake. This was about much more than snapping a two-game losing streak. This was about job security, which is why he seemed more agitated, more on edge, during the days leading up to the game. He needed to win in the worst way to silence influential alumni and donors who would be nipping at his heels if the streak continued.

Riding the skills of Wilmeth and a stout defense, he got his wish. Syracuse eked out a 7–0 victory. After the referee pulled the trigger on the final gun, pandemonium ensued as hundreds of delirious Orange fans tore down the wooden goal posts and lugged them in a conga-line procession to a raucous block party near the Hotel Syracuse that carried on into the wee hours of the night.

"Man, Ike, you would have thought FDR had shown up handing out hundred-dollar bills," Wilmeth said upon returning home. "Never saw such craziness. Never realized how important beating Colgate was."

The following week's game at Archbold against unbeaten and unscored upon Duke would be highly anticipated too. For all the wrong reasons. Sadly, Wilmeth was thrust into the spotlight of controversy once more, through no fault of his own. Seems several years earlier Andreas had signed a contract with Duke for two games. The pact included a clause stipulating the Blue Devils would not play against Syracuse if it had a Negro on its roster. At the time Andreas consummated the deal, there weren't any Blacks on the SU roster; Wilmeth was still in high school. Circumstances obviously had changed when it came time to play the game in the autumn of 1938.

"Can you believe this shit?" Daugherty said while getting dressed for that Monday's practice.

"Yeah, I can," Glickman said. "Andreas is a bigot. Hates anybody who isn't a white Anglo-Saxon Protestant."

"Thought we were done with all this malarkey after what happened last year."

"What's even worse this time, Duff, is they want Sing-Sing to sit out a home game. Christ sakes. Do this and they might as well pack up everything and relocate the SU campus to the Deep South."

Daugherty and Glickman were determined not to sit idly by this time. They needed to act, so they leaked the story to the local papers, and soon it was being picked up nationally by the wire services. Players, student leaders, and several members of the faculty threw their support behind Wilmeth. Some even called for a boycott.

Despite the heat, Andreas refused to budge. Fortunately, the situation was diffused in midweek, when Duke coach Wallace Wade telegrammed Andreas: "Duke will have no objection to Sidat-Singh playing in the game of November 12."

Several columnists, including some in the historically Black press, applauded Wade as a man of decency. But there was more here than met the eye. His seventh-ranked Blue Devils were charging toward a Rose Bowl bid, and Wade correctly surmised a win against an SU team without its best player might ring hollow with the folks in Pasadena who handed out the invites.

"Happy with the outcome," Wilmeth told Ike on the porch steps the night before the game. "But let's be honest, it has nothing whatsoever to do with decency. Duke has an ulterior motive here. They're only doing it because there's something in it for them, not because they're against racism. Hell, if they weren't racist, why would they ask for that clause in the first place? Believe me, Ike, if they were oh and five instead of five and oh, they would have been on the same page as Andreas."

Like with Maryland, Wilmeth wanted to make the Blue Devils pay with his play, but he wound up turning his ankle early in the game and couldn't return, giving Duke what it wanted—a 21–0 lead that continued their victory and shutout streak.

The Orangemen finished their 1938 season the following Saturday with a 13–12 victory over Columbia University at Baker Field in Upper Manhattan. The win was a sweet conclusion to Wilmeth's college football career because it had been played in front of friends and relatives just a few blocks from his home and had come against Sid Luckman, the quarterback whom he had been compared with—the college quarterback regarded as the best in the land.

CHAPTER 33

Basketball practice began the following Monday, and although *Life*, the world's most widely read magazine, predicted Wilmeth would be the surprise of the year in college basketball in 1938, he arrived at the first workout with mixed emotions. Lew Andreas had been a thorn in his side ever since finding out Wilmeth was a Negro, not a Hindu. And their relationship grew even more tense when Andreas used his power as athletic director and basketball coach to perpetuate the myth of Wilmeth's Indian roots. Andreas had failed to come to Wilmeth's defense in both the Maryland and Duke football games. But the toughest thing may have been the way Andreas limited his playing time in basketball.

"Damn guy's been lording over me like some slave owner," Wilmeth grumbled to Ike. "Throws me a bread crumb here and there and expects me to be grateful. 'Thanks, masser!'"

"I know, Wil. Sadly, nothing you can do about it. Got to keep playing the white man's game."

Despite looking like the best player on the floor, Wilmeth was worried he'd be forced to spend another season coming off the bench and would have to continue suppressing his futuristic hoops skills. This was his last shot to play college ball, his last chance to showcase his abilities and perhaps play-for-pay with one of the professional Negro barnstorming basketball teams. He hoped and prayed the stubborn, prejudiced, powerful Andreas would remove the shackles and allow him to not only play—but play to his strengths.

After that first practice ended, Andreas called him into his office. Wilmeth feared the worst; thought another bomb was about to be detonated.

"Just want you to know, son, that you're going to start this year," he said.

Wilmeth was caught totally by surprise. Pleasantly so for a change. "Well, thanks, Coach. I'll give it my best."

"I know you will," Andreas said. "We have the makings of a special team. Some of the stuff you do on the football field—the passing and scoring and anticipating—I think we can translate to the basketball court."

"I think so, too, Coach."

The two men shook hands, and Wilmeth walked out of Andreas's office dumbfounded.

"Did I just hear what I heard?" He shook his head, looked to the sky, and grinned from ear to ear. "Thank you, Jesus. Miracles really can happen. Thought hell would freeze over before Andreas would hand me the keys to his kingdom."

At long last, Wilmeth would get a chance to show Andreas just how ignorant and foolish he'd been. He couldn't wait to spread his wings on the court and carry Syracuse out of the game's dark ages. Basketball was still a stodgy game, really not that far advanced from the late nineteenth-century peach-basket-on-the-barn-days of founder James Naismith. There were no clocks requiring teams to loft up shots within a certain period of time. No requirements to advance the ball past midcourt. Scores were routinely low, with teams often putting up fewer than forty points per game. Stall ball was de rigueur. Get a lead and milk the clock. Some teams would hold on to the ball for more than two minutes before firing a shot.

Wilmeth and his Black peers played a different brand of ball on the courts of Harlem. A faster brand. A more exciting brand. They experimented with fancy dribbling, passes, and shots. They were masters of the improv. They forced the action, attacked the basket creatively, made scoring a priority. Wilmeth had met resistance when he attempted to play "Negro ball" in practice and games. But eventually he won over his stubborn coach and teammates. They saw the advantages and came to accept and embrace them.

Wilmeth felt emancipated on the court that winter, and it showed in his play as he wound up leading the Orangemen in scoring by a wide margin. Among his most memorable games was an eighteen-point performance against Penn State, a seventeen-point outing in a rout of Fordham, and a twenty-point outburst in a 49–38 drubbing of the University of Pennsylvania. With Wilmeth setting the pace, the Orangemen posted a 15–4 record, enhancing their reputation as an eastern powerhouse and padding Andreas's impressive basketball résumé.

The season wound up being everything Wilmeth had hoped it would be. With one exception. Before a February 11, 1939, game against the Naval Academy in Annapolis, Maryland, racism—and Andreas—would rear their ugly heads again. An hour before tip-off, Navy's coach John Wilson informed Andreas his team wouldn't take the court if Wilmeth suited up.

Without hesitation, Andreas honored their request. Wilmeth sat. Unlike the Maryland and Duke football games, this bigoted benching received no media play. No one raised a stink. Neither the Syracuse newspapers nor the student newspaper, the *Daily Orange*, bothered questioning Andreas about Wilmeth's absence. They merely accepted it, and so, to a certain extent, did Wilmeth. He was just three months away from his coveted diploma. He decided to let it be.

On the first of June 1939, he officially completed his Syracuse sojourn, walking across the makeshift stage at Archbold Stadium to receive his diploma. Interestingly, the sheepskin was presented to him by Chancellor

William Pratt Graham. That delighted Wilmeth to no end, because he was well aware Graham had not wanted him to attend SU in the first place and actually enacted policies to significantly limit the enrollment of Black students because he felt they had inferior minds.

Wilmeth resisted saying anything to Graham on stage but did apply a vise-grip hold to the chancellor's right hand, shaking it vigorously for several seconds.

"Could see the sumbitch wincing, and that made me feel good, made me smile even wider," Wilmeth told Ike with great satisfaction later. "That poor excuse for a human being couldn't have been more uncomfortable, having to hand me that premed diploma and shake my Black hand. Inferior mind, my fanny!"

Wilmeth bounded off the stage beaming. He had gotten the last laugh and his diploma.

When commencement ended, he and many others flung their mortar boards skyward.

"Well, Duff, we did it."

"Yeah, Sing-Sing, we did, though, we both know you never would have made it without my tutoring."

"Yeah, right. Had I relied on your tutoring, I woulda been gone my freshman year, if not sooner."

Wilmeth then spotted Glickman.

"Don't know where the time went, Sing-Sing."

"Me neither, Marty. A blur. Just like you racing round that track."

"I . . . ah . . . just wanted to say again how sorry I am about Maryland."

"Gotta let it go, my friend. Can't erase the past. But we can write the future. And I think we all may be looking at bountiful futures. Five, ten, twenty years from now, you, me, Duff, and the other boys from Syracuse will gather back here to reminisce about the good times."

"Hey, Sing-Sing, we might even have to reenact that roll down Crouse Hill."

"We'll have to see about that, Marty. Gonna be older. Not as indestructible. Could wind up getting hurt."

"Well, if we do get hurt, we'll have a doctor in the house—Dr. Wilmeth Sidat-Singh."

"Like the sound of that, Marty. If my MD shingle's hung, I'll tend to you knuckleheads for free. Or maybe I'll charge you a six-pack of Utica Club. Only this time we're gonna make sure that penny-pinching Duffy pays up with a six-pack of UC on ice and doesn't forget the bottle opener."

CHAPTER 34

The tears were inevitable, especially when Thelma wrapped her arms around him.

"Now, you promise you won't be a stranger," she said, holding on to him like she never was going to let go.

"I promise," Wilmeth said.

"Ike and I will be expecting a letter from time to time."

"You can count on that."

"All aboard!" boomed the conductor.

Thelma reluctantly released him from her powerful hug, and Wilmeth shook Ike's hand.

"Can't thank both of you enough. You and Thelma will always be my Syracuse parents, my Ward parents. I'll be staying in touch the rest of my days."

Wilmeth grabbed his suitcase and duffel bag and boarded the caboose just before the doors shut for good. He waved through the window as the whistle sounded and the train began chugging east, then south toward New

York City and the rest of Wilmeth's life.

Though it had been difficult that early June day in 1939 to say goodbye to Ike and Thelma, Pastor Carver, and others he'd met in the Ward, Wilmeth was ready to move on. He couldn't wait to get back to the Big Apple. Couldn't wait to get started on his new adventures. Bountiful future indeed. Med school definitely was in his plans, but he'd probably have to wait a year or two in order to raise the huge chunk of change needed for tuition. His stepfather had hoped to help out, but his Harlem medical practice had taken a beating during the Great Depression. With fewer and fewer patients able to pay for services and the costs for medical supplies skyrocketing, Samuel Sidat-Singh's finances had taken a hit. He was barely keeping his head above water.

Despite that, Wilmeth remained optimistic about eventually being able to afford med school. And when he did accrue enough savings, he intended to apply to Howard University, the alma mater of both his dad and stepdad, but he'd follow a different path than them by becoming a surgeon. He wanted to fix people. Put them back together. That would be his calling.

Wilmeth was looking forward to unwinding a bit. Figured the year away from school would do him good, give him a mental break. In addition to working for his stepdad, he had some other ventures he wanted to pursue, including some play-for-pay sports opportunities.

Sadly, the NFL wasn't an option, but he had been chosen for a Negro college all-star team that would play the all-white New York Yankees football club in a charity game at the Polo Grounds. There also was a vibrant semipro football league in the metropolitan area that paid by the game, and given his stature, Wilmeth might be able to negotiate his per-game pay to reflect his regional popularity—a drawing card, to be sure.

His senior basketball season had been a good one and attracted the attention of some of the professional barnstorming teams, including the Syracuse Reds, who believed it would serve them well on the court and in the stands if they could sign a marquee guy who had become a Central

New York sports legend.

"Got a lot of options, my friend," Pop Gates told him one night over gin and tonics at the Cotton Club. "World's your oyster."

When he wasn't working at his father's practice that first summer after graduating, Wilmeth could be found throwing the football around in preparation for that summer's college all-star game. He might not be allowed to play in the NFL, but he damn well could show those white owners what they were missing by not giving him and Negro football standouts like Kenny Washington and Brad Holland a chance.

The game would wind up having historical significance for pro football and for Wilmeth. Baseball exhibition games between Negro Leagues and white major-league teams had been commonplace for years, as Satchel Paige's All-Stars took on his Caucasian contemporaries Dizzy Dean and Bob Feller in barnstorming contests that regularly drew robust crowds in nooks and crannies throughout North America. But this football all-star game was the first integrated matchup of its kind, and a throng of more than twenty-five thousand spectators showed up at the Polo Grounds, high atop Coogan's Bluff, a stone's throw from Wilmeth's neighborhood.

The Negro stars more than held their own, coming up just short, 24–20. And Wilmeth put on the show he hoped he would, dazzling spectators and his NFL opponents with his powerful passes and elusive runs. In fact, he was virtually unstoppable for most of the game. Wilmeth felt if he had gotten his hands on the ball one more time, the NFLers would have tasted defeat.

"That Negro boy with the funny name sure can play," marveled Kip Hurt, one of the Yankees' star players. "Thought I had the SOB dead to rights a few times, and somehow he wriggled away like a trout off the hook. No doubt in my mind—he could play in our league."

Others echoed Hurt's sentiments. And when Wilmeth read their comments in the papers the next day, he felt simultaneously proud and disappointed, reminded for the millionth time that being good enough wasn't good enough in a world divided into skin colors.

In addition to the respect of his opponents, the scintillating performance earned him a contract with Harlem's premier semipro team, the Aces, and he played several games for them that summer and fall, adding to his reputation and his coffers.

That November, the Syracuse Reds made him an offer he couldn't refuse—$200 per game—and he spent weekends traveling with the hoops team on a barnstorming tour throughout the Northeast and Midwest. In those pre–National Basketball Association days, traveling town and industrial teams were all the rage. Their rosters usually were either all-white or all-Black, so the Reds signing of Wilmeth in 1939 was historically significant because they were one of the first professional sports teams to field an integrated roster.

Wilmeth was a pioneer again but thought nothing of it. He just wanted to keep playing ball. And doing so in his college town, in front of the Harrisons and other folks from the Ward, was an added bonus. It gave him an opportunity to renew old acquaintances and sink his teeth into some of Thelma's buttery salt potatoes again.

Old stereotypes and ruses, however, still died hard. When Wilmeth signed his Reds contract, the headline in the *Syracuse Herald* read: "Hindu Ace Aids Syracuse Title Quest."

"Sheesh," Wilmeth muttered, when shown the story. "Like a damn stain I can't wash off no matter how hard I try. I'm Negro, not Hindu. When are people gonna learn and move on?"

The basketball greatness he'd displayed during his senior year of college was carrying over into his professional career. On December 1, 1939, the Reds shocked the hoops world by upsetting the Original Celtics, the world's top all-white team, 40–37, at a packed gymnasium in Watertown, New York. Wilmeth set the pace, with a game-high fourteen points, prompting one scribe to describe him as "an unstoppable one-man team." The Reds would go on to record several more stirring wins, and it wasn't long before bidding wars for Wilmeth's basketball services broke out.

His goal all along was to play for the New York Renaissance, better known as the Harlem Rens, an all-Black squad famous for winning multiple world basketball tournaments, which featured Wilmeth's best buddies, Pop Gates and John Isaacs. After watching the impact Wilmeth had on the Reds, the Rens came calling, and in 1941 he would join them and help them win more titles.

Despite their success on the court and the sizable crowds they were drawing, the Rens started struggling to make payroll. A big reason for their business woes were the exorbitant rental fees charged by white arena owners. This was similar to problems faced by Negro League baseball owners when they played in major league ballparks. Eventually, the Rens folded, and Wilmeth was forced to seek other basketball employment.

One day, out of the blue, he received a phone call from Sam Lacy, the famous sportswriter who had outed him before the game against Maryland. Though Wilmeth had been pissed about the timing of Lacy's story, he never blamed him for writing about what amounted to an open secret. He even sided with Lacy when the scribe told ticked-off Black readers their anger was misdirected, that the real villains were the muckety-mucks at Maryland and Syracuse University, the ones who'd come up with their racist gentlemen's agreements.

"Hey, Wil, I know all about the hardships going on with the Rens, and I got a business proposition for you."

"Really, Sam? What's that?"

"Well, I've got a deep-pocketed promoter down here in DC—guy by the name of Abe Lichtman—who wants to put together the best basketball team in the world, and he asked me to help him round up some outstanding players. I immediately thought of you, Pop, and John."

Wilmeth's ears perked up. He'd been thinking for a while that a change of venue would do him good. Maybe returning to his hometown might be what he needed. It would give him an opportunity to reunite with his mom, who had returned there after a messy, public divorce from his stepdad . He could save some more money and finally fill out the med school applications to Howard. And he'd still be able to play basketball for pay with two of his best friends, forming the nucleus of a team capable of playing for a world championship.

"I'm intrigued, Sam. But I'm going to need to see some greenbacks to convince me to make any commitment. Don't want to be a jerk about this, but the Rens stiffed me and others, so I'm gonna want my money up front."

"That shouldn't be a problem, Wil. We can get you and the other guys some advance money as a show of good faith. Like I said, this guy Lichtman has some awfully deep pockets. He wants the best of the best, and I don't think he's gonna spare any expense."

"I could always move to the District, but it's not going to be so easy for Pop and John. They got jobs, homes, and family up here in Harlem."

"I know. But it would only be weekends—for tournaments and barnstorming games here and in New York, Detroit, Philly, and Chicago. Hardly ever a game on a weeknight. And they'll have access to a pretty snazzy new automobile you guys can use to get to games."

"OK. Let me think it over."

After hanging up, Wilmeth began smiling. The deal seemed good, the timing right. If Lacy delivered the advance money, he'd be in. When Wilmeth spoke to his mom about his intentions, she seemed happy. But something was bugging her, and it had been for some time.

"Wilmeth, when you gonna stop playing sports? Ain't no future in it. Ain't no money in it."

"Mama, it's just something I love doing."

"But it's getting in the way of what you said you were gonna do, what you should be doing."

"I promise you, Mama, I'm ready to apply for med school. I really am. Sports is just a side job. I was gonna have to work anyway. And this is a lot more fun than waiting on tables or hauling garbage."

"I 'spose."

A few days later, Wilmeth phoned Lacy. "Sam, you got a deal."

"Fantastic. Pop and John said they're on board if you are. And with a few other guys I have my sights on, we're gonna field one helluva team. Better than those great Rens teams. Maybe better than any team ever."

CHAPTER 35

Wilmeth needed to raise a thousand more dollars during the summer and fall of 1941 before he'd be able to foot the bill for med school tuition and books. So, in addition to playing for the Washington Bears—with whom he'd established a new single-game professional basketball scoring record with twenty-eight points and helped lead to twenty-two consecutive victories—he had secured a job as a recreation center director in his old DC neighborhood. The ravages of the Great Depression had hit the place hard, making the poverty much worse than what he remembered from his youth. He'd always loved working with kids, so the rec job was right up his alley. He hoped to mold and inspire them. He'd show them how dreams could come true. After all, he was the Walking Dream, right?

These were tumultuous times in the world, and as much as Wilmeth wanted to escape through sports, he couldn't. War was raging in Europe as one particular mad man sought to gobble up every country under the sun. Wilmeth believed President Roosevelt was doing his best to help allies Great

Britain and Norway while maintaining America's neutrality. The ill effects of World War I and the Great Depression were still being felt a generation later, so there was a powerful movement for America to remain neutral and avoid becoming involved in another great conflict.

But Wilmeth sensed that with each bomb pelting London, with each country surrendering to Hitler, the United States was drawing closer to war. And then, when the Japanese bombed the hell out of Pearl Harbor that infamous December day in 1941, the inevitable occurred, and America was neutral no more.

Suddenly, playing professional basketball seemed pretty insignificant, though Wilmeth did welcome the opportunities to reunite on weekends for games with Pops and John. They both had departed Harlem after landing jobs with Grumman, the huge munitions plant on Long Island that was revving up production of planes, guns, and ammo for the war effort.

"Doing our thing, Wil, for the good ol' US of A," Isaac told Wilmeth as the two nursed some beers in the locker room following a Bears game.

"How's that going?"

"Like gangbusters. You want to end a Depression and jump-start an economy? Go to war."

"What you making up there?"

"Everything you can imagine, war-related, and some things you can't imagine. Got shifts working 'round the clock. Nonstop."

"Gotta be rewarding, knowing you're making a difference arming the troops and fighting that maniac."

"Very rewarding. Can't be there aiding the cause, because they don't trust a Negro's soldiering skills. But this is the next best thing."

The conversation got Wilmeth thinking. He wanted to do something, too, to help the war effort. Something more important, something more meaningful than playing a child's game as a man when soldiers were dying, and the world was being blown apart at the seams. But what could he do? How could he help?

FDR had told Major League Baseball to keep playing games, even though the majority of the players had signed up or were drafted into the armed services, leaving just a watered-down version to pitch, hit, and catch. Ol' Franklin thought it would be good for the morale of the country and the soldiers fighting on foreign soil. Wilmeth wondered if he and his fellow basketball players were contributing in some small way, too, by entertaining folks, serving as a distraction.

Still, it didn't seem like enough. There had to be something more substantive he could do. One day he noticed an advertisement in the *Baltimore Afro-American*. Apparently, the draft had cut heavily into the ranks of DC policemen, and there was a huge need for cops to take their places. *That's what I can do*, he thought to himself. *I can become a policeman*. And that's what he did. He took the exam and soon was patrolling the streets. *Doing my patriotic duty*, he thought.

But he continued to feel unfulfilled, like he really wasn't doing enough.

One day his stepfather came to the capital to speak at a medical convention, and Wilmeth met him for lunch. Wilmeth updated him on what he was doing—essentially working three jobs—and how he had saved enough money for tuition and was going to apply to med school. He also told his stepdad how it gnawed at him that he wasn't doing enough for the war effort.

"Well, Wil, look at it this way. We don't know how long this war is going to go on. We don't know how many people are going to get wounded and injured. Gonna be a real need for more doctors at some point. So the sooner you get through school, the sooner you can help."

"I know you're right, but a part of me wishes I could be over there helping fight this thing. But they don't seem to want or trust Negroes. I'm sure they think we'd make inferior soldiers."

"I'd concentrate on med school. Go get the applications."

And that's what he did. He applied to and was accepted by Howard med school. He was ready to start in the fall semester in 1942, when he saw another newspaper ad that captured his eye.

A new training program for Negro fighter pilots had been launched at the Tuskegee Institute in Alabama. It said they were looking for college graduates, the best and the brightest of Black America. Wilmeth's heart began racing. For more than a year, he'd wanted to become part of the war effort. And now, in this black-and-white newspaper ad, he had finally found his answer. Med school could wait. Pro basketball could wait. He was going to become a Tuskegee Airman. He was going to do his part.

CHAPTER 36

A veritable boneyard.

That's how Wilmeth saw it when he arrived in Alabama in the summer of 1942 to begin military training. Tuskegee Army Airfield had been built on part of an abandoned cemetery—a plot of land the US government took over when a military appropriation bill laid a few million on the table. The grand experiment called for hiring Negro contractors to clear and grub the tract for a Blacks-only pilot training facility.

Wilmeth imagined the land had probably been a lot like the decrepit Columbian Harmony Cemetery back in DC, one of the five dedicated solely for African Americans. That old graveyard was over by Rhode Island Avenue, a shabby, rundown property a land agent would undoubtedly purchase someday in the future. And then probably just chuck all the dark bones they dug up into the Potomac.

The same kind of thinking probably took place in Alabama. Down here, Negroes didn't count as full humans. Dead Negroes counted less.

Back in January 1941, the War Department, or maybe it was FDR, sup-posedly decided against selecting land in Chicago, where most of the good Black pilots found themselves reliably inspired by Bessie Colman, America's first Black licensed aviator. Instead, the feds went about as far south into the land of prejudice and hatred as they could go.

Just like them, Wilmeth thought. *Picked an overgrown plot of land full of knocked-over headstones.*

Then again, maybe the land of the dead as a setting was fitting. Macon County was a nasty place, where getting cornered on a dark road could mean a Black man ended up hanging from a tree.

Tuskegee would also terminate a lot of Black fliers who didn't last long enough to get their wings. Bunch of brothers would get knocked on their butts when it came to learning the physics of aviation.

The important part in the best ghost stories was the rising back up. Returning with a vengeance.

Thankfully, Booker T. Washington's Tuskegee Institute was nearby, and that meant Black college-educated faculty and top-notch flight instructors, like Chief Anderson, living a stone's throw away. They would know the score. They'd know where it was safe.

According to the grapevine, information gleaned during his first day in the noisy mess hall, the first Tuskegee aircrew, thirteen of the best, with the class coding 42-C-SE, had started in June 1941 with Captain Ben Davis Jr. from Washington, DC.

Wilmeth already knew Davis had served as cadet commandant. That was no surprise. Davis had successfully soloed in September 1941, and along with five other men from the first thirteen easily passed muster. It could be done.

But it also wasn't hard calculating the success rate. Less than half of the thirteen made it through the gauntlet. Some of the fellows were already joking the brass were planning on eliminating as many as seven out of every ten from future classes.

Undoubtedly, Davis would come across as demanding, but to Wilmeth's way of thinking, he would get it. Davis would know how everyone in the whole country was waiting to see if Black "guinea pigs" could really fly. He'd make damn sure the boys of the Ninety-Ninth and any fliers who followed them were twice as good as the white pilots getting cleared elsewhere.

Chatter in the ranks was one thing, but Wilmeth had seen a reprint of a *Pittsburgh Courier* article in which a General Weaver, the man commanding the army's Southeastern Air Corps Training Command, was quoted saying the bar for getting into Ninety-Ninth Pursuit Squadron was purposely set high. Anyone wanting to accept the challenge would be required to ignore the coming storm. Social hazing, political dismissal, military mistreatment. In other words, the works.

Clearly, much worse than getting benched for one game at Maryland.

Weaver had called for men with superior aptitudes, attitudes, and abilities, telling the Black community to send their very best. "For their sake and for our sake."

In Wilmeth's mind, that use of the word *our* probably referred to the white command who occasionally stuck their necks out for Black fliers. Letting Blacks in was probably a career risk for a desk jockey.

Or maybe the use of *our* was intended for the whole US as it waited for a coming war. A massive fight where America took on the Germans. Maybe the Japanese too. God forbid Uncle Sam wanted to pick fights on two continents.

Who knew?

Wilmeth was quickly realizing that, in one respect, he was like a lot of the men he was meeting. He had no flying experience. Had never really thought about learning to fly during college. But soaring over the ground, zooming down on a target, that part seemed a lot more like running with the ball. Or attacking an opposing team through the air.

He had always been good at trajectories. Knew how to lead a receiver. There would be some of that in his becoming a pilot. As for the playbook, well, that was going to be massive.

Still, just having a chance to fly and fight was a fantastic concept.

Up north, there had been quite a ruckus made by the Black press about good young men wanting to join a Jim Crow pursuit squadron. The Negro media wanted immediate integration or no Tuskegee. Black men flying was a concept white America wasn't even remotely contemplating.

In the end, it came down to exclusion or segregation. Wilmeth knew he'd been included at Syracuse but also faced discrimination. He knew that bitter taste.

At Tuskegee that October, he found the sticky Alabama heat more oppressive than the District in July. It hung thick in the air, like a scratchy cotton shirt, particularly late in the day.

That meant living conditions in Tent City had been ripe with rich, sweaty aromas, which was another way for calling it primitive, like the cramped Archbold locker room after an early September game.

The first Tuskegee class had been forced to live in long rows of tents, the flaps always down, because the construction of barracks had been delayed. Now, with the arrival of Singh's unit, the third, the airfield was overcrowded. And stinking to high heaven under thick canvas sheets intent on holding stifling hot air in one place.

Plus, and perhaps this was intentionally designed for demoralizing the weak, there was no running water—it had to be trucked in. Meals were managed under field conditions. It truly felt as if the men were slaving on the fetid acres of some plantation boss.

The reason for this indignity?

Tent platforms were cheap to build, and there was nowhere for the first two graduating men to go. The army wasn't letting the newly minted pilots move out. That meant as new aircrews and support teams marched in, the quartermaster could get away with simply tossing squadron leaders a heavy bag filled with a tent, ropes, and stakes. Then, after a few choice words, he could angrily point them toward Tent City.

On the matter of finding beds, the de rigueur steel-frame double bunks with sagging springs and piss-stained mattresses meant the new fliers quickly learned they would need to scavenge or improvise. This was the army, not the Ritz.

On top of that grumbling, it was already whispered the overcrowding was another reason flight instructors were intent on washing men out. Flunk them at Tuskegee today and tomorrow they could serve as cooks or janitors somewhere else.

Still, despite the stench and usual military snafus, Wilmeth's first evaluation of the new cadets around him suggested every man selected for 43-C-SE was equally capable.

In the crowded mess hall, at their first evening meal, there were no Black waiters and white diners. Everyone was Black. Plus, what Wilmeth saw was the best of the best. Smart, educated, and talented. Men who wanted to prove they were good enough to fly and fight.

In some ways, they all looked the same. Like a football team. Everyone wearing the same green uniform. Dealing with the same itchy, ill-fitting fabric.

Thankfully, the usual complaining was mixed with some jive.

Humans always differed in hundreds of ways, but on this metaphorical court, Wilmeth felt comfortable sizing a man up. The loud ones—the braggarts, cutups, and clowns—always stood out. He was interested in the quiet men. The thinkers and observers. The calm, collected, and determined.

One thing about his incoming group was certain. Each was a college graduate or an existing upperclassman who would have to establish his bona fides and ability to fit in. But unlike his days at Syracuse or even during his time with the Rens, there were no veterans taking rookies under their wings and guiding them.

On white bases, there were men who had flown for years passing on their wisdom. At Tuskegee, most cadets had never flown. Some of the jokers boldly slapping palms had never even seen a plane up close.

It was like looking at a fresh batch of high school freshmen coming out for football on the first day. All goofy and gangly, running the wrong routes, making coaches scratch their heads and then start hollering about the basics.

Around him on the muddy parade ground, Wilmeth saw men covering up their fear or lack of confidence. That was a recipe for disaster, and in football, an unwillingness to hit or get hit always showed quickly.

If a man wasn't aggressive in the gridiron trenches, didn't square up and drive his shoulder into his opponent first, he'd get clobbered. Fear and uncertainty were logical, but the difference at Tuskegee was when they got into old planes men might die if Wilmeth didn't do his job.

"Hey, ain't you Sidat-Singh?"

The voice was low and came sliding over Wilmeth's left shoulder. It was just barely louder than a whisper and done in a way so as not to draw attention. The men had been filing out of the mess after the first so-called dinner of overcooked meatloaf, a few collard greens, and a pale slop of soupy mashed potatoes.

"Who's asking?" Wilmeth shot back, pivoting on his heels to face a slender, dark-skinned man with overly large hands.

"Charles Williams, at your service. Your new wingman."

With that overly confident introduction, a dark brown paw flashed into the short space between the two men. Wilmeth shook it and noticed the strength of the grip.

"I dunno about that," said Wilmeth, his face impassive, lest he give something away. "Nobody in our group has proved shit yet. Lot of these young men, maybe myself included, won't get their wings."

"But the two of us will get 'em. We'll see them pinned on."

"What makes you so certain, Mr. Williams?"

"I know all about you up at Syracuse, Wilmeth. I know you don't want to hear me calling you a hero and all, but playing at that white university, passing for all those touchdowns . . . you know, that was pretty impressive out where I come from."

"You're right about the hero rot. That football stuff won't matter a lick up in the air against the Germans. But since yo' ass is so forthcoming, where you from that you possibly heard about me?"

"Just outside Charlotte, North Carolina. God's country. But I had a family connection go to Howard. They sure write about you a lot in Washington."

"Ah, that stuff just lines birdcages. Howard U, huh?"

"Yep. Got to study under Chief Anderson. So I know a little."

"I heard about Chief when I got back home from Syracuse and the big city," offered Wilmeth, suddenly taking an interest in Williams. "Heard he's here with us now. Teaching at Tuskegee. As for the Almighty, seems to me God has got hisself set on a lot more people dyin' in the next few years. But I will say this much: I like your confidence."

"Yeah, well, I like your passing skills. You didn't get to do much in that Duke game, which by the way I almost got to see, but I figure you're going to need someone on your outside. Someone you can count on."

"Don't get me started on the Duke game, Williams. But listen, let's make ourselves a pact. We'll talk some football here and there, in exchange for you making sure I'm on top of these flying basics. I won't have any trouble with the books and manuals. But I'm gonna hound you if you know how these P-40s work."

"Not to worry. I got it down. The reason is partly 'cause of you. Y'all were a bit of an inspiration. To a lot of us."

"Oh, hell. I'll probably get your inspired ass killed. But I appreciate knowin' some part of my fame is helping us out. We gotta beat these Germans. Show that Negroes can do anything whites think we can't. Like throw the ball. Or fly. Fight for our country. Messed up as it is."

"Amen to that, brother," said Williams. "All right, let's get ourselves to this next meeting and start acquainting ourselves with the other eight pilots in our squad. I heard our motto is going to be 'Spitfire' and our call sign 'Percy.' Funny names, huh?

"Well, Mr. Williams, these are funny times."

CHAPTER 37

Syracuse, New York, April 2000

As she steered her rusty, old Honda Civic into the rectangular lot a stone's throw from the Carrier Dome, Breanna couldn't help but notice the knee-high banks of dirty snow and the road salt caked onto the sides of all the parked vehicles.

Ah yes, she thought, cracking a smile. *Welcome back to the 'Cuse. Good ol' Salt City.*

Though Breanna had spent the entirety of her young life in Upstate New York and had come to detest the endless winters that often spilled over into delayed springs, there was something about these refuse-to-melt snowbanks and weatherworn vehicles that comforted her in a strange way. Made her feel as if she were back home. Along with the Dome and other familiar surroundings, they greeted her like long-lost friends, had her yearning for her undergraduate days at Syracuse University—a simpler, more innocent time.

It had been several years since Breanna had been back on campus, so it was only normal memories would start pinballing around in her head.

After grabbing her purse and tote bag, she got out of her car and gaped at the Dome. The Teflon-bubbled stadium loomed large over everything—just as it had during her college days—dominating the campus skyline like some enormous, plopped-down UFO. The cavernous arena had been a second home. In fact, she may have spent more time in there than any classroom. She thought back to all those football, basketball, and lacrosse games she had covered for the *Daily Orange* beneath that big top. Breanna remembered, in particular, her interviews with Donovan McNabb, who had not only quarterbacked the Orangemen from 1995 to 1998 before heading off to National Football League stardom but had also played briefly on Jim Boeheim's basketball team, once coming off the bench to spark a stirring come-from-behind victory against hated rival Georgetown.

McNabb had been the biggest of "Big Man on Campus" players, and Breanna lost track of how many times girlfriends had asked her what he was like or if she was secretly dating him. Her answer never pleased anyone because even back then she'd kept things professional. There was no faster way to destroy journalism credentials, current or future, than to sleep with the star QB and have everyone on campus talking about it.

As she walked past nearby Hendricks Chapel and other ivy-covered buildings bordering the large green, grassy quadrangle, she felt as if she had been transported, like some *Star Trek* character entering the teleportation chamber, and had reemerged on top of her old footsteps. She was older and wiser. And perhaps a tad more jaded and cynical, but still striving. Still hopeful of achieving her career goals.

The puzzle that was Wilmeth Sidat-Singh had prompted her to return. There still were so many missing pieces to his story, especially with regards to his time at Tuskegee, and she'd hoped to fill in some of the blanks by combing through the archival files in the top floor of Bird Library, a six-story, slit-windowed, concrete fortress that architecturally reminded her of a low-grade federal prison. After cramming for her last exam and scrambling to finish her final paper years earlier, she vowed never to set foot in the building again. But, as she had learned, life can take one on unexpected journeys. She would gladly break her vow today if it meant fleshing out this story of a dead hero who had become an obsession.

While descending the sloping, brownish, green lawn toward University Avenue, Breanna stole a glance at the Hall of Languages. The oldest building on campus supposedly had inspired the haunted mansion depicted in the opening and closing credits of the *Addams Family* television sitcom. Breanna had loved watching reruns of that 1960s show as a kid, and she reveled in telling visitors to campus about the Hall's Hollywood connection.

When she reached the sidewalk at the base of the hill, she gazed at Newhouse I and II—the modernistic, cube-like, I. M. Pei–designed buildings where she first honed her newspaper skills. She remembered how manic professors would scribble an enormous *F* in blood-red ink on papers if they contained a misspelled name. As a student, she thought they were overly harsh but was now grateful they had been that way because they instilled the importance of getting things right.

"There is a trust a journalist builds with his or her readers," newspaper professor Steve Davis would harp in his classes to her and the other aspiring Woodwards and Bernsteins. "And when you get things wrong, even with something as simple as a misspelled word, you erode that trust and begin losing credibility. That's not to say you won't make mistakes. You will. We all do. Journalists are human too. But our work is based on maintaining public trust, so do everything in your power to be accurate, to get things right. Make that extra phone call. Do the painstaking, often boring research many avoid. Reread and rework your story several times before submitting it. Do whatever it takes to get it right."

Get!

It!

Right!

That's what I'm trying to do with Wilmeth's forgotten story, Professor Davis, she thought as she arrived at the entrance to Big Bird. *I'm going to keep digging and digging and digging until I get his story right.*

Breanna pulled open the library's heavy glass door and passed through the strange device that still radiated like a clicking Geiger counter. Those clicking sounds made her chuckle. The purpose of the device supposedly was to announce when students had "borrowed" books without checking them out. Or perhaps it was to determine how many students actually used the library each day. Either way, she wondered whose job it was to do something about it.

Wilmeth remained an enigma, a mystery, and Breanna had come back to Syracuse armed with the knowledge he'd left work as a Washington, DC, policeman and rec director in 1942, inspired in some way to serve his country by joining the Tuskegee Airmen. He'd survived and thrived in Alabama before shipping off to Michigan.

But was there anything of note about his final days at Tuskegee?

Pulling up a rolling plastic chair in front of one of the library's updated computer terminals, Breanna decided to hunt for anything she could find about Wilmeth's graduation. Perhaps someone of elevated military rank had presided over the commissioning of the Black pilots who had completed their flight training. Maybe that connection played a role in Wilmeth's placement at Arlington National Cemetery after he died.

The starting point for all things Black in the 1940s were the Black newspapers, especially the *Pittsburgh Courier* and *Baltimore Afro-American*, both of which had national circulations.

Breanna knew from memory Wilmeth graduated from Tuskegee near the end of March 1943. If she scanned microfiche pages from around the twenty-fifth onward, she held a decent chance of finding something that unwrapped the Wilmeth mystery. Something that might reveal a little about the commencement speaker or the individual responsible for pinning on Wilmeth's wings.

The existence of the Tuskegee "birdmen" had been news throughout 1942 and well into 1943, and so her needle-in-a-haystack exercise was not as random as it might have seemed. A Tuskegee dateline was all she needed.

There was nothing from the last week of March, and Breanna was just getting ready to switch to the more well-known Baltimore paper when the word *birdmen* seemingly flew off the page at her. On page eight of the April 3 edition, she saw the headline halfway down the right side of the page: *LARGEST CLASS OF BIRDMEN GET WINGS*.

It was placed next to a story about the British praising Negro antiaircraft units and a Guadalcanal hero. *Oh, bless them*, she thought. The Courier *was thorough*.

Just as she'd hoped, Wilmeth's class had been recognized for their March 25 graduation. The story was dated April 1, and the lede indicated that, after listening to "the brilliant wit of Lieutenant Colonel Noel F. Parrish, commanding officer of the Tuskegee Army Flying School, the latest contingent of Negro birdmen were elevated to the rank of flying lieutenants in the army air forces."

Hastily, Breanna wrote down Parrish's name before returning to the story. Would there be a mention of Wilmeth? Breanna didn't have to wait long. Her eyes racing down the page as fast as a guiding finger on the greenish glass monitor would carry them, she started seeing it. In the seventh paragraph, Wilmeth was noted for winning an aerial sharpshooter medal.

One paragraph later, he was singled out for graduating second in his class, with the handing out of cadet honors coming from Captain John Cooke. One sentence later, Wilmeth was recognized again as one of the most notable graduates.

Three mentions! But who else besides Parrish and Cooke was involved? Who hung those wings on Wilmeth? Running her finger back up the story on the blue-tinted screen, she saw an indent starting with the words *silver wings*. It read: *Silver wings were pinned to the flyers' blouses by Major Donald G. McPherson, director of flight instruction.*

Whoa! Now there's a wild SU coincidence, thought Breanna. The man who ceremonially certified Wilmeth as a pilot had the exact same name as one of Syracuse's most famous quarterbacks. Letter for letter. Even the same middle initial.

Breanna was certain of the *G* because during her career she'd done at least two profile pieces on the 1987 Heisman Trophy runner-up and captain of an undefeated Syracuse football team. It was almost like the universe, or maybe God, was playing with fun historical facts.

The first Black man to quarterback an SU team, Wilmeth had been pinned by an individual with the exact name as one of the great Black quarterbacks who would star at Syracuse fifty years later. McPherson would join a long line of Black quarterbacks. Names like Bernie Custis, the first Black professional QB, Avatus Stone, and Tim Wilson, who directed the Orange offense for an entire year in 1978. Marvin Graves, Kevin Mason, and McNabb came next, inspired by the exploits of the All-American McPherson. Breanna had never checked her hunch, but she guessed no major college football team, bar schools in the HBCU, had ever featured more Black QBs than the 'Cuse.

What made quarterback McPherson so interesting—compared to Major McPherson—was knowing number nine had announced himself, after playing professionally in the NFL and Canadian Football League, as a feminist. The most masculine of men, a strong Black Adonis, talented and smart enough to lead an almost all-white offensive unit, a hero to the masses for his strength, courage, and presumed virility, had taken up the mantle of trying to teach men to show more respect to women.

Breanna had captured all of McPherson's rhetoric on domestic sexual abuse, rape, and misogyny in her first major feature for the school paper, the *Daily Orange*. She'd marveled at the time this decorated Syracuse alumnus gave lectures all over the country, telling largely male audiences they needed to do better—that lovable boys were somehow morphing into pumped-up predators egged on by society to identify themselves via their sexual triumphs.

Her front-page story left no doubt she'd been impressed with McPherson's sincerity and willingness to challenge a prevailing way of thinking. For telling type-A man-boys they needed to grow up. That masculinity was not defined by screwing and keeping score.

She thought to herself the women's movement in America needed more men like McPherson because the number of women raped each year never seemed to go down. Somewhere out in America's urban and rural wildness, men were not catching on. According to McPherson, they weren't getting fed the proper narrative about compassion, honor, and love.

Looking at her watch, Breanna realized she'd taken longer than she wanted, and if she was going to get a slice of pizza at the Varsity, one of her old campus haunts, she'd better hurry. Late lunches only brought on late dinners, which, by their very nature, never did anything for anyone's digestion or weight management. Some gooey cheese at the Varsity would hit the spot.

CHAPTER 38

Syracuse University's famous pizza place sat like an anchor at one end of the unofficial main street of campus. Marshall Street, known to many as M Street, had long hosted a ragtag collection of T-shirt shops, fast-food eateries, bars (that frequently were shut down for underage drinking violations), and one upscale clothing store (for the well-heeled from Manhattan, Westchester County, and Long Island). At one end of M Street stood the Varsity, sandwiched between a head shop that sold leather goods, bongs, and rolling papers, and an Irish pub that looked very English.

It was hard to explain to someone who hadn't attended Syracuse what made the Varsity special. Much of its charm was attributable to the Dellas family, which had continuously owned the place since emigrating from Greece in the 1920s and had festooned the walls with historic photographs of Orange sporting greats like Jim Brown, Floyd Little, Derrick Coleman, and Roosevelt Bouie.

During Breanna's years, following a home win, the SU marching band would come tromping down South Crouse, raucously pouring into the Varsity, with horns honking and clarinets squawking. The crowd would erupt, and cash registers would jangle as large pizzas and sloshing pitchers of beer were sold by the armful to gleeful fans.

Having made the quick ramble over from the library, Breanna entered the pizza shop and immediately turned left. At the very front of the awninged building, skinny pizza makers were always evident through the front window, shoving black pans of dough, sauce, and pepperoni into huge steel ovens. This was the place for a slice and a cold can of soda.

After paying, Breanna knew it was a free-for-all for a table or booth. Luckily, on this day, the crowd was modest, and she had no trouble finding a seat. Around her, doctors and nurses from nearby Upstate Medical Center jostled with undergrads, grads, and faculty members for places in the cafeteria-style line for burgers and sandwiches or salads and wraps.

"Well, a few factoids down," said Breanna to no one in particular. "A few more to find."

"Hey, Breanna," came a voice she hadn't heard in years. "What are you doing back in town?"

Standing mischievously in front of her table was none other than her old journalism professor, Steve Davis, holding a bag with a small grease stain showing at the bottom.

"Professor Davis. This is so crazy. I was thinking about you and your journalistic wisdom earlier today."

"So that's why my ears were ringing."

"What a small world, Professor. I sneak back onto campus to do some research and we both end up at the Varsity. Must be fate."

"Avoiding my office hours again, I see. Well, no crime in that for a big-time sports reporter from Buffalo. Good to see you. What's the occasion?"

"Working on an involved five-part series of stories about an old SU alum. I don't want to say too much about it, but he was a Tuskegee Airman who lost his life on a training mission and wound up getting buried in Arlington

National Cemetery."

"Can't say I know too much about Arlington," said Davis, "other than the Tomb of the Unknowns was designed by a Syracuse alum. Guy by the name of Lorimer Rich. And I would never have known that except I just heard about Rich from someone in Maxwell the other day. Was up there for a Faculty Senate meeting and sat with David Bennett. You remember David, don't you? Great history professor."

"Sure do. Took one class with him my senior year. We gave him a standing ovation after the last class. He was that good."

"Indeed. He consistently amazes. A natural. Well, listen, I won't interrupt you while your slice is still hot. I'm gonna run. Was just grabbing a drink and a cheesesteak. Please call me the next time you come to town. Would love to buy you a coffee or a beer."

"I'll do it," Breanna said, smiling at her old teacher as he barely avoided tripping over a wayward metal chair.

With that, he was gone. Breanna pulled out her morning notes. She was thrilled she had stumbled upon that tidbit about Major McPherson pinning those silver wings on Wilmeth's chest. That research discovery was like prospector's gold. But she needed to find out more about Tuskegee, and that would be her afternoon's priority.

After wolfing down her two slices—just like the good ol' days, when she was always inhaling food between deadlines—Breanna decided to walk the length of M Street on her way back to Bird Library. Traversing the street running adjacent to Wilmeth's and her alma mater, she wondered if he, a "Hindu" star of the football team, would have been allowed to eat in the Varsity. Could he have gotten food or snacks, or would he have been turned away?

Back at Bird, she gathered more material about Tuskegee that would provide valuable background and context. Her research uncovered that in December 1940 the US Army Air Corps had suggested undertaking the Tuskegee Experiment and determined a small all-Negro fighter squadron was worth testing. The Ninety-Ninth Pursuit Squadron would feature just thirty-five pilots supported by a grounds crew numbering less than three hundred. As experiments go, it would remain inconsequential and as unobtrusive as possible. There was no need to get racist generals from southern military academies up in arms.

Naturally, the first officers of the Ninety-Ninth would be white, but the AAC's groundwork called for Black officers to eventually take command. Breanna found it interesting that in December 1940, a full year before America officially entered World War II, the military brass knew the storm was coming. They could sense it and were already building up troop strength for a battle they were itching to fight.

Hence, she reasoned, the War Department announcement just one month later, on January 16, 1941, that Blacks could become pilots.

A big part of that official decision, Breanna deduced, was a little-discussed lawsuit brought by Yancey Williams, a Black pilot who boldly sued the Secretary of War, Army Chief of Staff, the Adjutant General, plus Hap Arnold, the chief of the air corps, and Walter Grant, the commanding general of the US Army's Third Corps.

Williams's brief was aided by the presence of the NAACP and guided by a rising young lawyer named Thurgood Marshall, who later became the Supreme Court's first Black justice and, like Williams, was a Howard University graduate.

What made the lawsuit overtly powerful and opened doors for men like Wilmeth was the insinuation the President's top military advisors were actively derelict in their war preparation duties. They wanted war and knew it was coming, but kept turning away talented fliers like Yancey Williams.

As Breanna clawed through the case files, she smiled at Marshall's strategic courage in suggesting "such conduct on the part of these defendants, who, in their official capacity as officers of the government and of the Army of the United States and charged with the duty of the preparation for national defense in a period when the nation, according to its chief executive, the president of the United States, faces the gravest emergency in its history, is a violation of the duty and obligation of these defendants to the citizens and government of the United States and contravenes the fundamental principles of the American democracy."

That's some heavy shit, she thought to herself. *These brothers threw down on the establishment hard. Invoked the president, democracy in general, and called the white folk out. That is particularly badass.*

The more she looked into Wilmeth's era, the more she confronted truths about systemic racism everywhere and the unlikeliness a project like Tuskegee could have ever gotten off the ground.

More digging showed the pivotal moment on the path to Black aviation acceptance likely occurred in the spring of 1941 when Singh was back in DC. It appeared a Howard University educator named Alfred Anderson had started a civilian flight training program in 1939 and soon after got it bumped up to an official academic program.

One article in Howard's school paper, the *Hill Top*, suggested an engineering professor lectured would-be fliers on the fundamentals of flight. After the students took courses in navigation, flight theory and meteorology, Anderson took them over to a local, rundown, airport at Hybla Valley, Virginia, and let them reach for the sky.

Anderson's crowning achievement for Black airmen came in March 1941, when Eleanor Roosevelt, the country's vociferous First Lady, was touring Tuskegee's hospital but stopped to ask her aide about the Anderson legend. Her belief, it was reported, "was that colored people couldn't fly," but here she was in Alabama, and somewhere nearby a Black man was soaring and teaching others to do the same.

On meeting Anderson and liking him instantly, Mrs. Roosevelt announced, "I'm just going to have to take a flight with you." And Anderson, sensing a way to impress the "conscience" of the White House, jumped at the chance. Despite protests from the First Lady's security detail, Anderson loaded Roosevelt, still wearing a flowery hat, into his small two-seater Piper

Cub and took off to the amazement of all.

Breanna sat back and wondered about the incongruity of FDR's wife whipping around the skies of central Alabama with Montgomery, the former first capital of the Confederacy, barely visible just forty miles to the west. *How wild was that?* she thought.

A Black man in 1941 flying the president's wife and showing love for a country that didn't love him back because of his skin color. Her people never ceased to amaze. It was obvious Wilmeth and Anderson were the uncelebrated heroes she needed to bring to life in her multipart series.

It also was clear that almost overnight Anderson's historic flight propelled him into the Negro newspaper stratosphere. It made him a hero in the Black community and, with FDR thinking about reelection and Black votes, might've been what pushed the US military into more fully endorsing the Tuskegee experiment.

Anderson's daring move started a chain reaction inspiring smart, talented men like Wilmeth to believe he must serve his country in the sky. And why not? His most impressive feats at Syracuse involved making a football sail through the air. Could he not do the same in a fighter plane?

CHAPTER 39

Tuskegee, Alabama, March 25, 1943

My God, thought Wilmeth. *Nine months have gone by. We come here last fall, and it's already spring. A fine Thursday comin' down. And warm. Sweet kind of warm. Leavin' here soon. Headin' back up north. To who knows what.*

"Wilmeth."

No reply. The cloud of thought surrounding Singh was thick.

"Wil-meth! Boy, where's your head at?"

It was Charles.

Piercing the cumulus. Who else could it ever be? Whispering through clenched lips. Always thinking about something different from Wilmeth. Usually football, women, drinks, or weekend passes. About going into town to see some musician. Who was the last one? Dinah Washington? She wasn't bad. Barely nineteen. Come down from Chicago. A bit jazzy. Less of the country and Delta blues.

"Been thinking, Charles."

"'Bout all you do, Singh."

"Been thinkin' about where we're headed next."

"Where we headed is our graduation in a few short minutes. Out on those drill fields. In front of the bleachers. In front of Colonel Parrish. Graduating. Just like I told your sorry ass the first day we met."

"You told me lots of things the last few months. Told me we'd get our wings. That we'd survive von Kimble. I'll give you both of those. We surely did. And this cat Parrish, well, jury's still out on him. Shakes a lot of hands. Smooth. Took down the colored and white signs right away. That was progress. Hear he's talking about bringing in some celebrities like Joe Louis and Cab Calloway."

"Lena Horne too. Don't forget he mentioned her."

"We'll be gone by then. Heard we're shipping out Saturday. Ben Jr. says we're getting sent up to Michigan. To a base called Selfridge. Name of some cat who was the first flier ever killed on active duty. Was flying with one of the Wright brothers as a passenger. Ain't that a sad bitch? Dyin' at the hands of the man who went and invented the damn airplane."

"Well, we're gonna get our own selves killed here if we don't get the three hundred first lined up in formation. Cap'n Morse is doing the commissioning, and McPherson is pinning wings. You up for any awards, or is that just foolish talk? Me asking if the famous Lieutenant Wilmeth Sidat-Singh gonna get any special recognition?"

"Aww, you know. I might get mentioned for aerial gunnery. Some kind of sharpshooter medal. That's not counting my coming in second in the class to Alfonza Davis. At least I beat out McCreary, Leroy, and Pearlee."

"They pretty good, those boys. Pearlee in particular."

"Yeah. They are. All of us are pretty good. Pretty good at getting up every morning at six a.m. to that stupid bugler blowin' reveille. Just hope we're prepared for the next phase."

Wilmeth knew simply graduating from Tuskegee was only the start of their war service.

It was like playing pickup. Or the spring scrimmage for Coach Solem. They would still need to survive Selfridge before getting sent into the ultimate game. The one where they'd square off against Nazis.

Wilmeth noted Captain Ben Davis Jr., tops in the first class and the first to solo, had said he thought the Ninety-Ninth would finally move out sometime in early April. He wasn't sure where they were headed but thought they might land overseas before May. Possibly in North Africa.

Well, that was fine for them.

Today, on this warm Thursday in late March, April was just over the nearest hillside. They were living on the sunny side of the valley. The end of the beginning.

In the near distance, the US Army Air Force Band was warming up on their brass horns, bleating out triplets of notes. Within minutes, the underclassmen, in their crisply pressed dress uniforms, would start lining up for field formations in the cadet area.

The upperclassmen, nervous with the pride in their achievement, were glancing around, talking about just needing to avoid tripping going up the stairs to the platform. Some clumsy fool would probably still manage that indignity.

As it turned out, the ceremonies were less of a spectacle than Wilmeth had imagined. He'd never really seen the marching bands at Syracuse. Had always been up in the Archbold locker room.

On this day, while the military band pumped out their songs, Wilmeth appreciated a lot more the genuine recognition his unit was receiving. Seemed like it was about time.

Post chaplain Doug Robinson started the proceedings with his God-graced invocation before turning the ceremony over to Lieutenant Colonel Hazard, the EO and von Kimble's aptly named hatchet man. God and the Devil on the same stage. The same page.

Hazard gave the first address and acknowledged 42-C-SE was the largest graduating class to date. That wasn't too hard to achieve given there had only been two groups previously, but it clearly suggested Black pilots were making progress. Not that anyone would know it from Hazard's words.

Then, as Charles had suggested, Morse commissioned the second lieutenants and Major McPherson, looking sharp as he always did in his duties as director of flight instruction, pinned silver wings on every flier's dark green blouse.

His chest taut, Wilmeth enjoyed the moment he stared deep into McPherson's eyes as the Major lined up the pin and drove the medal's point through the thick cloth. Days before, Singh had made up his mind that even if McPherson went too deep, poked him, and drew blood, he would not respond to the pricking pain.

As it turned out, McPherson seemed more than practiced at the pinning protocol and having completed the task, he stepped back before sharply saluting. It was a measure of respect Wilmeth had long desired and here, finally, was the moment. Wilmeth returned the salute, his right arm snapping upward as it had on so many passes to Marty Glickman and Phil Allen.

Looking out at the crowd, Wilmeth was certain his mother was beaming with the same pride he'd generated with every touchdown pass.

The day's payoff speech came from Parrish, Tuskegee's CO, and even Wilmeth had to admit the smooth-talking Kentuckian knew firsthand what flying was about. He'd worked in a few jokes about his own training at Randolph Field in Texas, commented on the nominal quality of the training aircraft available in Alabama and the challenges the assembled men would continue to face going forward.

To Wilmeth, there was no question Parrish had grasped what a hellhole Colonel Frederick von Kimble had created and the ill will he left behind when he was promoted and replaced by Parrish that January. While Parrish might have been politically motivated, he seemed committed to desegregation and making things better for the incoming classes.

By the time the hour-long graduation was over, Wilmeth realized he'd been recognized a few times. The first came as the second-highest scoring cadet and the latter was handed out for his eagle eye with guns.

Now, with the final military strains echoing in his ears, the final notes dying softly in the breeze, Wilmeth suddenly saw clearly how another short phase of his life was finishing up. Seemed like he was always moving around. Hadn't he just turned twenty-five the month before and already lived in DC, Harlem, Syracuse, New York City (again), DC (again), and Alabama? And now, next up, he was pointed toward somewhere near Lake Saint Clair, Michigan.

That much had been formally announced during the festivities. They were headed north, to a different set of commanders and circumstances.

"What do you think the next place will be like, Wil? Good-looking women?"

"I think it will be cold, Charles. We're talking Detroit. That's practically Canada. And I imagine we'll be getting pushed right back down in the same old hole in order to show us who is boss. First thing every cracker wants to do is make clear where we stand in the pecking order."

"C'mon now. This is our graduation day. Lemme have one day to enjoy the sun. Tomorrow we gonna be packing and giving hell to classes Forty-Three E and F."

"No, you right. Tonight's a night for celebration. Time to enjoy a few cold beers. We did it, Charles. We sure as hell did it."

"I ain't ever been to Michigan. Did your Syracuse boys ever play out there?"

"Yeah, in 1938. We lost nineteen to twelve to Michigan State, in East Lansing. The week after the big game against Cornell. It was windy as hell. Made it tough throwin' the ball. Had one long one for a TD. But we fell behind early, like we did against Cornell. Just ran out of steam in the second half. Missed some extra points. One of our guys fumbled at a key point."

"What about Michigan? What was it like?"

"Hmm . . . I saw a little bit through the bus windows. Looked a lot like Upstate New York. Farm fields mostly. Hadn't started snowing yet. It was the middle of October, so it was pretty much brown already. Leaves were gone."

"You run into any name-callin'?"

"Nothing out of the ordinary. Never did hear the crowd much. But some of the Spartans gave it to me on the field. Standard stuff. By then I could tune it out. If I ever responded, it only got worse. And I couldn't afford some idiot jumping on my ankle when I was down."

"Man, I still don't know how you did it. That's a rough enough game even when it's Black on Black. Takin' on eleven white guys? That's crazy."

"Well, Charles, I'll say this—and I hate to keep bringing everything back to fightin' and flyin' against the Germans—but it pays to be quick. I always wanted to keep from getting caught from behind."

"Your mama stayin' around? Must've been a long trip getting down here from DC. How long you figure she was on the bus just to see you get your wings?"

"I dunno. Let's see. Stops in Richmond, Greensboro, Charlotte, Atlanta, Tuskegee. More'n a day. But she all-day tough. Ridin' in the back of that Greyhound. Said she wouldn't have missed it. Not for anything. Said it was one of the proudest days of her life. Don't know if you know this, but for a while I toyed around with doing medical school. Even enrolled at Howard. But somehow getting accepted by the US Army and selected for Tuskegee, she said that even beat becoming a doctor."

"She can stay with my kin in Carolina on the way back, you know. If she wants to break up the trip."

"Mighty kind of you, Charles. I'll mention it to her tonight."

The two men were walking back to Tent City to change uniforms. All around them men were caught up in the spirit of the day. It seemed to Wilmeth like the newly minted pilots were floating over the dusty tracks leading from the grounds back to their living quarters.

Already flying in their minds. No talk of war or dying. Only, for this one night, of living large. Of soaring over the land like immortals. Toasting each other on what was coming next. Of challenging the great unknown.

CHAPTER 40

Selfridge Air Field, Michigan, March 30, 1943

Wilmeth knew immediately.

Could smell the racism in the air. Could practically see it like his frosty, crystalline breath as he became familiar with his new surroundings.

He'd seen discrimination all his life, but it was going to be different here in Michigan. Palpable. This was no college campus. No cityscape. The joint felt like a prison built specifically for segregation. Whites and Blacks separated. White women, the WACs, never allowed near the 332nd. Not under any circumstances.

Selfridge might sit near Detroit and its nightclubs, but the base reeked.

"Charles, this shit ain't gonna be right."

"Whatcha mean, Sing-Sing? It's just another base. This one is Selfridge. Been here since World War I. Probably looks like every other airfield."

Wilmeth looked out at the billowing pine trees just beyond the base perimeter and guessed from the look of the thin green needles they were pitch pines. His eyesight had always been that good. Now as he stared at them, he saw thousands of ramrod-straight trunks walling off the outside world. A brown-and-green barrier.

Beneath the pines stood a group of stiff white MPs, all of them showing menace. Each of them offering their contribution to a collective sneer. They meant some kind of business. But what were their orders? To protect or bust heads? Their hatred likely had nothing to do with Nazis.

"Naw, that ain't the point, Charles. This place is different. Black airmen and mechanics arriving pretty as you please, but all the officers here are white. What I see is Black pilots and white guards. And they don't like us getting to fly. Makes us look uppity. Got a feeling we're gonna see it a lot different than what we saw down in Alabama."

"Lissen, I don't know what they taught you up at Syracuse, but any kind of fool knows that's how it is. White folk in charge."

Wilmeth shook his head in sly disgust and realized just how tired he was. The troop trucks were taking forever to park. It was only a matter of time before some fool with stripes started ordering them to line up by rank, in squadron formation, for a formal welcome.

Closing his almond-brown eyes, Wilmeth thought how the process of transferring Tuskegee Airmen from Alabama to Michigan's Selfridge Army Air Base had taken the better part of three days. At every stop, the proud Tuskegee Airmen had faced segregation and discrimination. In the South, the open hatred was always easy to see. But most northerners hid their feelings, disguised their distrust, distaste, and disdain. They were a lot better at their racism. He'd seen it in Syracuse and knew he'd see it his whole life.

It would be so easy to just give in. Let the world spin off its crooked axis.

The transfer, the whole relocation process, had gone as well as could have been hoped for, given the wartime restrictions of 1943. Under the direction of Colonel Ben Davis Jr., the first Black officer to graduate from West Point, the new class of pilots and its support team had been safely delivered.

Both Wilmeth and Charles felt Davis was a good, kind man. He hadn't sold out to get his stripes. Used to be that stripes came from the whip. The new stripes came on shirts, but to Wilmeth it still meant the Black man was serving.

Davis was no mystery to Wilmeth. Both men had been born in DC, with Davis only six years older than SU's ex-quarterback. It was no surprise they had found each other and their commonalities.

Both had dealt with family tragedy early. Wilmeth lost his father at a young age, then had to adjust to a stepfather whose name he took. He'd lost some of his identity on that one. Davis faced much of the same.

His mother had died when he was four, and he'd come of age trying to please an often-absent father, Benjamin Sr., the US Army's first Black general.

Where Wilmeth had gone to Syracuse University and joined the Orangemen to play football, Davis Jr. had gone to the prestigious University of Chicago. From there, under the recommendation from the only Black member of Congress, Davis had been nominated for admission to West Point.

Over drinks at Tuskegee, Wilmeth learned just how completely Davis had been isolated at the US Military Academy. They'd given him the silent treatment as a highest priority. No friends. No one to eat with. No one to study with. No roommate. For four years! The bastards had tried so hard to run Ben Davis out. In the end, they'd failed miserably.

At least for Singh, while he'd initially been forced to hide his race in order to play football, he'd been accepted on his campus. Made friends with guys like Duffy and Marty, who'd faced his own challenges for being Jewish.

Accepted all right, but only enough to get by as a valued football player. Majoring in zoology made it clear he was smart. Still, despite his heroics against Cornell and others, SU's true colors were such that he hadn't been allowed to live on campus his first three years, in one of the dorms. And, of course, the frats would never have even allowed him onto their gleaming white steps.

That turned out fine because he'd simply gone downtown to the juke joints, where the whites felt uncomfortable. Down in the hood, he was somebody. A cat who could cut it.

It wasn't lost on him that he was always moving between worlds. He often was treated as a hero on Piety Hill, but five steps off Mount Olympus, M Street, or the Quad, his status often changed, swiftly, dramatically. How many times had he heard the N-word as he trekked down Irving Avenue before making his turn onto Adams Street and striding off to find one of the clubs, where the music reminded him of sweet times in Harlem listening to Duke Ellington or Cab Calloway?

In his fatigue, Wilmeth moved around in his colliding worlds. Nothing was linear.

There was no question Davis Jr. had taken the tough route, stuck on West Point's sprawling campus that ran alongside the dark Hudson River and yet unable to get so much as a weekend pass to go into the city. Still, he'd graduated, endured their shit, determinedly kept his focus. Got himself assigned to a buffalo soldier unit in racist Georgia, where the half-wits who ran the base wouldn't even allow him into the officer's club.

Wilmeth kept his eyes closed and blocked out the truck's grinding gears. He made things quiet. It was a trick he'd learned playing in roaring stadiums. Single-minded focus on the ball and his receiver.

"Wilmeth." There was a pause and then the whispered voice again. "Wilmeth. Wake the fuck up. Colonel Colman is coming."

Wilmeth immediately blinked his eyes wide. Colman was trouble. Ben Davis had said as much during drinks.

"Nastiest racist drunk motherfucker we'll see in this war, Wil. Worse than the Germans. Worse even than Hitler."

Wilmeth knew it was true because he'd asked Davis what they should expect in Michigan. It was all secondhand, Davis said, but Bill Colman's reputation easily preceded him. Wouldn't allow a Black driver. Was lazy.

Drank heavily. And his base always seemed to lack the proper equipment. Rumors started circulating the colonel was deep into the black market. Tied somehow to Henry Ford.

In fact, Ford's grandson, Benson, had just gotten transferred to Selfridge from Fort Custer near Battle Creek. That kept the Fords close to their automotive interests and fashionable Grosse Pointe estates. Allowed them to see what kind of machinery could be sold to the US government.

"Listen to me," Wilmeth whispered to his friend. "Ben Davis said this prick is nasty business. Tell the others. No side looks. No eye-rolling when we think he isn't watching. Quick. When we line up, this corn cracker will be looking for something. Don't let it be you."

"That's just like you, Wil. Always careful. Looking out for us. Trying to huddle us up for the next play. Like that Cornell game I read about. The one where that writer compared you with Sid Luckman and somebody else. Skips my mind. But, shit, when I heard you was joining up, I knew we'd be sweet."

"Stow it."

Piling out of the olive-green, one-ton truck, the pilots began assembling on the snow-scraped parade ground. The wind was stronger out in the open. Clearly, their quartermaster hadn't calculated the difference between Mobile and Mount Clemons in March.

Within seconds, an overweight colonel, his medals evident, was walking unsteadily among the ranks with his adjutant, hunting for someone. He seemed hungover.

"Willie Singh. That's who I'm looking for, Captain. He's here among us. And what I want to know is, well, will he?"

"Will he what, sir?"

"Will he sing?"

"I can't rightly say, sir."

"Well, find him. Where is this famous Black boy I've heard so much about? Played football for those pissants at Syracuse. I'll tell you certain, them Orange boys couldn't beat a Michigan team when we had someone like Stanley Fay running the ball. Now that sumbitch could carry the weight. Twice they ran the damn table. Undefeated national champions in thirty-two and thirty-three. And he's rose up through the ranks, working for Henry Ford right here in Detroit."

"Yes sir, he has."

"Well, bring this Willie Singh forward. Our very own celebrity. Rubs shoulders with all them famous Negro entertainers and boxers. I want to meet him and let him know right off the bat that he will not get special attention here. This is the United States Army."

Wilmeth knew what was coming. His fame, great in the Black community, modest to some degree with whites, was about to get used against him. He'd have to hit it head-on at the start, but it soured his stomach like curdled milk.

"Lieutenant Wilmeth Sidat-Singh, reporting, sir."

Wilmeth stepped out of the even ranks, turning smartly to face Colman. His crisp salute showed every evidence of military order and respect.

"C'mere, son. You can approach your colonel."

The distance to Colman was no more than five yards, but if both men advanced toward each other, Singh would come in hot. This was not the day to appear overly aggressive. He wondered if Ben Davis would intervene or let the situation play out.

"Sir, Lieutenant Wilmeth Sidat-Singh, Three Hundred Thirty-Second Fighter Group, Three Hundred First Squadron, sir."

"Well, yes you are, I reckon. A pilot in a Black fighter group. Come up here to fly our P-40s and P-39s. Yer smaller than I thought, Mister Willie Singh."

"Begging the colonel's pardon, sir?"

At just a hair over five ten, Singh knew he wasn't a towering presence. But the colonel was probably five seven, at best, and Wilmeth's solid athletic build gave off the appearance of physical superiority.

"I told your commanding officer, Mister Davis, that I wasn't much in favor of colored pilots being trusted with our valuable equipment. And I'm even less impressed with your news clippings and exploits. They don't mean shit here. Am I clear, son?"

"Yes sir."

"That'd be right. That's what I expect to hear from every one of you sonsabitches. You come up here from Alabama to fly my planes out of my base. And you will do it my way. Am I understood, Mister Willie Singh?"

"Yes sir."

The rest of the 332nd's initial engagement with Colman—a near-drunken tirade—offered little more than a hawkish dressing down from a racist white man clearly out of line. Wilmeth had been returned to the ranks when Davis intervened, but the message was clear. Tuskegee Airmen might want to push a civil rights agenda forward, but in doing so, they'd take orders and die for a country intent on holding them down.

Finally assigned to their spartan quarters, Wilmeth quietly let his anger seep out. He'd need to be extra careful at Selfridge and make sure the men around him had each other's backs. This base was toxic. And wings earned in Alabama would surely get tested up here.

"Did you hear that crap, Charles?" Wilmeth asked. "Calling Ben Davis 'mister' instead of by his rank. And going on about *his* valuable equipment and *his* base. He'd be all for us dying while he's lying up there in his fancy house drinking his gin. Man's dangerous."

"Wil, that might be an all-day fact, but it don't change nothin'."

Charles made it clear he wasn't through with his thought.

"He's got to let us fly. He knows that. But it be up to us to make sure we're always checking our own equipment. Packing our own chutes. I got a quick glimpse at our planes, and I tell you they don't look like much. I believe training will be as deadly as the missions we'll see in Europe or North Africa. I tell you this, those P-40s they got out there are as tired as my old granny."

Wilmeth thought about that. He thought back to his times with his mom after his father died. She'd tell him to go for a walk. Stow his gear. Get his bearings. Clear his mind. Keep his temper under control. Keep from boiling up his blood.

From what Wilmeth started to see, Selfridge was tired. The opposite of crisp. He saw peeling paint, cracks in pavement. Someone was skimping on maintenance. And that someone was undoubtedly getting their orders from the colonel. If he had to guess, someone was profiting on the side.

The camp dated back to World War I and had evidently been built around something called the Joy Aviation Field. It was one of the first military airfields in the US and connected with the Packard Motor Car Company. Henry Joy had been president of Packard and wanted to make aircraft engines.

The source of the wind for those early biplanes had clearly come off Lake Saint Clair, which got its source water from Lake Huron. That was before LSC unceremoniously funneled everything down the Detroit River, past the Motor City and Windsor, and south into Lake Erie.

The existence of Lake Saint Clair made Selfridge bombing runs or target practice on fixed targets less of a civilian risk, although the international border between the two countries, the one bisecting the lake and running right down the middle of the river, meant pilots needed to avoid veering into Canadian airspace. Wilmeth imagined they'd do most of their flying over Saginaw Bay and Huron's massive sea-size waves.

According to Charles, who'd done some Selfridge snooping on his own, the Seventeenth Pursuit Squadron had left for the Philippines and then, at the start of 1940, several pilots left to serve with the Flying Tigers under General Claire Chennault in Rangoon.

At that point, the US wasn't even in the war, but the First Air Force's VIII Interceptor Command had come through Selfridge in early 1942. Things stayed quiet until the Tuskegee men arrived in March 1943. That was where things stood.

But what should Wilmeth do about Colman? He certainly wasn't going to get the Ted Williams or Jimmy Stewart treatment. Wilmeth knew those white stars were more famous, but fame was a strange burning flame. In the Black community, because of his Syracuse heroics and then playing for the Rens, Wilmeth had gotten pretty recognizable. Didn't hurt with meeting girls, and the army liked using him to inspire guys like Charles to join up.

Funny thing, that. Finding the brightest and best young Negro men and giving them a chance to fly hand-me-downs. What was it that Charles had called the Tuskegee pilots? The best, brightest, and bravest, with each man offering himself up as a flying guinea pig.

Ben Davis had said he would meet with Colman that day so the men could start checking out their "rides" in the morning. That would relieve some of the stress. Get the men thinking about flying. It would lift them up and over the racism of men like Colman.

CHAPTER 41

By early the next morning, Wilmeth was ready to join Sergeant Moses Downing, his favorite Tuskegee crew chief, to have a look at their "little friends." That was the term bomber pilots used to describe the fighter planes that protected them, and it suited Wilmeth just fine. Because up in the sky, he imagined he and his comrades, white and Black, would care more about saving each other's skin than the color of it. They would fight together for America.

Charles would probably give him grief for wearing rose-colored glasses on that one. He'd say Wilmeth should know better. He would remind his friend the Tuskegee Airmen were mostly an "experiment" because white air command still had little confidence that colored men were capable of flying.

Hell, thought Wilmeth, on December 7, 1941, *there had been less than 125 Black pilots in all of America. Less than three per state.*

That meant Negro men who were accepted into the Civilian Pilot Training Program in 1939 or had gone to college could raise their hands, offer to fly, and join up. But it also meant those same men got screened, double-screened, poked, rescreened, challenged, back-screened, provoked, and shown any other kind of barrier and hazing the US Army Air Corps could find. The men who met that racist challenge had arrived in Tuskegee with confidence. They were smart, physically robust, and more than competent in the cockpit.

They still wanted to fight for their country. Even if their country didn't want them, primarily because Negro men giving orders to enlisted whites would create what General Henry "Hap" Arnold, senior CO of the entire US Army Air Forces, called "an impossible social problem."

So the problem wasn't just "hazing."

Colored pilots starting in Alabama made do in bi-wing Stearman Kaydet trainers, crappy little Piper Cubs, and retired P-36s before graduating up to secondhand Curtiss P-40 Warhawks made in Buffalo starting around 1938. They were robust planes—faster than a Japanese Zero, but the Zero could outmaneuver a P-40 in combat.

The Tuskegee men arriving at Selfridge were prepared to fly, fight, and if necessary, die.

Wilmeth was living proof of the first two. He'd performed well earning his wings, instrument rating, and mastering the nuances of flight. On this first morning at Selfridge, it was time to get back in the air. To harness a P-40 in flight.

"I'm telling you, Mo, takeoff is just about the best feeling in the world," Singh said to Moses as they walked along a silver line of parked planes, each angled smartly toward the main runway. "You get this anticipation. Concrete's rushing past, speed increasing, and then the bump—it's like a little hop—and then you're up there."

"You ever scared?" Downing asked with interest. "I mean, like, you know, worried if something could go wrong."

Wilmeth paused on the tarmac and looked at the 332nd panther insignia on his uniform. He wondered how many eyes were tracking two Negros walking along a line of planes while the morning mist lay low to the ground. The quiet was sweet, like praying in an empty church just before folks started coming in.

"Listen, Mo, it's all a risk-reward thing. Like when I was playing football. I knew I'd get hit. And it would hurt. But I was always trying to think like a cat. Twitchy-like. You know? Eyes in the back of my head listening for that defensive end. Same thing with planes. I'm watchin', listenin', calculatin'. All of 'em. But I know what I'm doing. And I like the reward."

"You know which plane you been assigned?"

"It's got a Z2 on the nose. Hasn't been named yet."

"I heard somebody named a plane *Tondelayo*, after that girl in the *White Congo* movie came out last year."

"Hedy Lamarr. Yeah, she's supposed to be native in that movie, like half Egyptian, half Arab. But shit, she ain't nothin' but a white girl actin' colored. Guess I can't give her too hard a time though. I had 'em thinkin' I was a Hindu for a couple of years at Syracuse."

"I know. I wondered about that."

"Wasn't a big thing. Made it easier to play."

"So what you thinkin' about naming your bird?"

"Dunno. Still pondering whether I might use something Cab Calloway would appreciate. Something like *Jumpin' Jive*."

"Why Calloway?"

"Got to know him. Played against him in some of his exhibition basket-ball games that he staged with his band. He needed opposing teams to pick up some side cash. Pretty hep cat."

"You ought to go with *Minnie* for a name, then."

"Nah, that's old school. What's Lieutenant Dickson naming his?"

"*Peggin*. Could have something to do with baseball. But I doubt it. His wife's name is Phyllis, but maybe he calls her Peg."

"Larry's a good joe. I'll check with him on that. Meanwhile, let's get us a look at this Z2. See what kind of hand we've been dealt."

As the men arrived at the hardstand, there was no question that if this was Wilmeth's plane, it needed work. Downing went straight for the engine's portside cowling. He would need a ladder if he was going to get at the V12 Allison block or the propeller housing.

That would have to wait. By now Wilmeth felt he knew the P-40 playbook by heart.

Two Browning .50s firing through the nose propeller and two more .303-caliber machine guns in each wing. Six pieces of firing power tied to an in-line liquid-cooled engine. That was about the Warhawk's only true advantage against the lighter Mitsubishi A6M, the Japanese Zero.

The A6M had a faster rate of climb, could go higher in the sky, and from what Wilmeth had gathered, far better maneuverability. It supposedly could turn on a dime and go straight up.

The Zero's weakness was its armament, and in Burma, General Chennault and his Flying Tigers, with their painted-on shark-teeth noses, had advised fighting the Japs at close range and then diving away. Fire off short bursts and get out of Dodge. Trying to outrun a Zero was worse than engaging it head-on.

Wilmeth left Downing scouring the P-40's bow and started running his finger along the fuselage. He ducked under the left wing, moving his hand up into the port wheel well, where the ship's tires retracted after takeoff. The tire looked tired. Slightly underinflated.

He shook his head but didn't stop his survey. In five quick steps, he'd reached the tail.

All up, the Warhawk's length was almost equal to its width. The wings were just over twelve yards and the body, from bow to stern, about thirty-one feet. He knew only too well the distance from the line of scrimmage to the first-down marker.

It seemed so many things in life were measured in ten-yard increments.

Here at Selfridge, it wasn't far between the Operations Hut, checkerboard-roofed hangars, the equipment hut, the mess hall, and the barracks.

More than ten yards in some places, but compact nonetheless. Having quietly looked around, Wilmeth knew the beating heart of the base was no bigger than the walk from Syracuse's quad to Archbold Stadium.

The barracks were set up like street blocks, with the flight lines running perpendicular to the main avenues. There was even a baseball field and two tennis courts, but there was no way Colman was going to allow free time for sports. Not given the victories the Germans and Japanese were racking up in Europe, Asia, and the Pacific.

Thank God the navy had prevailed in the Battle of the Coral Sea and Midway. The Japs were tough, but the American sailors were finally getting a watery toehold. Wilmeth looked around and wondered about the world he was marching into. Less than five years ago, he would've been peacefully prepping for an early morning biology class or walking to practice from his apartment in the Ward.

This world was on fire.

With spring weather looming, the Nazis were again attacking the Russian front, while the English army, with help from the Aussies, were pushing the Germans around in Tunisia and North Africa. Maybe the tide was turning.

In Michigan, there were trace remains of snow in the shadowy sections of the base and out around the pines. If he listened closely, he could hear more weather in the wind, coming in off the lake, mingling with the sound of truck motors.

Nature and machines trying to work things out. It was quieter in the sky. Still, despite his fondness for the troposphere, the sounds of a base coming to life was one Wilmeth never grew tired of hearing.

Looking over his shoulder, he saw the sun making headway in the predawn gloom. Off in the muted distance, the cooks were getting ready to mix up their powdered eggs and start brewing the black coffee men everywhere needed to attack another day.

By now his fiancée, Marjorie Webb, was probably up at her apartment in DC and getting ready for her day. He tended not to dwell on their rushed engagement, but every now and then she crept in or sent a letter, lifting his spirits. Wilmeth didn't bother with fatalism, but a flyer's reality, like a race car driver's, was simple enough. Airmen died. He was a lot safer in Michigan than in Burma or flying over the English Channel, but every flight was a roll of the dice, especially if the equipment wasn't maintained.

Staring up at the cantilevered tail, his rudder, Wilmeth called out to Downing. "What are you seeing, Chief? You feelin' good about her?"

"Listen, Lieutenant, I'm seeing a little more oil smear around the starboard side of the cowling. I can't get in there right yet, but somebody's wiped off the spillage pretty fast and left enough for me to know something's greasy. Ain't right. Imagine they'll do some kind of pilot orientation-type stuff with you today, but you don't go up in this bird until I can get at her. We clear on that?"

"No problem from me, Mo." There was a reason Wilmeth trusted Moses Downing. His life at Selfridge depended on his mechanic. "Rest of her looks acceptable. I want to see how she responds when I get up to ten thousand feet. Put her through her paces."

"That's fine, sir, but I wouldn't be counting on whoever worked on these 40s most recently to care if they stay up in the air. Might've been some incentive for them to be a bit sloppy. What with colored pilots coming in. We knew what we were dealing with at Tuskegee, but we controlled our crews and aircraft. Different story up here. At least for now."

"That's true, Chief. I'm guessing you heard Colonel Colman made a show of me yesterday. So I expect every man and his dog on this base knows what plane I'll be in. We'll want to be careful."

"Very much so."

"All right, Chief. Think we've seen enough for our first morning. Let me buy you your first cup of Selfridge java."

"Mighty white of you, Sing-Sing."

The two men laughed at the insult and turned to make their way back to the warmth of the crowded, noisy mess hall.

"What were you thinking 'bout back there at the tail?" asked Downing as they walked side by side. "You seemed pretty far away."

"Oh, mostly about my girl back in DC. Wondering what she's doing. If she is still asleep. But some of my thoughts were about this war and folks holding us back."

"I hear ya."

"See, I think Blacks are looking for leaders. Like back in the day. Harriet Tubman, Booker T., Frederick Douglass. You ever read the speech he gave in Rochester, New York? Back in 1852."

"Can't say I have. Doubt anyone has."

"He gave it on the Fourth of July to a Ladies Anti-Slavery group. Almost ten years before the Civil War started. Told 'em Fourth of July was for white folk. And I was just wondering who our Frederick Douglass is when this war ends. Who steps up come 1945 or whenever?"

"Man, you one deep thinker for this early in the morning."

"Well, you saw the shit we faced in Alabama at that hellhole. What von Kimble and Hazard did to us on the base. The segregation and prejudice. Keeping Black officers out of the officer's club. No promotions. Whites getting posts we shoulda gotten."

"Way it's always been."

"Yes, but see, Mo, we gotta stop taking it. We need to rise up and get our respect. And somebody—maybe it'll be Ben Davis—has got to be that leader."

"From what I see, Negro leaders tend to get knocked back."

"They do. But then they get up off the dirt and try again. I know it firsthand. We're making progress just having Tuskegee exist. When Chief Anderson took Eleanor Roosevelt up in that Piper last October, well, that had to have influenced the president. That single act was big-time leadership."

"And . . ."

"Well, I'll say this much: Because we stood our ground, they took von

Kimble away from Tuskegee in January. And they'll get Colonel Hazard next. For now, though, we got to deal with Colman. And watch that he doesn't try to get some of us killed."

"How you going to do that?"

"Well, I'm not sure. Beyond Big Ben watching over us, we're going to need to deal with Sam Westbrook as the Three Hundred Thirty-Second's CO. Not sure he'll last very long."

"Well, our call sign is Percy. And we'll find out soon enough how these Charlies react to us."

"Charlies they are. Some are Chucks, and some are Charles, but white folks pretty much the same whatever we call them. For now, let's get some chow and find out how today is shakin' out. I'm sure our very own Charles Williams will have something interesting to say about this war."

"I'm sure he will. That cat sure can talk. And then talk some more."

Both men laughed, nodding in unison.

CHAPTER 42

Wilmeth's first reaction—his gut instinct—was usually his best first indicator. It was like a sixth sense. Like the way a cat always landed feet first. Even if you held it upside down six inches off the ground, a cat knew up from down and somehow made the adjustment in midair.

On this day, May 9, 1943, Wilmeth's intuition told him he'd need feline quickness to get back safely. The reason was simple. Something was wrong, and he'd need a truckful of the "old black magic" the Glenn Miller Orchestra had most recently started honking out on their trumpets and trombones.

Initially, he couldn't put his finger on it. This unnamed P-40, the one lettered Z2, was still new to him. But he'd had enough solo-seat experience to sense when an engine was running ragged. What his brain was registering, was filtering, were tiny, unsettling vibrations, gyrating like a human seismograph. It was the opposite of smooth. Down in that twisting pit of his stomach, a familiar sensation was rumbling.

Wilmeth didn't know how he'd developed such a perceptive early warning system, but somewhere along the way, whether it was judging people, playing football, or training in Alabama, he always understood the innate harmonics of his situation. When not to talk about music at the Ellington home or timing the exact moment to get rid of the ball. When to avoid going into a bar with Orange teammates and when not to speak confidently, or even challenge, a racist base commander.

This moment in the cockpit was certainly shaping up as one of those occasions. His Allison V-12 engine was out of sync and not purring like it should. He needed his panther ready to prowl.

Outside his fighter's cowling, he observed three six-by-six cargo trucks idling, the doors adorned with a single white star. The big six-ton vehicles had carried the flight crews, ammunition, and fuel to the oil-stained hardstand, and Wilmeth smiled, inwardly, at the good-natured kidding his men had thrown around from the back of the rig. Now the sixes, their work done, sat detached from the runway. Unusually, the assigned ground crews, white and Black, were still standing around, waiting for something, eyes intent on Wilmeth's four-man ensemble to head out.

It was another audience witnessing Wilmeth in action. A crowd waiting for a performance. Women wanting to dance with him. Men who wished they were fast or smart enough to take the field. Yet those very same people didn't want to get hit in the face or shot at by an enemy. Fueling and loading ammo was just fine for them, staying safe while others took on the challenge.

Wilmeth's issue today, and it was unfolding quickly, was knowing there was a barge target on the lake to light up and weekend passes waiting for his team. If he could nurse the P-40 through one last routine, a milk run, he'd turn it over to Moses for a full inspection. Now was not the time to scrub a practice mission and get Colman's ire up.

"Gentlemen, I want a quick, efficient effort today," Wilmeth said gruffly into his microphone. "Nothing fancy. We get over the target and line up four across. Then each of us unloads his four hundred rounds. Shoot 'em clean. Lieutenant Williams will lead us up to twenty thousand. From there, we'll form up on him. I'll come in last. Remember: we keep radio chatter to a minimum. Let's go."

The assured confidence in his voice would've fooled his three wingmen as well as the desk jockeys listening up in the tower. Everything was as it should appear. Inside, though, Wilmeth furiously debated whether he should risk continuing or call them off.

Unfortunately, it was already too late. With the sun strengthening in the early eastern sky, Charles Williams had hurtled down the runway, smoothly lifting off for the flight north to Lake Huron. The moment for canceling had passed. Wilmeth would have to monitor his gauges closely. He'd miss out on feelings of joy as he looked out over the flat landscape of trees, lakes, and in the distance, auto industry smokestacks belching out the remnants of hot iron ore.

In that moment, images of Wilmeth's life started flashing past his eyes. It was like watching a *News of the World* movie treatment. Just the other night he'd been holding court in the uncomfortable barracks, talking about Harlem and sneaking into the smoky jazz clubs when he was fifteen. Of playing hoops in the big city. Policing and recreation work in DC. It had all gone by so quickly.

What was wrong, he asked angrily, vigorously hand-cranking the P-40's canopy into the closed position. If the engine wasn't "right," what was the issue? He remembered on an earlier practice mission, Charles's plane had suffered an oil leak, and his confident wingman had just barely survived a fiery crash. There had been no way of knowing on that morning if an old plane had simply sprung a leak or if something far more concerning, more sinister, was afoot.

Wilmeth hated thinking white maintenance men or ground crew would even consider purposely damaging a plane such that it might kill the pilot. Weren't they fighting the same enemy? But another thought swirled like the clouds rising on the portside of his fighter. Was it possible someone could have acted on orders from Colman? Did whites, especially Colman, hate

Negroes so much that, given the chance, they would engage in subterfuge and murder their own men?

Checking his multifaced control panel, he squashed those thoughts quickly. There were eleven circular dials immediately in front of him, just beyond his perpendicular stick. Each one provided essential information and, not unlike a football playbook, revealed exactly what role they'd been assigned to perform. Altitude, trim, pitch, roll, airspeed, fuel capacity, manifold pressure, RPMs, and an emergency contactor that could emit a signal every fifteen seconds. Of all of them, if there was trouble, the manifold pressure gauge would probably reveal itself first.

As soon as it lifted off, knowing the exact instant his wheels had left the earth, Wilmeth was multitasking. Watching his speed, ensuring the proper trim, squeezing the right-hand controls to engage his gearing. He would need to be very careful, constantly observing and judging the tightness of his unit's performance in the air. Formation flying demanded super sensitivity to wind shear, air density, blinding sunlight, and flight procedure. Vectoring in on a stationary target at speed was challenging enough, even for a single craft. Bringing four of them in line without touching wings or shooting up a fellow pilot required something completely different.

"Let's watch that cumulus bank off your port wings and tighten our spirals as we climb. We stay out over Anchor Bay until we're assembled."

"Roger that." It was Williams still out in front. "Will confirm when I have a visual on the target."

Wilmeth knew Williams had been solid since their first days at Tuskegee. He smiled to himself, lips pressed tight. The pride of Charlotte. Educated at Howard. Flew with Chief Anderson. Knew aeronautics all the way around. Had kept their pact.

In exchange for some you-are-in-the-Syracuse-football-huddle moments, Charles had passed along his flying expertise. He quizzed Wilmeth relentlessly on the tech manual and the engineering precepts of fighter planes. They'd made a great team, and with Smirk Smith and Leonard Johnson, the four had dominated target competitions.

For the better part of the first hour, as the four silver birds climbed in unison to their desired altitude, Wilmeth found himself believing he'd been mistaken about his engine. That Z2, soon to get its name as *Jumpin' Jive*, was fine and his sensitive intuition wrong. But the nagging sensation, moving from his stomach up to his mind, was not letting go.

Navigationally, the route had been simple. They'd headed due west out over Lake Saint Clair before cutting NNE, always keeping the Saint Clair River, the blue line flowing raggedly out of Lake Huron, off their starboard wings. It was simply a beautiful morning, and with each incremental one thousand feet they gained, the panorama of Michigan and Ontario, Canada, spread beneath them. Far to the south of them, the sun creating a shimmering mirage-like glow, lay Lake Erie.

"Tighten up, gentlemen. Watch your heading indicators."

Reaching the target, Wilmeth's watch showed 08:24. In the moments that followed, in rapid succession, each of the four made quick work of the barge. This being practice, there were no gun crews protecting the sitting duck and no other fighters chasing them. But that wasn't the point. Even for top graduates from Tuskegee, Wilmeth's patrol needed to show they could shoot straight. Could be trusted to unload the quartermaster's finest bullets into a target.

Time and time again, Williams led the four planes down into a safe firing range, and inside of ten minutes, each member of the quartet signaled they had emptied their ordinances. Despite his concerns, Wilmeth was impressed with their accuracy. Smirk had fired wide at first but corrected. The rest had been all on target amidships.

"All right, gentlemen," radioed Wilmeth to the other three, "nice work. Let's get home, pronto. Detroit City, that little town over there in the distance, comes next."

That was the moment Williams cut in.

"Hey, Sing-Sing, you've got a problem. You're smoking pretty good."

So he'd been right.

Wilmeth was not surprised. In fact, his premonition, the one that had been lurking like an unseen phantom, had finally announced itself. He'd held back for the last hour, but now the hour had arrived. The time of insurrection and revolution was revealed.

Rigorous training required Wilmeth remain calm and factor in everything he knew about a P-40. About what would happen if his engine cut out. How to eject. What to remember. What to mark as far as his exact location.

"Thanks, Charles. I'm good. I should be able to reach Selfridge."

"Negative, Sing. You're on fire, man. Bail out."

Wilmeth was just about to counter when he realized he'd run out of time. The plane was stalling, tilting forward into a very dangerous dive.

"Roger. I'm abando—"

He hadn't even finished the sentence when the Allison's fiery heat started enveloping the P-40's narrow cockpit. There was no time for more words. Only action.

With the same fine motion he'd once used in throwing a football, Wilmeth lunged forward with his strong right hand to crank open his canopy. Simultaneously, he unsnapped his harness, coiled his legs into a lifesaving spring, and moving his hand into position on his parachute, bolted up through the raucous, wind-whipped opening.

Yanking on the handle, Wilmeth instantly felt his silk chute unspooling, and for a moment, he imagined everything would work out just fine.

In his mind's eye, in a slow-motion dream, he saw himself dropping away from the plane, tumbling madly at first but then floating down toward the lake. Once he got within thirty yards of the water, he'd cut himself loose from the chute. The water would be cold, and he'd need to tread some for a while, but his Mae West flotation vest would keep his head above the surface long enough for the rescue crews to reach him. Above him, the others would have his back. Would follow him down and radio in his exact location.

Hopefully, the rescue boats weren't too far away, and Huron's temperatures had reached the fifties. He'd endured more than a few cold showers after games at Archbold, and while this would feel like an ice bath, he'd tread water to keep warm.

One thing was certain: His crewmates and the women they would meet in Detroit this weekend would want to hear this exciting escape story over and over. How the great Wilmeth Sidat-Singh—football hero, basketball star, friend of famous musicians, stalwart of the Black community—had leaped from his plane just in the nick of time.

CHAPTER 43

Buffalo, May 2000

Erik usually didn't come over to Breanna's apartment.

It wasn't that they didn't want to be seen together in public on her side of Buffalo, although an interracial couple was still a rarity in conservative Upstate New York. It was just that his place was closer to the office, and if they were both honest, it was nicer. He'd enjoyed a few more years of salaried work to build up a collection of appliances and accoutrements that Breanna had not. Of greatest value was his Italian espresso machine.

Here, on Breanna's turf, Erik always felt he saw a slightly different side of this woman he was falling in love with more fully each day. In her own den, the lioness was a little feistier, a little more confident. It was evident in how, having cleared the dinner dishes together, she moved. And how she could so easily return their discussion to her overarching mission of unlocking the vexing mystery of Sidat-Singh.

"Erik," she said, after they had finished dinner at her apartment one evening that spring. "I'm still at a loss about how Wilmeth died. I mean, it's just a training mission over Lake Huron. A walk in the park. He knows his plane. Had done everything right at Tuskegee. This is a smart guy. No way he just flames out."

"Well, remember, and I think Charles told you this: These are hand-me-down P-40s. And they have a drunken commanding officer who didn't like the Black men populating his base. Flying *his* planes. Not exactly a recipe for high-quality maintenance."

Erik had emphasized the word *his* to infer Colonel Colman thought of Selfridge as his plantation. The base was his antebellum mansion.

Breanna thought about that very inference.

She and Erik had previously discussed whether Colman—someone later brought up on charges for shooting his Black chauffeur and ultimately relieved of his command—could have been murderous. There was no proof, but like the Gene Hackman movie *Mississippi Burning*, it was certainly possible 1940s racism ran so deep just north of Detroit that someone could've actually taken matters into their own hands.

"Colman himself couldn't have rigged a fighter plane," she said. "And I don't think the plane gets off the ground or even out over the lake without Singh knowing something's wrong."

"OK, maybe, but based on what you've told me, the plane just flat-out fails in midflight. If that's right, it means Wil has barely a few seconds to make his next move. He knows he can't nurse it back to the base. There's no ejector seat. So he's sliding back the cowling, rolling it over, and releasing from his harness."

"So you're saying his engine just completely seized up. How does that happen? I mean, the plane is good enough at first to take off, get to altitude, but then stops working?"

"You're asking the wrong guy. The reason I'm a writer is because I wasn't a car guy like everyone else I knew. But think about the Indy 500. Car is running fine, and then it blows a piston or a gasket. Something pops, puff of smoke, and boom, you're out of the race."

"That's what I need right now. A puff of smoke, like when they're picking the next pope. I need one of these guys, Wilmeth or Charles, to get me through this roadblock. But wait a minute. Couldn't he also have mysteriously run out of fuel? That would also shut you down."

"Yeah. But usually you'd get some knocking. Like in a car. Coughing. The engine misfiring. If Singh had gotten any of those telltale signs, he would've radioed his wingman. Would've suggested something was wrong. For that to happen, someone would've had to tinker with his fuel gauge to ensure it looked full but really only had an eighth of a tank. From what we know, Singh didn't indicate he had a problem before he had one."

"And that's the problem. We don't know."

Erik went back to drying Breanna's plastic dishes and putting them away when suddenly he heard Breanna speaking. But not to him.

"You got to help me with this, Wilmeth. Talk to me. You too, Charles. Either one of you fools could lend a hand."

"Back to the ghost again?" Erik loved how Breanna's passion for the project did not dismiss otherworldly ways of getting into her subject's head. She'd sensed, or imagined, Wilmeth's ghost before. This was new though. She was also speaking to Charles as if either man were present.

"Do you have any other ideas?" she asked.

"Well, have you tried going back through Charles's letters and papers? Singh was his idol. I mean, Wil didn't leave word for you, but maybe his wingman did. He seemed pretty knowledgeable when you met with him."

"I've been through that box of stuff he gave me. And other than one thick envelope that looked like it was all old newspaper clippings, which I skimmed through, I've read all of Charles's stuff. His letters. The certificates. You know he tried for a lot of years to get Singh the Medal of Honor. But it was no dice, because Singh never got into combat."

"Wait a minute. Our star reporter left one stone unturned? You got to dig that file out again and sift through it. You never know. And one other thing: There's a reason it's called buried treasure. If it were easy, everyone would find it."

Breanna knew Erik was right but suddenly didn't feel like making the evening a research night. Their jobs at the paper were hard enough, and there was only one night a week when one of them wasn't working. Plus, it was a lot easier being romantic at night with a glass of white wine than at lunchtime over a break-room Diet Coke.

"I thought tonight was going to be about us, baby," she said.

"It can be, but I want you to show me that stack of papers where this envelope is hiding. I've known more than a few folks who got into that patron saint guy. Jude, I think. Patron saint of lost causes."

"No, you mean Anthony. The Catholics pray to a dead guy to help them find things. Craziest shit I've ever heard."

"Fine, fine. But pull that bad boy out and let's spread the clippings out," Erik said. "It will only take a minute. I always feel like the answer to something is right in front of me, and I'm just not starved enough. Gotta stay hungry in this journalism game."

Retreating to her desk with just a hint of a frown on her face, Breanna reached down into a corrugated box with the word *WILLIAMS* written in Magic Marker across the side. The papers and letters were stacked horizontally in a pile, and that meant with each handful of yellowed pages and No. 10 envelopes, she needed to create a stack on the floor.

"I know you mean well, Erik," she was saying when her hand unearthed the brownish manilla envelope. It was so stuffed Erik could see why she hadn't originally bothered to pull things out. They would never go back in again.

"I do," he protested meekly, wondering if he would ever use those very same words on another occasion.

He smiled, thinking how his late mother used to save his bylined articles and place them in a scrapbook. She'd build up a thick collection of papers before grabbing scissors and cutting out his stories. Laughably, that bugged him. His own mother was defacing the sports section and removing the very place where his story sat on the page. Her kindness also eliminated recognition for everyone who had been alongside Erik writing that day.

Well, she meant well.

"I'm going to do this quickly, and then we're going to get down to . . . whoa! Look at this. Stuffed in here like nobody's business."

Eric came over to her quickly and rested his elbows on her desk. He could see she was holding a clear-plastic binder with what looked like a college term paper.

"Whaddya got?"

"Looks like a paper he wrote for a creative writing class at Erie County Community College back in 1977. It's called *The Last Mission*. I don't know how I missed this the first time I went through this stuff."

"Whaddya wanna bet it covers his memories of exactly what happened that day?"

"I think you're right. Damn, boy, you are good."

"Well, I try. How long is it?"

"Looks like ten to twelve pages, long as the chapter of a book," she said, riffing the pages through her fingers. "Written in first person. The first page has a dateline reading, 'Lake Huron—May 9, 1943.'"

"I think one of your invisible friends just stood up for you. Get yourself a glass of wine and tell me what Charles has to say for himself."

CHAPTER 44

It quickly became apparent to Breanna and Erik this wasn't merely an essay for a community college creative writing class; this was a baring of one's soul, a spilling of ink—and guts—onto paper. For decades, Charles Williams had kept the horrific memories of his friend's death suppressed deep inside, but on these pages, they gushed forth explosively, like lava from a once dormant volcano. The assignment to write from the heart about a personal experience had to have been cathartic, must have brought Williams some much-needed and long-overdue relief. In the end, that had to have been more important to him than the professor's notations of praise or the large A-minus grade scrawled in red Sharpie atop the cover page.

By essay's end, Breanna and Erik were in tears.

The Last Mission

Charles Williams

Creative Writing 101—Professor Oglethorpe

Erie Community College

May 22, 1977

Lake Huron—May 9, 1943

The nightmares still haunt me on occasion. Once or twice a month I'll wake up drenched in sweat, gasping for air, feeling as if my heart is trying to punch its way through my chest. Like a young Joe Louis slugging his way to another knockout.

And I'll start screaming: "What are you doing, Sing-Sing? Release from your chute! Release from your bleeping chute!"

But all along, I knew he couldn't. He was out cold. Maybe dead already.

This first-person memory is from almost 35 years ago. About the day I saw my best friend, my real-life hero, die.

There was a time when my dreams tormented me almost nightly. Had to go see a therapist who convinced me to take pen to paper and sort it out. Try to find some peace. I've come to realize the dreams will never go away completely. I'll never stop wondering, "Why? And what if? Could I have done more?"

To this day, I think my friend Wilmeth Sidat-Singh did everything right.

It just didn't end the right way.

That bright, crisp, early May morning back in '43 remains as vivid as five minutes ago. I can still see it. The four of us out over Lake Huron.

I'll never forget how the sun rose brilliantly over those fifty-foot-high pine trees that surrounded the airstrip in Selfridge, Michigan. The smell of those pines was particularly pleasant that morning as we made our way to the hanger for our daily assignments. Used to love that aroma. Now, I hate it. Triggers those demons—even in the light of day.

Can still see my buddy Wilmeth—Sing-Sing, to many of us—the Negro kid with the unusual Indian name—springing from his army cot like some excitable kid on Christmas morning.

"Come on, Charles," he bellowed across the room as I wiped sleep from my eyes. "Time to rise and shine. Time to save the free world."

"Man, you're nuts!" I'd protest, pulling my pillow over my head. "They ain't even blown revelry yet, and you're already acting like some damn fool. Go back to sleep. Shine your shoes or something."

Pretty much every morning started that way with Sing-Sing.

He couldn't wait to pull on his fighter pilot's uniform and get on with his day. For some unexplained reason, he seemed more hyped than usual that morning. It was like he'd already downed several cups of that nasty army-issued coffee we drank. Stuff had enough octane to power a B-17. And once Sing-Sing got going, look out!

Everything was a damn competition, though usually in a good way. He loved challenging himself and others. I remember him double-timing from the barracks to the hanger that morning like a bat out of hell. Would have thought his damn shoes were on fire.

I had known about Sing-Sing since his days as a football and basketball star at Syracuse University. Me and just about every other colored person in America was familiar with him. He was the first Negro to play quarterback for a big-time college football program. And that was a big deal for us because Negroes weren't supposed to be smart enough to handle decision-making positions like quarterback or fighter pilot or—God forbid—president of the United States of America. But I think he could've done that too.

Sing-Sing destroyed all those myths. Gave us reason to puff out our chests, burst with pride. He played QB so well that famous sportswriter Grantland Rice compared him to Sammy Baugh and Sid Luckman, which was like saying Terry Bradshaw or Johnny Unitas. Pretty heady company, if you ask me. He also was quite the basketball player. Reminded me of a Harlem Globetrotter with his fancy dribbling and passing.

So I guess it's no mystery why he became a hero to me and thousands of other young colored boys from the 1930s who couldn't wait to read about his exploits in the Afro-American. *When I heard he was signing up for the Air Force's all-Black pilot school in Tuskegee, Alabama, I didn't hesitate; I signed up, too, even though I was still a teenager. I wasn't the only one who wanted to follow his lead.*

I know for a fact our heroes often disappoint when we meet them.

Not Sing-Sing. There was just something about the way that cat carried himself. He oozed charisma. Made you feel good in his presence. And he was one of those rare dudes whose appeal went beyond his race.

It was like what they said later about Jackie Robinson—how he was a credit to his race, the human race.

Through the years, I got to talk to and know some of his Syracuse teammates, and you could tell by the way they spoke about him just how much they respected Sing-Sing—not just as an athlete but as a person too.

And boy, was he sharp. If they ever tested him, his IQ must've jumped off their charts. He told me he'd been a zoology major at Syracuse. Wanted to become a doctor. Or maybe it was a veterinarian. Several of his teammates said he tutored them. That was Sing-Sing. Always helping people, always sharing his blessings.

I also learned he was as tough as an old leather football helmet. And I guess a lot of that had to do with what he had been forced to overcome. He lost his dad when he was young. And from what he told me at Selfridge, that was devastating, because he loved his Pops. Mr. Webb was one of the first Black pharmacists. Bright and caring.

As if overcoming that loss wasn't enough, later on, at Syracuse, Sing-Sing was forced to hide his identity, when the school's coaches and officials passed him off as a "Hindu" rather than a Negro. Wilmeth had taken on his stepfather's name when his mom remarried a guy by the name of Samuel Sidat-Singh.

The folks at Syracuse believed mistaken identity would enable them to keep their star player in the lineup for those football and basketball games against the lily-white schools south of the Mason-Dixon Line that wouldn't play teams with Negroes on their rosters.

Being an Indian was acceptable for white America in those days; being Negro was not. Sing-Sing really had no choice but to go along with the ruse. It actually started in high school, when the sportswriters referred to him as the "Manhattan Hindu."

The thing is, Wilmeth never denied being a Negro. In fact, he was proud of the fact he was. And all of us African Americans knew the truth too. We felt bad he had to play this game, but that's the way it was back then. Kind of sad you couldn't be who you truly were, but I guess in some ways it's not much different from today. There are people still afraid to be themselves because there might be hell to pay.

I admired the way Sing-Sing handled it. Don't know if I could have done the same. Like I said, in some respects, he was like Robinson with the Dodgers, only Sing-Sing faced the racism crap ten years before Jackie broke baseball's color barrier. Unlike Jackie, he was never going to get the opportunity to play as the National Football League's first Negro quarterback, because the league had outlawed Negroes. And there was no National Basketball Association in those days, just barnstorming teams like the Harlem Rens and Washington Bears.

All that stuff most definitely prepared him for hard times we encountered at Tuskegee and later in Michigan. Most of our white instructors were good men, realized we were all fighting on the same side. But some of them could be brutal. Would mark us down for the smallest infractions. The back-seat trainers would jerk the control stick into your knees until you had bruises. People forget the armed forces were segregated back then. Wasn't until after the war President Truman integrated the US military, made us all one.

I recollect nights in Jim Crow Tuskegee when I would return to my bunk totally demoralized after a day of intensive training and browbeating. I sometimes questioned fighting for a country where, despite what the Declaration of Independence said, not all men were created equal.

I won't lie. Was near tears on occasion, wanting to put my fist through a wall or one of my instructor's faces. I'd be cussin' and cursin', and Singh would talk me off the ledge, calm me down before I did something I'd regret.

"Charles, believe me, I know what you're feeling, because sometimes I feel that way myself," he'd say. "It stinks. Not fair at all. But we got to stick it out, my friend, and we got to stick together. Got to keep hoping if we persevere, prove ourselves, then people one day might change. I might not believe in the system the way it is, but I refuse to stop believing we can't get to 'all men created equal.' All airmen too."

I quickly learned Sing-Sing wasn't only a smart man; he was a wise man. He helped guide me and others through some—pardon my profanity—shitty times. Thanks to his encouragement and sense of humor, I survived those eight months in hell, and he and I became part of the third class of pilots to graduate as Tuskegee Airmen. You wouldn't believe how proud we were when they pinned those wings on our chests. We had to endure twice as much crap as our white counterparts. Had to be twice as competent.

We wound up being assigned to Selfridge Airfield, on the shores of Lake Huron, about twenty-five miles northeast of Detroit. Legend has it Thomas Selfridge was killed in 1908 while flying as a passenger with Orville Wright of Wright Brothers fame, making Selfridge the first military person to die in the crash of a powered aircraft.

The 332nd Fighter Group of the Tuskegee Airmen began in-flight training at Selfridge in late March 1943. We were placed under the command of Colonel Benjamin O. Davis Jr., the first Black to graduate from West Point in the twentieth century and later the first Black air force general. He also was one of us, so he could empathize with what we had been through. He told us he was a hard-ass because he wanted us to become the best fighter pilots in the world—and I'd like to think we achieved that goal.

Although we had a Black commander, that didn't mean Selfridge was a sanctuary from racism. Far from it. In fact, not long after we arrived, scandal rocked the base when Commander Colman, a white man, was charged with shooting Private William MacRae, a colored chauffer who had been assigned to drive him. We heard the incident occurred because Colman's regular driver—a white guy—was off duty, and the dispatcher was unaware of Colman's standing order that he never have a Negro driver.

After that incident, we learned about several other problems with Colman. Apparently, the commander liked to put his hand in the cookie jar when nobody was looking. Wound up being accused of stealing weapons and ammunition and selling them on the black market. And he also accepted bribe money in exchange for illegal transfers of men.

Our morale wasn't exactly boosted when a court martial found Colman guilty of careless use of a firearm rather than MacRae's first-degree murder. He also was conveniently acquitted of 23 other charges. His punishment was demotion to captain. What a bunch of bull! That miscarriage of justice caused us to be even more anxious and on guard.

Wilmeth was shaken mightily by the events, but he somehow remained optimistic in spite of it. He told me if we could survive Alabama, we could survive anything.

We felt like the Germans weren't our only enemies. We also were fighting Jim Crow. The US Army Air Corps had given us the old Curtiss Hawk P-40s to fly, but they were suicide machines. I remember springing an oil leak during one of my first times piloting a P-40 at Selfridge. That Texas tea came gushing back at me like water from a fire hydrant. I had to keep one hand on the throttle while using my other hand to keep wiping the oil from my goggles so I could see where the hell I was going. Somehow I found my way back to the base.

Everybody talks about Ted Williams, the baseball legend, being one of the greatest fighter pilots because of his superior vision, great hand-eye coordination, and fearlessness. Well, that's how it was with Sing-Sing. The great athletic skills translate. Sing-Sing had that ability to make split-second decisions on the move, similar to what he did on football fields and basketball courts. There was no panic in him.

A day before the morning that still haunts me, Sing-Sing, me, and two other pilots in our group—Curtis "Smirk" Smith and Leonard "Jack" Johnson—competed in a gunnery match against our fellow pilots. The four of us were as competitive as all get-out and hell-bent on taking home first-place honors.

A number of floating docks were set up in Lake Huron, a few miles from shore, with enormous swastikas painted on them. Sing-Sing, Smirk, Jack, and I blew our targets to smithereens to win the competition.

When we landed back at the base, we let our fellow airmen have it, talked trash about how we couldn't possibly have lost with a quarterback like Sidat-Singh leading the way. Colonel Davis told us not to get too cocky, because there was plenty of work to be done in a short time before we shipped out and began shooting at German ships and planes that would fire back at us.

The next day just so happened to be a Friday, and we didn't think anything of it until Colonel Davis made an announcement to an assembly of pilots.

"Men," he yelled loud enough to shake pine combs from branches, "I just want to let all of you know that as a result of winning the gunnery

competition, Lieutenant Singh's group has been granted a weekend pass to Detroit City."

We leaped to our feet and hugged one another, while most of the other pilots good-naturedly booed and said the competition had been rigged. The colonel restored order and reminded us we needed to refocus on that's day's assignments. The orders were fairly routine.

Head twenty thousand feet above Lake Huron and empty four hundred rounds into a floating dock a few miles from shore before heading back to Selfridge. We knew it shouldn't take more than an hour and change. As we walked briskly to our planes, Sing-Sing and I took a few more drags on our cigarettes before flicking them away.

"Hey, man, I know about this cool club in Detroit," I said enthusiastically.

"Sounds like a plan to me, Charles."

Upon arriving at our planes, we reviewed our flight plan. Intent on turning everything into a competition, Wilmeth suggested the pilot who scored the fewest number of hits on the target would buy the first round of drinks.

"Sing-Sing, looks like your wallet's gonna get light in a hurry," I remember Smirk saying.

"Yeah, right," Wilmeth responded. "That'll be the day."

We buckled our Mae West flotation vests and our parachutes, grabbed our helmets and oxygen masks, and shook hands before climbing into our cockpits. Since I was flying point that day, I would lead the attack but not return to the base until the other three had completed their assignments.

At eight o'clock sharp, I advanced the throttle to the full position and began rumbling down the airstrip, pushed back in my seat by the engine's power. I could see the runway disappear beneath my wing and stole a quick glance at my air-speed indicator. It read 130 mph.

At ten-second intervals, Sing-Sing, Smirk, and Jack followed. We made one circle of the airfield and then started climbing in a close formation, just three to five feet separating our wingtips. It was a clear day with little turbulence, and I couldn't help but notice the beautiful contrast of the light blue sky with the dark blue lake.

We reached our target at 08:25 and began making our firing passes five minutes later. By 09:00, Smirk and Jack had finished shooting, so I radioed for them to return to the base. As Sing-Sing turned his plane for home, indicating he had emptied all his rounds, I noticed a trail of black smoke coming from the tail of his P-40.

"Hey, Sing-Sing, you've got a problem," I radioed. "You're smoking pretty good."

"Thanks, Charles," he responded. "Doesn't seem too bad. I think I'll be able to make it back to Selfridge."

A few more seconds passed, when I noticed flames.

"Screw getting back to base!" I yelled into the radio. "You're on fire, man. You need to bail."

"Roger. I'm abandoning ship."

"I'll radio the rescue boat. Sing-Sing, remember to release from the chute just before you hit the water, just like we trained. You don't want to get tangled up in the drink."

I watched as Sing-Sing slid back the cockpit cowling, undid his shoulder straps, and brought his legs up under him. Then he leaped out of that flying inferno just in the nick of time.

But then the worst possible thing happened. Within a split second of bailing out, before his P-40 spun out of control, his chute caught on the tail of the P-40, and I'm guessing Sing-Sing must've smashed his head on the stabilizer because he looked dazed. He was just hanging there, getting pulled toward the lake, tethered to his crashing plane.

I radioed our position to the rescue boat, which was about four or five miles away, but I knew if Singh didn't get a miracle, he'd smash into the water with his plane.

"Bust your ass, boys," I said. "That lake's still ice cold. He won't last long in there."

I chased Sing-Sing's plane all the way down from three thousand feet, watching the smoke and flames. The bright white silk of the chute was turning black. At one point Singh seemed to shake his head. Like he was coming around. I wondered if he could unbuckle his chute and chance the drop.

As the P-40 neared the water, I could see he wasn't making any moves to unbuckle from his parachute. I started yelling, "What are you doing, Sing-Sing? Release the chute! Release your fucking chute!"

But for some reason, he didn't. He couldn't.

That plane was nose-diving. He had no chance.

"Come on, Sing-Sing! Keep fighting, boy! Keep fighting! Please, God! Please, God! Please, God! Help him."

When Singh's plane hit the water, there was an enormous smash and splash. It was horrific, but within seconds the big white spot in the lake grew smaller and smaller, until the P-40, with Singh still snagged, was sucked under the surface and disappeared completely. At best, there were only a few pieces of wreckage that stayed on the surface.

Just then my plane began to chug and lurch. I noticed the arrow on my fuel gauge had settled limply on the E. I wanted to keep circling until the rescue boat arrived, but I had no choice but to try to get back to the base before I ran out of gas.

My propeller started sputtering, an indication I was flying on fumes. I wrestled with the wheel and somehow managed to reach the airfield. I came down so hard that I blew out my right tire, causing my wing to scrape against the concrete runway as I skidded to a halt.

I dragged myself out of the cockpit and wobbled several feet before collapsing to my knees. I was delirious.

I started punching the runway, pretending it was God's face in hopes of paying him back for what he did to my friend. Smirk, Jack,

Colonel Davis, and the medics ran up to me. I was so enraged, so crazed, that I began whaling away at them, too, with my bloodied, broken knuckles. Took four guys to subdue me, to prevent me from doing further damage to myself and to them.

They pinned me to the ground. I tried with all my might to break their grip, to keep punching, to take out my anger on anyone and everyone. After about a minute, I had nothing left—my fight was gone. I was as drained and broken as that dammed P-40 I had just crash-landed.

"Why, God?" I sobbed as I was helped to my feet. "Why? He was the best of us."

CHAPTER 45

After composing herself, Breanna shot Erik a look that suggested hundreds of questions were now rolling through her journalist's mind. Curiosity was having a field day under her many tightly coiled curls.

"Can you believe that? That's incredible. Singh's body was still attached to his plane by his chute. He was suspended. Floating under the surface. Man, that is eerie."

"Do you remember that song by Gordon Lightfoot?" Erik said. "From back in the seventies . . . 'The Wreck of the Edmund Fitzgerald'? My father used to sing that to us kids. It had two lyrics that always stuck with me. The first went: 'The lake, it is said, never gives up her dead.' Well, he was wrong in Singh's case."

"Un-huh. What was the second?"

Breanna was not really interested in old white folk singers at the moment.

"It was something like, 'Lake Huron rolls, Superior sings, in the rooms of her ice-water mansions.' That was where Singh was standing guard. Over his plane. Loyal to the very end."

"No, that's not right. They needed to find him. But here's my next question: If Singh died that day in May, was he the first Tuskegee Airman killed in training? He couldn't have been, could he? I mean, some of the first men in training must have crashed down in Alabama."

"Dunno. But like you just said, Singh went to Arlington National. Maybe he was the first from Tuskegee buried there. That would have been something meaningful for the 1940s. Could he have been the very first Black man buried there?"

"He wasn't. I already checked into that. There were Civil War Blacks buried there, but way off in a segregated section. I know Singh was buried in section eight. That's in my notes somewhere. But section eight is not the point. Singh dies in Michigan, is finally recovered seven weeks later, and somehow his remains, whatever they looked like, got moved to Virginia. At taxpayer expense. That's a pretty notable expense and outcome for a Black man dying during training."

"Well, you're right about that," Erik said, his enthusiasm clearly waning.

In truth, Erik didn't like where the supposed romantic evening's plot was headed. Instead of wine and some time on the couch, Breanna was about to get consumed by facts and World War II questions. He'd have to move quickly or give in and let her fully satisfy her intuition.

"Any chance we can let Singh rest in peace for the night and come back to him tomorrow?"

"Is my baby worried he might get overlooked tonight?"

"Well, if I know one thing about you, Bre, it's that there's no quit in you. Listen, I'm good with us kicking this around. But how about we fly this couch together and hash out a plan. My Spidey-sense tells me you're going to want to do some research on Arlington. Find out who brought enough juice to the table to get Wilmeth buried there."

"Erik, I'm going to get to the bottom of this if it kills me. I'm going to find out the how and the why."

The next day Breanna placed calls with the chief historian at Arlington, but quickly discovered this was going to be a lengthy process, bogged down by bureaucratic request forms she couldn't wait for. Later that week, she was back at Syracuse University, hunkered down in the sixth-floor archives department, rifling through files, trying to solve the mystery of how Wilmeth had wound up in one of the most sacred cemeteries in the world. She found evidence President Truman had ended burial segregation at Arlington in July 1948—five years after Wilmeth died in 1943—and was buried in section eight. Something told her Singh's commanding officer, Ben Davis Jr., or maybe Davis's father, the first Black general in the US Army, Ben Sr., had something to do with the special treatment. After all, Wilmeth had been a celebrity. At least in Black circles.

The rest of the day proved rather fruitless. Brigadier General Parrish was marginally interesting in that, as a southern white man from Kentucky, he had commanded the Tuskegee Airmen. Most pieces on Parrish suggested his commitment to his men aided their early success and later helped them land their first combat assignments.

Unfortunately, Breanna's bigger story couldn't afford to go too far afield on Arlington, when Wilmeth's sporting prominence and death was the piece that would interest readers the most. Still, she refused to let the Arlington thread evaporate.

The death of a Black fighter pilot in World War II, even in a training mission, was historic. Plus, if Wilmeth's funeral brought out celebrities like boxing champion Joe Louis and big-band leader Cab Calloway, then this was a death the US Army had been unable to ignore.

Luckily, the files revealed a few texts that laid out the basics of Arlington's history as well as detailing some of the notables who found themselves as nearby neighbors for Sidat-Singh's bones. In death, Wilmeth was not alone.

One compatriot was Henry Lincoln Johnson, a man Theodore Roosevelt Jr., the founder of the American Legion, had called "one of the five bravest men to serve during World War I."

Johnson, originally a railroad porter, had served in the all-Black 369th Infantry, which was, in the racism of the day, assigned to the French army. The short version of Johnson's later story was found not on the battlefield but in his coming back to America. It was there, after talking about bigotry in the trenches, that Johnson was arrested for wearing his uniform in public beyond the expiration date of his commission.

"Unbelievable."

Breanna clenched her fists at the reality of Black life in America. Here was a soldier, not unlike Wilmeth, a hero of his age. He received the Croix de Guerre, but it took until 2003 for him to win the Distinguished Service Cross—long after his death in 1929 at age thirty-six. He suffered for ten years with more than twenty wounds he got single-handedly fighting off thirty-six Germans so others could live.

"When will America stop killing us? When do we stop offering to die for a country that doesn't love us?" She spit the words out to no one in particular, but knew people around her were staring. Breanna didn't care. At the moment, she despised a lot of folks. And institutions. Syracuse University. The US military. The media. Her own paper.

Hatred would eat her alive if she wasn't careful.

She walked back to her car, got in, and drove back to Buffalo in a funk. The happy nostalgia she felt each time she was back on campus had been shattered. History and every one of its impertinent facts could go straight to hell.

CHAPTER 46

John Isaacs had just boarded the Long Island Railroad heading to Harlem for a Mother's Day celebration in his old neighborhood that mid-May day in 1943, when he was startled by a familiar voice shouting the nickname he had earned on the basketball courts and sandlots of his youth.

"Boy Wonder! Boy Wonder!" Eyre Saitch called out. "Look at this."

Saitch handed him a copy of the *Pittsburgh Courier*, and Isaacs felt his heart sink as he read the story beneath the bold headline:

ANOTHER AVIATOR KILLED ON LAKES

DETROIT, Mich. May 13—Wilmeth Sidat-Singh, second lieutenant in the Army Air Force, and former football star at Syracuse University, was reported missing Sunday night at the Army Air Force base at Selfridge Field after an eight-hour futile search in the waters of Lake Huron.

"Doesn't sound good, Boy Wonder. Can't help but think he's dead."

"Shut the fuck up, Eyre! No way Sing-Sing's dead! No freaking way."

"But—"

"But nothing. We both know what a great swimmer Sing-Sing is. Guy swam like a fish. Like a Negro Johnny Weissmuller. He had to have made it back to shore. They just haven't found him yet. That's all."

"Pray you're right."

"I *know* I'm right."

In the days and weeks that followed, Isaacs held steadfast to his belief, refused to consider the alternative. And anyone who suggested otherwise, he quickly shouted down. But deep down, he knew he was in a serious state of denial. Each passing day, hope faded.

The news he never wanted to hear finally surfaced, along with Wilmeth's corpse, on the shores of Lake Huron six weeks after the crash. The first thing Isaacs did was call Wilmeth's mom in Washington.

"John! John! John!" Pauline Sidat-Singh sobbed over the phone line. "I still don't believe it. He was indestructible. Can't be. Just can't be."

"I know, Mrs. S. I know. Now, don't you worry about the arrangements or anything else. I'm gonna hop a train. I'll help you with everything."

"The army told me it's going to be weeks before they get the body here by train. I want to make sure my boy has the funeral he deserves."

"He will, Mrs. S. You need not fret about that. Wilmeth's gonna get his proper send-off, a hero's send-off."

After hanging up, Isaacs immediately rang Wilmeth's fiancée. Marjorie Webb's voice was lifeless, barely audible. No sobbing. No emotion. Just a listless monotone.

"John, don't know if Wilmeth had a chance to tell you, but he proposed to me on the way to Selfridge. He was gonna be home on furlough in a few weeks. We were going to get married before he shipped out to Europe. Nothing big. Just us and the justice of the peace. We'd have a big ceremony when he came back from the war. We just wanted to make it official."

"Yes, he told me about those plans, and you wouldn't believe how excited he was. Kept saying how you was the one. His soulmate. The love of his life."

"Tell me, John. How do I go from planning a wedding to planning a funeral? How do I do that?"

Isaacs was at a loss. He hadn't a clue what to say.

"Wish I could tell you, but I can't. Wish I could remove the hurt and the emptiness we're all feeling. We're gonna be there for you, Marjorie. These next days and weeks and months are going to be brutal. We're all going to have to figure out how to get through this."

"There are no answers, John. There is no getting through this for me. Not now. Not ever."

On the ride down to DC, Isaacs peered through the window and back in time. So many special memories. Playing ball. Clubbing. Laughing so hard they cried. Just several weeks earlier, on his way from Tuskegee to Michigan, Wilmeth spent a day in the Big Apple, joining Isaacs, Gates, Mercer, and the rest of the neighborhood crew at the Morris Tavern for beers and merriment. Near the end of the evening, the tall tales ceased. The conversations turned serious. They all knew the danger Wilmeth was preparing to face, but they left those fears unspoken. Instead, they discussed dreams, talked about what they would be doing after Wilmeth helped vanquish the Nazis and returned home to a hero's welcome.

Isaacs remembered how Wilmeth became animated when he mentioned his plans to continue playing professional basketball even after becoming a doctor. Wilmeth's smile became incandescent when he said he couldn't wait to get married and start a family. They talked about how bad things had gotten in Harlem. The police brutality had turned the hood into a tinderbox. Wilmeth wanted to heal those racial divides and make Harlem a vibrant place once more.

If anyone could have done it, Isaacs thought to himself, *it would have been Sing-Sing.*

As Isaacs reflected on his late friend's shattered dreams, he felt something eating away at him. He recalled the time Wilmeth told him, Gates, and the other neighborhood guys working at Grumman how they were building the planes Wilmeth and the other Tuskegee Airman would soon fly.

"You guys better not let your minds wander to basketball or the ladies when you're working on those assembly lines," he joked. "Don't want any loose rivets, my brothers, or I'm gonna be the first to come back from the grave and haunt you."

Isaacs shivered in his seat.

He knew he hadn't worked on any of the planes that Wilmeth and his comrades flew at Selfridge, but it bothered him to no end that his best friend probably met his fate flying a plane he never should have been flying. An unsafe, defective plane he'd been ordered to fly. A suicide machine.

CHAPTER 47

Washington, DC, July 1, 1943

It seemed like half of the District had gathered around Pauline Sidat-Singh's house on the morning of Wilmeth's funeral. And as John Isaacs worked his way through the throng to get to the steps where Pauline was standing, he was struck and heartened by how many people Wilmeth had touched in his short life, particularly people in the Black community, where he had become a hero the instant Sam Lacy "outed" him and turned him into a civil rights cause before that infamous game in Baltimore six years earlier.

When he finally reached Pauline, the two hugged. There was no holding back the tears.

"How's my second son?" Pauline said between the sobs.

"Doing OK, Mrs. S. More importantly, how are you doing?"

"Better than I thought. Look at all these people. Most of 'em I don't know from Adam. Total strangers. But they come up to me and tell me stories about Wilmeth and his kindness and how he inspired them. Makes me feel real good."

Pauline dabbed at her eyes with a handkerchief, grabbed Isaacs's hand, and began leading him into the row house.

"Got some people I want you to meet."

When they walked into the living room, Isaacs's jaw dropped when he caught a glimpse of the familiar face towering over most of the people in the crowded room.

Holy shit! he thought to himself. *That's Joe Louis.*

"Joe! Joe! I want you to meet someone. This is John Isaacs. He's like a son to me and was like a brother to Wilmeth."

The world-famous heavyweight boxer extended the enormous right hand that had knocked many a man to the canvass and offered his condolences.

"Thank you, Mr. Louis. It's an honor to meet you."

"Honor's all mine, young man. Any friend of Wilmeth's is a friend of mine."

Louis turned to Pauline and updated her about the funeral arrangements.

"We're all set. They've agreed to bury Wilmeth in Arlington Cemetery. Full military ceremony."

"Joe, that's such an honor. How in the world did you ever pull that off?"

"Let's just say I was owed some favors. Remember when FDR said, 'Joe, America sure could use your muscles when you have your rematch with Max Schmeling'? Well, after I took care of Hitler's heavyweight, the president congratulated me and said if I ever needed anything to contact him. So I did."

"Can't thank you enough, Joe."

After saying goodbye to the boxer known as the Brown Bomber, Pauline dragged Isaacs into the kitchen. He was pleased to see Cab Calloway, whom he had gotten to know through Mercer and Duke Ellington.

"Hi dee, hi dee, hi dee, ho!" the famous jazz musician joked while shaking hands.

"Hi dee, hi dee, hi dee, ho!" Isaacs responded, smiling.

Despite a capacity of more than five hundred people, Holy Redeemer Catholic Church on New York Avenue in northwest DC could not hold all the mourners who had showed up to pay their respects to Wilmeth at his funeral the next morning. Those who couldn't sardine themselves into the pews stood in the outer aisles or the choir loft in the balcony at the back of the cathedral. Still others stood outside and planned to accompany the horse-drawn caisson that would carry Wilmeth's body a mile down the road for his burial in Arlington National Cemetery.

Louis was among several asked to eulogize the fallen airman and spoke emotionally about how Wilmeth's impact on the war effort would not end with his death. He mentioned how Wilmeth had inspired scores of young Negroes to sign up for segregated armed forces units and how he would be featured in an upcoming campaign to get more Blacks enlisted while also raising money for war bonds.

After a priest spoke of Wilmeth's ultimate sacrifice, Dr. Samuel Sidat-Singh walked up to the pulpit to deliver some closing remarks.

"It is our hope," he said, in a voice choked with emotion, "that Wilmeth and thousands of others like him shall not have died in vain. That when this war is won, America will be a safe place for all people, Black and white. That there shall emerge from these sacrifices an emancipation from racial bigotry and prejudice, from the inequalities of opportunities, both civic and economic, and that there shall be a just recognition of true merit, not based upon the color of one's skin."

He paused for a moment to compose himself before resuming. "We are certain he would feel that his life was not in vain if it served to put a spark into the lives of aspiring youngsters and to impress upon them that ability, slowly but surely, receives recognition."

The doctor then returned to the pew and embraced Pauline. Despite an acrimonious divorce that had played out publicly and embarrassingly on the pages of New York's Black newspapers a few years earlier, they felt a closeness they hadn't felt in quite some time. United, sadly, by the death of a son they both adored.

The priest said a final prayer and instructed Louis, Duke Ellington, Isaacs, and the other pallbearers to carry Wilmeth's casket down the main aisle. Up in the loft, Calloway raised his hands for the choir and parishioners to start belting out the verses of "Amazing Grace."

Grabbing on to Samuel's left arm, Pauline followed the coffin to the vestibule. For the next hour, the couple stood there, exchanging hugs, handshakes, and stories with the hundreds who had packed the pews. After the procession ended, Pauline asked the commander of the honor guard that would escort her son's coffin to the cemetery if she could have some time alone with her family and friends.

She leafed through several scrapbooks people had compiled about Wilmeth. Newspaper clippings and photographs told stories of a robust life—a life of great promise cut short.

She walked over to the life-size painting the Tuskegee Institute had commissioned of her son. He looked so dapper in his army uniform, with the shiny wings emblazoned on his lapel. Beneath the portrait was an inscription: "HE WAS A MAN'S MAN—WHAT MORE CAN ANY MAN SAY."

There was a poster from his high school teammates celebrating his achievements at DeWitt Clinton High School and several floral wreaths, including an orange one from Syracuse University. A huge box contained scores of letters and cards.

"You should read this one, Pauline," Sam said, handing her a handwritten note.

It was from a young man who had just enrolled at Syracuse. He mentioned how he was from the Fifteenth Ward, where Wilmeth had lived while attending college there.

We were shooting baskets one day, and he told me he was getting ready to climb that Hill. And I thought to myself, no way is a Negro going to be allowed to climb that steep Hill. But he did. And he told

me I could, too, one day if I put my mind to it. Well, Mrs. Singh, I'm
standing on your son's shoulders, and I'm standing atop that steep Hill.
   Sincerely,
   Jacob MacAlister

"Wow, Sam! Just, wow!"

"I know. Short as it may have been, his life definitely wasn't in vain."

As she and the others prepared to leave the church, Sam Lacy and several other reporters from the local Black newspapers walked into the vestibule.

"Can we get a few comments about Wilmeth, Mrs. Singh?"

"Lacy, haven't you gotten enough comments through the years?" the doctor snapped.

"No, it's all right," Pauline interjected. "I'd like to say a few words about my boy."

She cleared her throat and stared at the nearby portrait—the one with the visage of the handsome soldier destined to remain forever young.

"We loved him, but God loved him more. I really don't feel so badly now, after seeing and feeling this outpouring of love. Wilmeth really crammed a whole lot of living into his twenty-five years."

She ran her fingers over Jacob MacAlister's heartfelt note.

"I'm sure a lot of little boys can get a bit of inspiration out of just looking at these things," she said, pointing to her son's portrait and the scrapbooks and the medals and the silver wings someone had affixed to a dark green army blanket on a nearby table.

With that, she, her ex-husband, and the others walked out the door and followed the riderless, horse-drawn casket across the bridge to Arlington.

Her son wound up receiving the send-off she had prayed for. A hero's send-off. As Joe Louis, Cab Calloway, and Duke Ellington stood by her side, members of the US Army honor guard and several DC policemen with whom Wilmeth once served fired their rifles in unison. Pauline couldn't help but notice that Black cops and white cops were standing side by side.

Wilmeth would have loved that. Despite all the indignities, all the injustices, he never became a cynic. Never stopped believing in the goodness of people, even the bigoted ones who had done him wrong.

"Mama, some day we all are going to learn to get along and to love one another," he would tell her often. "Still many miles to travel to get there, and probably more heartache to come. But I truly believe we'll get to that destination someday. I really do."

A bugler playing "Taps" jolted Pauline back to the awful present. After the final note had faded into the distance, a B-24 thundered just ten feet over the treetops. It scared the bejesus out of everyone while dropping a wreath near Wilmeth's newly dug grave. The casket was then lowered. Pauline tossed a flower onto it. She gazed tearily one last time at the hole in the ground that would be her son's final resting place, and whispered, "I love you, Wilmeth. You made us proud."

Lacy and the other reporters from the historically Black newspapers covered the story as if FDR himself had died. On the other side of the journalistic ledger, the white mainstream press barely acknowledged the funeral. The *Washington Post* ran just three paragraphs, burying them at the bottom of a story about the death of a sixty-seven-year-old patent attorney and office manager from Epping Forest, Maryland, named Horace Chandlee.

At Louis's urging, a poster depicting Wilmeth as a pilot and athlete was commissioned and ran in Black newspapers across the country in an effort to increase enlistments in the segregated armed forces and raise African American dollars for the war efforts.

That was pretty much the last anyone outside Wilmeth's circle of family and friends would hear of him. The world was at war, with the outcome still very much in doubt. Hundreds of American soldiers were dying daily. Wilmeth was gone, and soon would be forgotten. For a long, long time.

CHAPTER 48

Buffalo, April 2001

Bucky Abramoski called everyone to the center of the newsroom.

"Got a special announcement to make, everyone," the managing editor of the *Buffalo Express* hollered as reporters and editors slowly gathered around him.

"Where's Breanna?"

"Over here, Bucky."

"Oh, there you are. Please, Breanna, come and join me."

Abramoski pulled two letters from his folder. "The reason I wanted you all here is so we can celebrate a couple of bits of great news regarding some superb journalism by Breanna."

"You the woman, Breanna!" hollered one of her colleagues. "You rock!"

Breanna smiled, feeling somewhat embarrassed at being the center of attention.

"Both announcements relate to Breanna's marvelous three-part series on Wilmeth Sidat-Singh. First, we received word from the Associated Press Sports Editors that Breanna took first place in feature writing. And then we were notified that her series was a runner-up for the Pulitzer Prize."

Applause filled the newsroom.

"Speech! Speech! Speech!" called out assistant sports editor Victor Arucci, patting her on her back.

A beaming Breanna shook her head side to side. "No speech from me," she shouted.

Her colleagues started chanting, "Speech! Speech! Speech!"

She had no choice but to say a few words. "OK, OK. But I promise you this is gonna be one of the shortest speeches on record. I just want to thank Bucky for believing in me when I first broached the story idea. And I want to thank Colonel Charles Williams—God rest his soul—for tipping me off to Wilmeth. And I want to thank Erik Allen for being a sounding board and a shoulder to cry on. And believe me, there were plenty of times during this journey when I needed that shoulder."

Her colleagues began applauding as Abramoski handed her a plaque from the APSE and the letter from the Pulitzer committee.

After the impromptu festivities ended, Stash Malinowski stopped by Breanna's desk and asked her to come to his office. She had tried, like the plague, avoiding visits there, but she figured she was safe this time around, given what had just occurred.

"What's up, boss?" she asked.

"Close the door and have a seat. Breanna, I want you to know how happy I am for you. Remember how you were pretty angry with me when I first assigned you that story on the Tuskegee Airman? Well, I guess that worked out pretty well, now, didn't it?"

"It did, so thanks for suggesting it."

"No problem, young lady. No problem. Breanna, the reason I called you in is I want to offer you the Bills beat. I know it's something you've dreamed about, and I think you've earned it."

Breanna forced a smile. This indeed had been a dream assignment, but so much had changed in the past year. Wilmeth's story had opened doors for her. Big doors. Several newspapers had come recruiting her to join their staff, including the *Washington Post*, which was offering her the Redskins beat with the potential of becoming a sports columnist. That would make her a pioneer of sorts, one of the first Black women to hold such a prominent job at a major newspaper.

"What's the matter, Breanna? Cat got your tongue? I'm offering you the most desired beat at the paper."

"Um, Stash," she stammered. "That's always been my dream job, but . . . um."

"Um, what?"

"Well, I just got this great offer, and I've accepted it."

"Really? Can I ask where?"

"Yeah, I'm going to cover the Redskins for the *Washington Post*."

"Wow! That's a pretty big jump, isn't it? From Buffalo to our nation's capital. Much larger market. Much bigger demands and expectations. That's a lot of pressure, given your circumstances."

Breanna couldn't believe her ears. She'd heard similar stuff from Malinowski's mouth before. She thought her work might have truly opened his eyes a bit, shown him the error and hatred of his ways. But no. Deep down, he was the same guy who wondered if she was truly qualified.

"I'm ready for the circumstances, Stash. I'm going to embrace them."

"Why not the Bills instead of the Redskins? This is the team you've followed all your life."

"I know, but I think the timing's just right for me to test myself in a major market. And they've talked about other opportunities too. Maybe even a columnist's job someday."

"You really should think about this some more. Why not sleep on it and let me know tomorrow?"

"I appreciate that, Stash. I really do. But I've already accepted the job. Thanks again for thinking of me."

"Well, all right, young lady. Good luck."

"Thanks, Stash," she said, shaking his hand.

As she made her way out of his office and through the newsroom and back to her desk, she had mixed emotions. Yes, the Bills beat had been a lifelong dream. And as much as she hated to admit it, Stash was right: the *Post* assignment would bring added pressure. Breanna would be forced to prove herself all over again, but that was cool. She needed a fresh challenge, a change of venue. Needed to start anew. Not only in her professional life but in her personal life.

"Hey, Brenda Starr, superstar, wanna grab some celebratory brews at O'Loughlin's?" Erik asked when she arrived back at her cubicle.

"How 'bout someplace quieter, like Salvatore's, just down the block? Someplace where we can talk?"

"That's cool. When do you wanna go?"

"Now's as good a time as any."

Breanna had been dreading this moment for some time. Had been putting it off, as if doing so would somehow make the problems disappear. There was a time when she truly loved Erik. Or at least thought she did. He was such a good soul, had always been her biggest booster. In times good and bad. But in recent weeks and months, they had been quarreling more and becoming less intimate. The flame in their relationship was flickering— was on the brink of being extinguished. As one of her favorite oldies songs lamented, she had lost that loving feeling.

Salvatore's, as she had hoped, was nearly empty, and after grabbing some merlot from the bar, they settled into a quiet booth in the corner.

"Here's to you, Bre," Erik said, hoisting his glass. "Your talent and hard work have paid off."

"Thanks, hon," she said. "You played a role in that happening. And I can't thank you enough. Plenty of times when I wanted to give up, and you refused to let me."

"Thanks, but I had little to do with it. It was you, Bre. All you."

Breanna felt like such a jerk. Doing this to such a sweet guy. And on a day they should have been celebrating.

"Erik, I have some breaking news."

"We journalists love breaking news. Bring it on, babes. Bring it on."

"Erik," her voice quivering, "I've accepted a job with the *Washington Post*."

"Wow, Bre! Um . . . um, that's great. I hadn't realized you had been in contact with them."

"Yeah, they first reached out to me about a month ago. Even flew me down there for a day or two."

"You mean the day or two you told me you were visiting an old classmate in DC?"

"Yeah, that day or two."

Erik's heart began palpitating. The joy he had been feeling was turning to anger. He couldn't help but feel as if he had been betrayed.

"Geez, Bre, I thought you would have at least told me about this from the start. I mean, that's a huge decision. A decision affecting both of us. Thought you would have confided in me."

"Well . . . I . . . uh . . . I uh, didn't want to bother you with it."

"What the hey! Didn't want to bother me with something as important and life changing as that? We've never kept any secrets before, especially not with something that big. Thanks for keeping me in the loop. Talk about being blindsided."

"I'm sorry, Erik. It's been such a whirlwind in recent months. And if we're both being honest, things haven't been great between us for a while. I swear this came out of the blue, but maybe there's a reason why it happened when it did."

"Yeah, whatever."

"Look, I was wrong not to tell you, and you have every right to be pissed.

You deserved better. And I'm sorry."

"Save your sorry for someone else."

Tears welled in Erik's eyes as he extricated himself from the booth and began walking toward the front door.

"Erik, wait! Please don't go."

He stopped briefly and stared back at her with daggers in his eyes.

"Guess our relationship was a farce, huh, Bre? Can't help but feel as if I were used. I now understand what I was to you. I was just a shoulder to cry on."

"Erik, please! Please!"

"Go have yourself a wonderful life," he said, storming out the door.

CHAPTER 49

The movers had loaded the last of Breanna's boxes into the van, and before leaving her apartment a final time, she walked through the rooms for a final inspection. All her possessions had been removed. Nothing remained but memories. She thought of all the parties she had hosted there and how she and the other young reporters, who called themselves the Brat Pack, had downed beers, busted chops, bitched about editors, and danced to music, sometimes till the sun rose.

She remembered the times she had spent with Erik, how the two of them had made love in every room of that apartment. She thought about all the deep conversations they had, how they discussed everything under the sun, even broaching the idea of someday getting married. Her heart ached at the thought of what might have been. She felt as empty as the rooms.

Breanna and Erik hadn't spoken since he'd bolted out of Salvatore's, even though they had crossed paths a few times in the newsroom while she boxed up her belongings in the adjacent cubicle. Breanna wanted so badly to pull Erik aside and hug him, but she could see how wounded and angry he was. He wanted nothing to do with her.

She hated herself for the way it had ended—so abruptly, so callously. Erik deserved much better than this. He was such a good person. She understood completely why he felt like he had been used.

As she gazed out the bedroom window, she thought back to the first time they met in the newsroom at the *Buffalo Express* and how welcoming and friendly he was. He had treated her with total respect and acceptance. As an equal. He wasn't like the others, many of whom, through threatening looks and body language, made her feel unwanted and unworthy. Erik, though, never gave off those negative vibes.

He had always been encouraging, especially during her moments of despair and self-doubt, when she wondered if this obsession, this story of a lifetime, had become too consuming and had taken over her life.

Somewhere along the way, their relationship had blossomed from colleague and friend into something much deeper. No question Breanna had come to love him, but she occasionally wondered if it was romantic love, or rather a special bond between two close friends and confidants.

And, of course, there was that other matter they often had to deal with—the matter of race. Would they be able to make this work, be a true couple in a world that, for the most part, was still unaccepting of interracial relationships? Breanna thought back to that conversation they had in this very same apartment after she had learned in a phone call with John Isaacs about Wilmeth's torrid, verboten relationship with Nan Maris. The parallels between those relationships, six decades apart, were strong—and painful.

Breanna remembered sobbing so hard she gasped for air that night, and Erik rushed over and hugged her, thinking for sure there had been a death in the family.

"They say love conquers all," she told him after composing herself. "But I think there are some things love can't conquer."

"Whaddaya mean, Bre?"

"I mean us, Erik. I mean us."

"I don't understand."

"Come on, Erik. You understand. Think about the shit we've put up with because our skin's not the same color. We go out and people stare at us, and sometimes we hear things being said behind our backs. Even in the newsroom."

"So what, Bre. Screw 'em. It's none of their fucking business."

"Wish it were that easy, Erik. Hell, even our own families don't want us together. Your parents and my parents keep telling us, 'Stick to your own kind! Stick to your own kind!' Just like Ike Harrison told Wilmeth when he had an affair with a white coed."

"What do we care? As long as we're happy."

"It's not that simple, Erik."

"I know it isn't. Bre, the world's changing. It's not like it was in Wilmeth's day, thank God. People are more accepting. Not as hung up on this stuff as they used to be. Many are finally starting to realize that love's deeper than skin color."

"Yes, it's changed, Erik. And it hasn't."

As she finished replaying that conversation in her mind, a loud knock on her apartment door jerked her back to the present. She figured it was one of the movers.

"Erik!" she screamed, upon opening the door.

"You didn't think I was going to let you leave town without saying goodbye, did ya?"

The two hugged for the longest time, then walked over to the bay window and sat on the ledge.

"Erik, I'm so sorry. I'm so sorry. I'm such a self-centered ass."

"Well, I'm not going to argue with that last statement," he said, cracking a smile. "Look, Bre, I've been doing a lot of thinking these past ten days, and you were right. I was kind of in a state of denial the last few months, acting as if everything was the same when it wasn't. Time passes. Circumstances change. Relationships change."

He looked at the vacant room. "Lots of memories here, huh?" he said.

"For sure, Erik. For sure. Great memories. Unforgettable memories."

"Well, Bre, no use in making this more difficult than it already is. Things change, but one thing won't ever change. I'm always gonna love ya. You'll always be a part of me."

"And you'll always be a part of me, too, Erik. Ain't never ever gonna forget you, hon. Couldn't if I tried."

CHAPTER 50

Washington, DC, October 2004

"Breanna Shelton here. Can I help you?"

"Hey, Breanna, it's Sean Kirst, from the *Post-Standard* in Syracuse. Left you a message the other day about Wilmeth Sidat-Singh."

"Oh yes, Sean, yes. How ya doing? Sorry I didn't get back to you sooner, but we had a crazy day here, you know, with word coming down that the Montreal Expos are relocating to DC."

"No problem. Figured things were pretty hectic with that bombshell being dropped. Good for DC to finally be getting baseball back. Hey, the reason I called is that I know you've done so much on Wilmeth through the years, and I thought you'd like to know that Syracuse University is finally going to acknowledge him by retiring his basketball jersey."

"Really? Wow, that is great news."

"Yes, it is. And obviously several decades overdue."

"So, Sean, how'd this all come about?"

"Well, I credit you, Breanna. I read your stuff, which was sensational, and it got me thinking about the SU connection. Seemed sad to me the school had never done anything to honor him. Go around campus, and you'll see plenty of stuff recognizing Jim Brown, Ernie Davis, and Floyd Little, but nothing for Wilmeth."

"You're right, Sean. And it's a damn shame."

"Well, you know we columnists like to stir things up. So I started writing about it, how this should be rectified, and fortunately there's a guy at the university—guy by the name of Larry Martin—and he really picked up the ball, pun intended, and ran with it."

"Very cool."

"Larry and I thought the timing was right, given Syracuse just won the national championship in hoops two years ago. We talked about how there had been so many great Black athletes who really put Syracuse basketball and football—not to mention the university itself—on the map. And Larry pointed out that all of them owed a debt of gratitude to Sidat-Singh because he paved the way. As Larry put, 'All of 'em—Brown, Ernie, Floyd, Dave Bing, Carmelo Anthony—stood on Wilmeth's shoulders.'"

"True that. Heck, Wilmeth was Jim Brown before Jim Brown."

"That's what Larry said too. So he went to Chancellor Cantor and said, 'We got a wrong here that we, as an institution, need to right.' And she was in total agreement. So mark your calendar for February 26, 2005. Going to be a historic day in the Dome when they get around to unveiling his jersey during halftime of the SU-Providence basketball game."

"Thanks, Sean, for the heads-up. And thanks to you and Mr. Martin for championing Wilmeth's legacy. I'm going to get ahold of some of his relatives. I know they are going to be thrilled. I'll try to head up there on the twenty-sixth to write about it. Folks in DC will be interested hearing that one of their forgotten brothers is going to be remembered."

***

Though she had spent much of her life in Buffalo, dealing with winter wind and cold, Breanna's blood must have thinned considerably since moving to the nation's capital and its more temperate climes several years earlier. Despite having been in the Dome for more than two hours, she was still attempting to thaw from the wintry February Syracuse weather that had chilled her to her core.

"Man, I do not miss these Upstate winters," she joked to Kirst.

"Hey, after a few days here, you'll get used to it."

"Maybe." She smiled. "But I have no desire to see if that's true. I'll be back in DC after filing my column today. I'm told it's forty-five and sunny there."

"Beach weather in Syracuse," joked Kirst.

Just then their banter was interrupted by the booming baritone of public address announcer Carl Eilenberg, who asked the crowd of twenty-seven thousand to direct their attention to the large video board above the Dome's upper deck. A ninety-second film highlighting Wilmeth's extraordinary career and life was shown before Syracuse athletic director Daryl Gross took the microphone. He introduced several of Wilmeth's relatives, then asked the crowd to look up at the jerseys of former Syracuse All-Americans Derrick Coleman and Sherman Douglas that were affixed to a wall just beneath the stadium's billowy white roof in one of the end zones.

"We pay homage to a forgotten hero who is forgotten no more," Gross told the throng. "Today Wilmeth Sidat-Singh takes his deserved place among all the great athletes who ever played at Syracuse University."

Those who hadn't headed for the restrooms or concession stands began applauding when Wilmeth's No. 19 jersey was unveiled.

Breanna knew immediately that Syracuse had blundered because nineteen was Wilmeth's football, not basketball number. But she wasn't about to quibble or remind school officials of their error. She was just happy to see Wilmeth finally acknowledged along with all the other legendary athletes who had played basketball and football there.

After the ceremony, she pulled Martin aside to talk about Wilmeth.

"This is intended both as a tribute and as a means of healing some old wounds," Martin explained. "When we won that national championship back in 2003, and everyone was offering credit, I immediately thought of Wilmeth Sidat-Singh and how he paved the way for generations of African Americans at SU. I think this will be a fitting tribute for an extraordinary individual who up until this point has almost been hidden from us."

Breanna thanked Martin for advocating on Wilmeth's behalf, then walked over to speak to Wilmeth's cousin Yvonne Jenson. "For him to go down in Syracuse history is a most comforting thing," she told Breanna. "He may not be as well known as many of those other guys up there, but his jersey is going to cause some people to try to find out more about him, and that's a good thing. And once they do, they're going to realize just what a big deal he was."

"Yvonne, I imagine this brings you and your family some closure, doesn't it?"

"Sure does. Brings closure and makes us feel damn proud."

Breanna had all she needed to write her column. She wound up filing it just as the final gun sounded. That meant she'd be able to catch her seven o'clock flight back to Washington.

On her way out the doors with the hoard of fans, she couldn't help but eavesdrop. Two guys in their fifties were talking about Wilmeth.

"Never heard of that guy with the funny name," remarked one of them.

"Me neither."

"They say he was a multi-sport star, like Jim Brown."

"Well, if that was the case, he must have been pretty damn good."

"My interest is piqued. I'm going to do some research on him when I get home. I want to know more."

Breanna smiled as she veered toward her rental car in a nearby parking lot.

CHAPTER 51

Her years at the *Washington Post* had been fruitful and memorable. She had accomplished so much. Made her mark. Thanks to her extraordinary storytelling skills, perseverance, and the encouragement of a few open-minded editors and colleagues, Breanna was able to spread her wings and flourish. Yes, she still encountered BS based on race and gender, but she—and society—had made some progress since her early days as a journalist when several Neanderthals sold her short, and she thought seriously about chucking her aspirations.

Breanna's rise since that pivotal moment in Buffalo had been meteoric. She swiftly advanced from covering the Washington Redskins beat to regularly writing long, in-depth features and investigative stories to becoming one of the first Black female columnists at a major newspaper.

In June 2011, her lifelong dream of writing for *Sports Illustrated* came true when the magazine hired her away from the *Post*. As a young girl, her father had gotten her a subscription to that bible of sports journalism, and

Breanna couldn't wait for the weekly magazine to arrive so she could devour it front to back. She would read every single word, not only for information but for writing style. She especially loved the long, soulful features by Frank Deford, Gary Smith, and Steve Rushin, as well as Rick Reilly's off-the-beaten path pieces at the end of the magazine, which occasionally caused her to laugh and cry—sometimes within in the same column.

She also loved the magnificent photography of Neil Leifer and Walter Iooss and often taped the covers they shot to her bedroom walls. While looking at Michael Jordan, Muhammad Ali, or Hammerin' Hank Aaron staring back at her, she would dream not only of one day appearing on one of those covers as a groundbreaking athlete but also producing the kind of literary prose for which the magazine had become famous. Parallel dreams definitely were at play there. She wanted to become a star athlete—and a star writer.

Butterflies fluttered in Breanna's belly when she reported for her first day of work at the magazine offices inside the iconic Time-Life Building on Sixth Avenue in Midtown Manhattan. Dick Friedman, a seasoned editor and kindhearted man, immediately took her under his wing and put her at ease.

While they discussed future story ideas, Friedman brought up the work Breanna had done on Wilmeth for the *Express* and the *Post*.

"You know, I'd love to reprise that story for *SI*," he said. "We'd just have to find a new angle, a new hook, but it's one of those lost-history stories we love to share with our readers."

"That would be fantastic," she said. "Despite all I wrote, there still are so many people who've never heard of the guy. Having a story about Wilmeth in *SI* would bring it to a new and much wider audience."

"Well, if you can find a fresh angle," Freidman said, "I think I can sell it to my bosses."

"Thanks, Dick. Let me give it some thought."

Breanna hadn't thought about Wilmeth for a while, but Freidman's suggestion rekindled the embers. She decided to ring Wilmeth's cousin Lyn

Henley to see if there was anything new. If there was, he'd definitely know because he had been the keeper of Wilmeth's flame ever since he first heard tales of his famous but forgotten relative.

"Hi, Lyn, this is Breanna Shelton calling. How ya doing?"

"I'm doing great, Breanna. So good to hear your voice. I know you've only been gone a month or so, but we miss seeing your smiling face in the *Post*'s sports section."

"Thanks, Lyn. I would have been content spending the rest of my career there—the people there were so good to me—but working for *Sports Illustrated* was a lifelong goal—that and playing point guard for the Chicago Bulls—so I'm really looking forward to this new adventure."

"That's super. If you're happy, I'm happy. What can I do for you, young lady?"

"Well, Lyn, it's about Wilmeth. One of my editors at the magazine read a bunch of stories I wrote about him through the years and said if there was something new he'd like to see if I could do something on Wilmeth for *SI*."

"You aren't going to believe this, but your timing couldn't be better. There is something new and exciting, but it's still in the planning stages."

"I'm all ears."

"For the past few years, there's been something gnawing at me regarding my cousin's legacy. Me and my family were overjoyed back in 2005, when Syracuse got around to retiring Wilmeth's basketball jersey, though they probably should have retired his football jersey, too, but beggars can't be choosers, now can they?"

Breanna laughed.

"I was thinking that while Syracuse made amends for not sticking up for Wilmeth during that Maryland game way back when, we still haven't heard jack from the Terrapins. No apologies. No nothing. So, being the royal pain that I am, I wrote a few letters to some of the bigwigs there and told them about this injustice.

"Now, I'm a man of faith, so maybe there was some divine intervention here, but last week I received a call from my cousin Kumea Shorter-Gooden, who recently was appointed chief diversity officer at the college.

"After reacquainting ourselves, she told me she had never heard of Wilmeth's story, even though she's a distant relative by marriage. Long story short, she said her new employer definitely needed to do something to atone for this wrong, so she took my letter to the president of the university, and they've come up with the great idea of officially apologizing to Wilmeth's family during a ceremony at a football game this fall."

"Wow! That's definitely a new angle!"

"Yes, it is, Breanna. Yes, it is. And what makes the timing even more relevant is that Syracuse is scheduled to play at Maryland this fall. So everything will have come full circle."

"Lyn, I can't tell you how happy I am for you and your family. This is fantastic news, and long, long overdue. And, selfishly, it gives me a way of telling the story to a whole new audience."

"I'm so glad you called, Breanna. I'll let you know once I know more."

"Please do. You know me. I'll do anything I can to spread the gospel of Wilmeth."

CHAPTER 52

To the day he died, Benjamin Henley carried with him the hurt from that damp day in Baltimore in the fall of 1937, when racism benched Wilmeth. He and several other relatives had traveled to that Syracuse-Maryland game in hopes of seeing his nephew perform his football magic. Instead, they watched Wilmeth standing on the sidelines, towel wrapped around his head. That image would be forever seared in Henley's memory, never to be erased.

"They didn't just bench Wilmeth that day," Henley once told his young son, Lyn. "They benched the whole damn Negro race."

Henley often regaled his son with tales about how huge a hero Wilmeth had become—not only in DC, where he was born and spent his formative years, but throughout Black America, where African American newspapers and magazines championed him the way they championed the likes of Joe Louis, Satchel Paige, and Josh Gibson.

"Didn't take long for Wilmeth to become my hero, too, even though he died years before I was born," Lyn would later tell Breanna. "Dad and other relatives, plus all the scrapbooks I gathered up, painted a picture of someone I wanted to emulate."

And someone he wanted others to remember.

Resurrecting Wilmeth's achievements wound up becoming a lifelong crusade for Lyn. His persistence prompted Syracuse University to recognize its forgotten hero. That jersey retirement ceremony in the Carrier Dome was one of the greatest days of Henley's life—a day when he felt the strong presence of the father who had turned him on to Wilmeth.

Though Henley basked for some time in the glory of that jersey retirement ceremony, he couldn't help but feel as if the story hadn't come full circle and that there still was some unfinished business to mend.

When his dad told him about the benching back in 1937, Henley developed a hatred for the University of Maryland.

"Right or wrong, I spent the rest of my life rooting against them," he told Breanna. "My favorite teams were Syracuse and any team playing Maryland."

For him—and more importantly, Wilmeth's legacy—to experience closure, there would need to be some sort of recognition and apology for what that university had done to Sidat-Singh.

And that finally came in 2013, thanks to the perfect alignment of the planets and stars.

"It was personal for Lyn, and after he educated me about Wilmeth, it became personal to me too," Shorter-Gooden told Breanna. "But it went beyond personal. What happened to Wilmeth Sidat-Singh is an example of the worst of America's racial history. We can't undo the past, but we can recognize it and apologize for it and try to ensure it never happens again."

Shorter-Gooden met with Maryland athletic director Kevin Anderson. He, too, was unfamiliar with the Sidat-Singh story and told her, "We've got to address this."

Notepad and recorder in hand, Breanna made her way down to the Byrd Stadium tunnel just before the end of the first quarter of the SU-Maryland game that November 9. Upon spotting Henley, she sprinted over to him, and the two embraced.

"Can you believe this, young lady? Never in a million years did I expect this moment to occur."

"So happy for you, Lyn. All your hard work has paid off."

At the end of the quarter, Henley, his mom, and several other family members were escorted onto the field. The public address announcer called attention to the stadium's jumbotron, high above one of the end zones. As photos of Wilmeth as a Syracuse football player and Tuskegee pilot flashed across the screen, the announcer told the crowd about the forgotten hero's legacy. He then mentioned how Wilmeth had not been allowed to play against Maryland seventy-six years earlier, and how the university was now apologizing for that horrible injustice.

A framed Wounded Warrior football jersey was then presented to Henley, who joyously held it aloft, prompting the majority of the spectators to rise to their feet and clap their hands.

Syracuse coach Scott Shafer came over to shake Henley's hand and was joined by several players, who had affixed blue number-nineteen decals on their orange football helmets.

After returning to the suite Maryland officials had provided Wilmeth's relatives, Breanna pulled Henley aside. His eyes were still glistening.

"Pretty emotional, huh?"

"Yes, it was. Yes, it was. Somewhere up there, Wilmeth's smiling."

"Lyn, they billed this the Forgiveness Game. Can you forgive them?"

"Yes, I can. We can never forget, nor should we. But we can always forgive. It gives us the strength to move forward and to heal. Like Dr. King said, 'It's always the right time to do the right thing.' Today, all these decades later, the University of Maryland did the right thing, and me and my family are at peace. And Wilmeth can rest in peace."

After Syracuse put the finishing touches on a 20–3 victory, Breanna headed to the postgame press conference. She was interested in hearing what Shafer had to say because he had been quite emotional and eloquent about the significance of this gesture in the days leading up to kickoff.

"The thing I was most proud about wasn't the big hits, wasn't the rush yardage," the first-year head coach said before any questions were asked. "It was during the game when our kids said, 'Remember what we're doing this for—[Wilmeth's] family.' And these young men kept saying that throughout the game, and that's far more important than a football game on a Saturday afternoon.

"Seventy-six years isn't very long ago, but that injustice was in some tiny way cleaned up today."

CHAPTER 53

After saying goodbye to Lyn Henley, Breanna grabbed a cab back to her hotel to put the finishing touches on the ten-thousand-word story she would file that night to *Sports Illustrated*. Once back in her room, she checked her emails and noticed one from Dick Friedman.

"Hey, Bre, just wanted to give you some good news," he wrote. "At least I think it's good news. Had something fall through at last minute, and the ME decided to make your Wilmeth piece the cover story. So add in those final touches. I'm sure this will be the first of many cover stories for you."

Breanna's pulse quickened. She read the email again, just to make sure she hadn't become delusional from the fatigue of recent days.

"Oh! My! God! This is effing awesome. You in the high-rent district, girl. Now don't screw this up."

She began reviewing the notes she had jotted down that day. Ninety-five percent of the feature chronicling Wilmeth's extraordinary life had been written. It's prose she could have written by heart. She just needed to weave in the full-circle event that had transpired hours earlier on the Maryland campus.

At about eleven o'clock that night, she hit "send," and the tome was transmitted to *SI* headquarters in Manhattan.

She thought about heading downstairs to grab a celebratory drink or two at the hotel bar but was too exhausted. The instant her head hit the pillow, she was visiting la-la land. The next morning she checked her phone. There was a text from Friedman that included a photo.

"Congratulations, Breanna, on a job marvelously done! Hope you like your first cover."

Like it?!

She loved it!

With several hours to kill before checking out and boarding the train back to Manhattan, she decided to tend to some unfinished business. There were two old friends she needed to visit. So, after showering and dressing, she caught a taxi to Arlington National Cemetery.

The sun was shining brilliantly that November morning. *What a great day for a reunion*, Breanna thought to herself as she paid the cabbie upon arrival at the front gate. When she reached Charles Williams's grave, her mind raced back to that day years earlier when she met the old Tuskegee Airman for the first time. She recalled how pissed she was about losing out on the Buffalo Bills beat and how she didn't really have her heart in Charles's story when she showed up at that warplane museum in the middle of nowhere.

"You were right, Captain Williams," she said out loud. "Man, were you ever. Telling me this might be the story of a lifetime, and it was. Can't thank you enough. Hope you're pleased with how everything's turned out, including yesterday.

"I just want you to know I couldn't have done this without you. I'll always be beholden to you, my friend."

Breanna said goodbye, then walked briskly down the circuitous path leading to Wilmeth's burial site in section eight. When she reached her destination, several hundred yards away, she was beaming.

"Well, Lieutenant Sidat-Singh, we did it. Got your story out there for the world to read, hear, and see. You're anonymous no more. And maybe, just maybe, you'll be having a few more visitors in the coming weeks, so be prepared.

"This truly was a team effort, Wilmeth, and you were the leader, the commanding officer, the quarterback. Been quite the journey since we first met here many moons ago, hasn't it? I'm sure you were looking down and grinning ear to ear yesterday when those Maryland folk finally got 'round to saying they were sorry. Better late than never, right? And I'm sure you took some pride when your alma mater unveiled your basketball jersey way back when. So what if they got your number wrong? At least they spelled your name right.

"And come this Wednesday, your handsome mug is going to be splashed on the cover of a national sports magazine, and people will read the story you, Captain Williams, and so many others helped write."

Breanna pulled her phone and punched up the text from her editor with the photo of the cover.

"See," she said, turning the screen toward Sidat-Singh's tombstone. "There you are, for all the world to see. Hope you don't mind me saying this, Lieutenant, but you were one good-looking dude."

After putting the phone back in her coat pocket, Breanna knelt in front of the grave.

"Most of all, I want to thank you for inspiring me not to quit. I was ready to dump my notebooks and my career into the trash, till Captain Williams and you showed up in my life. Like two damn guardian angels, and then off we went."

Tears streamed down her cheeks.

"I warned you from the git-go this sister was going to be bugging the hell out of ya, and as you saw, I was true to my word. I can be a royal pain when I set my mind to something. Well, you can rest in peace now, 'cause

I'm all done pestering you.

"But I won't ever forget you. Never, ever, never. And I won't ever stop being grateful to you. You're still completing passes, still scoring baskets, still flying planes, still inspiring souls like me.

"Funny thing is, you were lost, and I was lost, and now we're found. 'Amazing Grace,' huh? A pretty damn cool final chapter, if you ask me. Especially if you like happy endings."

Breanna rose to her feet and patted Wilmeth's marble marker one final time before trudging up the long, hilly, curvy path toward the cemetery's main entrance and the rest of her life.

A slight breeze blew. Leaves rustled. Off in the distance, Breanna heard the echoes of rifles firing in unison twenty-one times. Three fighter jets thundered over the cemetery in formation. She looked skyward and smiled as she thought about how a dead man she never met had taught her how to live.

AUTHORS' AFTERWORD

Our circuitous trek from discovery to novel began roughly a quarter century ago. The instant we became aware of this man time forgot, we were hooked; there was no going back. We knew somehow, some way, we needed to tell the real-life, tragic-hero, multilayered story of Wilmeth Sidat-Singh. It wasn't a matter of if but of when and how.

Each newspaper clip we unearthed and each interview we conducted only whetted the appetite and led to more "Can-you-believe-this?" moments. It spurred us on. Over time our pursuit became an obsession. Even while we wrote other books, even while we lived crazy-busy lives, Wilmeth was always lurking, never far from mind and soul.

As journalists and historians, we initially planned to write this book as a biography, as nonfiction. There was just one problem with that approach: Despite Wilmeth's prominence in the Black community—by the late 1930s he was almost as celebrated as world heavyweight boxing champion Joe Louis and Olympic gold-medal sprinter Jesse Owens—there was little on the record from Wilmeth. The pioneering football quarterback and All-American basketball player from Syracuse University was rarely quoted in the historically Black newspapers or in the mainstream white press. There weren't any radio or television interviews to listen to—no treasure trove of letters or diaries to leaf through.

We had little to go on that would reveal Wilmeth's innermost thoughts about how he felt while being forced to hide his African American identity. We didn't know what it was like internally for him to accept a ruse concocted by white sportswriters, coaches, and administrators that he had Indian roots and was—in the parlance of the times—a "Hindu."

Through the years, we attempted to piece together the puzzle by speaking with relatives, coaches, teammates, and fellow Tuskegee Airmen. We scoured hundreds of newspaper and magazine articles, several of which revealed vibrant, telling anecdotes. In particular, the works of newspaper scribes Sean Kirst, Dave McKenna, Luke Cyphers, and Sam Lacy, along with James Roland Coates's 1970 master's thesis about Wilmeth's racist benching before the Maryland game, were rich in background and detail and offered valuable insights into our lost hero's personality and character.

Deeper dives into the circumstances that shaped our protagonist, such as the death of his biological father at age seven and his mother's subsequent remarriage to the man whose surname Wilmeth took, connected more dots. So did our research into his Washington, DC, roots, his college years living in Syracuse's predominantly Black 15th Ward, and his formative years in New York City, where he experienced firsthand the enormous energy and vitality of the Harlem Renaissance and forged friendships with famed musicians Duke Ellington, Cab Calloway, and several future Basketball Hall of Famers.

In order to develop a greater appreciation about the circumstances that shaped and molded him and put his story into historical context, we also studied what was going on in society and the world during Wilmeth's lifetime.

The unpeeling of numerous layers brought us closer to his core, his essence. Our probing enabled us to reach a point where we felt as if we knew

Wilmeth on a personal level. By the time we sat down to write the novel, we could hear him speaking to us, answering our questions, baring his soul. It was almost like we were having conversations with his ghost, his spirit.

The fact Wilmeth died so young (age 25) and so long ago (1943, during a Tuskegee training mission) both complicated and added poignancy to the story of a life cut tragically short. Sadly, our hero's legacy disappeared not long after his death. It got lost. And that made our efforts to revive his story more difficult. One prominent person we pitched the story to actually told us Wilmeth had been "dead too long. Nobody knows him; a modern audience won't care, won't relate."

But we cared. We related. And we believed others would too. His tale of courage and perseverance was so powerful, so human. How could they not care and relate?

Here, after all, was a person who was an aspiring doctor, who became an unwitting civil rights pioneer and a World War II patriot who paid the ultimate sacrifice for a country in which he didn't have full rights because of the color of his skin. Here, also, was a guy who was the greatest athlete people never heard of: Jim Brown before Jim Brown; Bo Jackson before Bo Jackson; Deion Sanders before Deion Sanders.

Wilmeth's trailblazing exploits prompted Grantland Rice, the most influential sportswriter of the day, to wax poetic and liken him to Sammy Baugh and Sid Luckman, the Tom Brady and Peyton Manning of their times. Decades later, Wilmeth would draw Steph Curry comparisons when inquiries were made about his basketball prowess for the world champion Harlem Rens, the greatest team of the pre-NBA era.

Wilmeth clearly was an athlete ahead of his time, who sadly was denied opportunities because of the times. The National Football League had policies banning the employment of Black players in those days. Had Wilmeth been born decades later, he likely would have flourished during this golden age of Black quarterbacks, joining the likes of Patrick Mahomes, Jalen Hurts, Russell Wilson, Lamar Jackson, and other African Americans in reinventing and dominating the position.

Given the rampant racism of his time, it is remarkable Wilmeth was able to do what he did. In an era when Blacks were treated as second-class citizens, here was a man of color serving as a field general on the gridiron and basketball court at a predominantly white university. He was giving orders to white peers—something unheard of in those days.

In his own, small, unintentional way, Wilmeth helped lay the foundation for the Civil Rights Movement a decade before Jackie Robinson broke baseball's color barrier and sixteen years before the seminal *Brown v. Board of Education* Supreme Court ruling integrated schools. And Wilmeth did so while being forced to hide his identity and suffer excruciating indignities because much of America wasn't ready for Black classmates, teammates, and neighbors, let alone Black leaders.

Research and interviews taught us Wilmeth was both charismatic and empathetic. People gravitated to him. He transcended race and earned the respect of both Blacks and whites. He even won over some of the bigots bent on seeing him fail.

In some ways, he reminded us of another transformative Black athlete, Ernie Davis. In 1959 Davis led the Syracuse football team to the national championship, and two years later he was shaking hands with President John F. Kennedy after becoming the first African American to win the Heisman Trophy. Sadly, Davis's story, like JFK's and Wilmeth's, would end tragically and prematurely. In May 1963, after a courageous two-year battle with leukemia, Davis died at age 23. Six months later, Kennedy would be assassinated at age 46. In the case of all three, we were left to wonder what might have been had they lived. Those unlived years, those unwritten chapters, those enormous voids that had a ripple effect on so many others add to the pathos and appeal of their stories. But unlike the glorified lives of JFK and Davis, Wilmeth's legacy would vanish for decades.

Though set in the 1930s, Wilmeth's story is very much a 21st century story. Sadly, all these years and tumult later, people continue to live in fear because of their race, gender, national origin, and religious and/or political beliefs.

One of our biggest challenges as authors was how to tell this story to a modern audience. And that's where our character, Breanna Shelton, came into play. Though a creation of our imaginations, Breanna is a composite of several Black female reporters and editors we got to know during our daily newspaper careers. We witnessed firsthand how these strong women were forced to deal with racism and misogyny while breaking into a field at a time when sportswriting was dominated by white males. Breanna is a compilation and celebration of determined women who refused to allow glass ceilings stop them from chasing their dreams. Wilmeth's story would strike a chord with Breanna, just as it had in real life with us. For her, like for us, it would become a tale that resonated deeply and had to be told.

In essence, *Invisible No More* boasts two protagonists in parallel pursuits. Both must plow through societal and cultural roadblocks in order to realize their passions. Breanna is our literary vehicle connecting past to present and bringing Wilmeth's story to life.

License was taken to get into Wilmeth's head and soul—to understand what he was up against, what he was feeling, and what coping mechanisms he employed that enabled him to endure and flourish. Imagine the pain he experienced not being allowed to live in campus dorms or eat in dining halls with his classmates and teammates at Syracuse. Think about the humiliation and devastation he felt after being forced to sit out games against the University of Maryland and the Naval Academy because colleges south of the Mason-Dixon Line had policies forbidding contests versus opponents featuring players of color.

Wilmeth and Breanna's fictitious conversations are predicated on facts culled from voluminous research and interviews about real events. These include

- the discovery of Wilmeth's passing prowess by assistant coach Roy Simmons Sr. during a college intramural football game;

- the "outing" of Wilmeth as Black, not Indian, by Hall of Fame sportswriter Sam Lacy, which subsequently led to the star quarterback's racist benching;

- the failure of Syracuse football teammate Marty Glickman to stand in protest and solidarity with Wilmeth before that 1938 Maryland game, just two years after Glickman was denied an opportunity to compete in the Berlin Olympics because he was Jewish;

- the national praise heaped on Wilmeth by Rice following the quarterback's stirring upset of national football powerhouse Cornell;

- the uptick in Tuskegee enrollments after Wilmeth signed up for the pilots' program;

- the full-honors burial at Arlington National Cemetery in 1943, attended by luminaries such as Joe Louis and Cab Calloway;

- the basketball jersey retirement ceremony in 2005 at Syracuse University's Carrier Dome; and

- the 2013 Forgiveness Game, in which University of Maryland administrators officially apologized to Wilmeth's relatives for the school's refusal to allow him to play seven decades earlier.

Of the scores of sources for this book, four stand out. The aforementioned Kirst wrote extensively about Wilmeth during his years as a columnist for the *Syracuse Post-Standard* and was a driving force behind getting Syracuse University to finally recognize their pioneering scholar-athlete.

Syracuse administrator Larry Martin wound up nurturing the seed Kirst planted, convincing then university chancellor Nancy Cantor that the great athletes in Syracuse history all "stood on the shoulders of a giant named Wilmeth Sidat-Singh," and that a historical oversight needed to be corrected, hence the jersey retirement.

Wilmeth's cousin Lyn Henley has spent a lifetime as caretaker and advocate of the Sidat-Singh legacy and has been a valuable resource throughout our journey, enabling us to know our hero on a deeper level. Wilmeth truly is fortunate to have someone carry the torch for him the way Lyn has.

We're also grateful for Coates's work, which drilled deeply into the racist gentlemen's agreements among college athletic departments in the 1930s, 1940s, 1950s, and 1960s. His exhaustive research and interviews provided telling context and perspective, as well as greater insight into Wilmeth the athlete and person.

The book *Black Knights: The Story of the Tuskegee Airmen,* by Lynn Homan and Thomas Reilly, filled in numerous blanks from Wilmeth's time in Alabama, as did an interview with Tuskegee Airman Herb Thorpe of Rome, New York. Thorpe was one of many inspired to follow Wilmeth's lead and sign up for the program.

Many thanks to Syracuse University Archives and the SU Athletic Department for fulfilling numerous requests for files stuffed with reams of newspaper clippings and photographs, and to Margie Chetney from SU's David Falk College of Sport and Human Dynamics for her kindness and tireless problem-solving abilities. We also are indebted to Syracuse chancellor Kent Syverud for his continuing support and faith in us.

The folks at Arlington National Cemetery, particularly Timothy Frank, were helpful in providing background information on Wilmeth's burial.

And we'd be remiss if we didn't give a shout-out to former Syracuse quarterback Don McPherson for his steadfast encouragement. A 1987 consensus All-American and Heisman Trophy runner-up, Don is joined at the historical hip with Wilmeth. A half century after Wilmeth paved the way, Don courageously refused to kowtow to college recruiters and NFL coaches who wanted him to switch positions because of their prejudices that Blacks "weren't qualified" to play quarterback at those lofty levels. We admire Don for his fortitude and friendship.

You will notice the use of certain words in the novel that may be offensive to some. We did our best to be sensitive about language, while attempting to be true to the times and the story and the way people conversed back then. It's often a delicate linguistic balancing act between accuracy and sensitivity when writing about history.

It should be noted that Wilmeth's position at Syracuse was listed as "halfback." This merely is a matter of semantics. He played the position that today is known as "quarterback." Wilmeth was the primary passer in the Syracuse offense and the person in charge of calling and executing the plays, diagnosing defenses, and making sure the other ten players on offense were in the right positions each snap.

We will be forever grateful to our underwriter, Andrew Siegel, for believing in us and in Wilmeth. Andrew admired our passion and saw the need to tell this story to a larger audience. We are also indebted to the Amplify Publishing Group, particularly CEO Naren Aryal and editor Myles Schrag. Like Andrew, they recognized our fervor and the story's power, and along with caring and deft copyediting by David Baker, they improved what we wrote and helped our obsession come to fruition. Thanks also to graphic designer Shannon Sullivan for bringing the images of Wilmeth to life, providing a powerful glimpse of the Renaissance man on the front and back covers.

We hope you were moved by Wilmeth—and by our messenger, Breanna, our amalgam of strong women.

Speaking of strong women, we need to mention our spouses: Beth Pitoniak and Barb Burton. This book never would have crossed the goal line without their love, encouragement, and understanding. They immediately grasped why this story meant so much to us.

While traveling this long and winding road, we experienced moments of doubt and desperation. There were times we considered punting. Fortunately, Wilmeth wouldn't let us quit. He kept speaking to us, kept touching our minds and souls in ways he once lifted the spirits of friends, relatives, classmates, teammates, coaches, teachers, airmen, and total strangers. It is our fervent hope we did him justice—that he's invisible no more and will never ever be forgotten.

ABOUT THE AUTHORS

Scott Pitoniak is a nationally honored journalist and bestselling author of more than thirty books. The Syracuse University graduate has worked as a sports columnist for the Rochester *Democrat and Chronicle*, *USA Today,* and Gannett News Service (150 newspapers nationwide), and has written scores of magazine  and website articles, often focusing on the human side of sports. He also has been an on-air NFL analyst for CBS television stations, cohosted an ESPN-affiliated radio talk show, and authored scripts for the Great Courses educational series. Scott is a member of six Halls of Fame. The Associated Press Sports Editors and the Professional Football Writers of America named him one of the nation's top columnists. He was chosen as an honorary torchbearer for the 2002 Winter Olympics. The former college professor's nonsports books include *Juke Box Hero*, a collaboration with rock 'n' roll legend Lou Gramm.

🐦 @scottpitoniak

Rick Burton is the David B. Falk Professor of Sport Management at Syracuse University and chief operating officer for Playbk Sports. Burton is a frequent contributor to publications such as *Sports Business Journal* and *Sportico*, and coauthor of numerous books, including *Business the NHL Way*; *Forever Orange: The Story of Syracuse University*; *20 Secrets to Success for NCAA Student-Athletes*; and *Sports Business Unplugged*. His latest World War II historical thriller, *Into the Gorge*, was published by Subplot in June 2023.

 @RealRickB